Copyright © 2022 by I. A. Dice

Cover Design by CoversbyJules

Interior Design by Feel-Good Smut

Edited by Dave Holwill

All rights reserved.

No part of this publication may be reproduced, distributed, or transmitted in any form or by any means, including photocopying, recording, or other electronic or mechanical methods, without the prior written permission of the publisher, except in the case of brief quotations embodied in critical reviews and certain other non-commercial uses permitted by copyright law.

This is a work of fiction. Names, characters, businesses, places, events, locales, and incidents are either the products of the author's imagination or used in a fictitious manner. Any resemblance to actual persons, living or dead, or actual events is purely coincidental.

All brand names and product names used in this book are trademarks, registered trademarks, or trade names of their respective holders.

A ROMANCE
NOVEL

TOO WRONG

Hayes Brothers Series Book Two
I. A. DICE

Also by T. A. Dice

HAYES BROTHERS SERIES
A sries of interconnected standalones
Too Much
Too Wrong
Too Sweet
Too Strong
Too Hard
Too Long

BROKEN DUET
Broken Rules
Broken Promises

DELIVERANCE DUET
The Sound of Salvation
The Taste of Redemption

Playlist

"Swim" by Chase Atlantic
"Too Good At Goodbyes" by Sam Smith
"Drinking with Cupid" by VOILÁ
"Right Here" by Chase Atlantic
"Over" by Honors
"Feeling You" by Harrison Storm
"Easier" by Mansionair
"Movement" by Hozier
"Playa (Say That) by Dennis Lloyd
"Meddla About" by Chase Atlantic
"Therapy" by VIOLÁ
"MVP" by Rhea Raj
"Chills – Dark Version" by Mickey Valen
"Church" by Chase Atlantic
"No Scrubs" by Unlike Pluto, Joanna Jones
"Safari" by J. Blavin
"I Feel Like I'm Drowning" by Two Feet
"Into It" by Chase Atlantic
"Power Over Me" by Dermot Kennedy
"All Mine" by PLAZA
"Addicted" by JON VINYL
"Make Up Sex" by SoMo

Dedication

To the girls who found their worth
and fought for what they want.

ONE

Logan

"Why are you making such a big deal out of this?" I ask, helping my younger brother rearrange his living room to accommodate the fifty-odd people he invited to his wife's birthday party. He's been married for two years, but it's still unnatural to think of my baby bro as a *husband*. "It's not like you threw a party last year for her twenty-fifth, and that was more significant than twenty-six."

Theo grabs one end of the sofa, prompting me to do the same with the other. I'm honestly not the guy for this fucking job. I've got muscles, alright, I work out in my home gym four times a week to stay in relatively good shape. I swim fifty lengths of the pool in my backyard when the weather permits. That's why I've got a swimmer's body and a swimmer's strength. Lifting couches isn't my strongest suit.

Besides, I'm lazy as fuck.

TOO WRONG

The only reason I'm here, suffering through the joys of helping Theo, is that he's my brother. A long time ago, I made it a rule not to say *no* to either of the six assholes I'm related to if they need help. That's not to say I won't sue if I throw my back sparring with this monstrous couch.

Theo dropped the ball calling me for help with heavy lifting instead of asking our younger brother, Nico. That crazy so-and-so would throw the couch over his shoulder and go for a run.

No biggie.

"We were on holiday for Thalia's birthday last year," Theo reminds me, walking backward down the hallway to stash the three-seater, heavy as a cow, bright orange couch in one of the guest bedrooms for the duration of the party.

I guess I'll have to stand all evening. This party just keeps getting better and better, doesn't it?

"This year, I want everyone here. Thalia and Mom still don't get along, and we don't have many chances to fix that."

Inviting fifty people won't give them the best opportunity to bond, but I don't waste my breath pointing it out. I also don't remind him about the last unsuccessful Mom slash Thalia bonding time. A get-together at our parents' house last month didn't go down well. Poor Thalia stormed out halfway through dessert after Mom insulted a strawberry cheesecake which, according to Theo, took Thalia six hours and four tries to make.

Internally, I sided with Mom when she chirped in an artificially playful tone that the cake looked like something a toddler threw up, but I hadn't said a word to Thalia.

If I'm perfectly honest, she scares me a little. She's beautiful, caring, and all-out amazing, but there's a side to her I don't enjoy so much: fiery, Greek attitude; a living, breathing volcano. The colorful, thick accent flares whenever she's angry, rendering English words impossible to understand.

Mom's reluctance to accept her as a part of the Hayes clan surprised all its current members. Dad included. Even more so because when Theo and Thalia started dating, the two were on the right track to winning a mother and daughter-in-law prize of some sort... right until Theo decided to marry the girl in Las. Fucking. Vegas.

Once Mom found out a big Church wedding wouldn't happen, she changed her tune.

Theo and Thalia dated for a few months before Thalia's surname changed from Dimopopololu or Dimopopus or Dimo-something or other to Hayes, so that probably didn't help their case either, but it's been almost two years of T&T's unbridled, sickening happiness that makes me want to double over and puke a rainbow half the time.

I thought Mom would get over herself by now.

She always wanted a daughter—hence seven sons—but now that she technically has one, she has morphed into a stereotypical monster-in-law. Jealous, petty, and ostentatious.

Theo has a lot more patience than I do. I'd chew Mom's head off if she treated my girl with the same cool, harsh restraint for no apparent reason. Not that I have a girl but case in point.

In Dad's words, Mom realized that one by one, all her sons would be snatched by a woman, leaving her alone and unwanted. Cue in operation *"Make Mom feel needed."*

The seven of us visit more often and ask for help with anything that springs to mind. It's incredible how calling her at seven in the morning, asking for a pancake recipe, lifts her mood. Unfortunately, the trick does little to warm her up to Thalia. *Civil* is as warm as they get.

"I bet it wouldn't hurt if you took Mom out to dinner and

just talked to her," I say, trying to pirouette the sofa through the door, my mind flashing with Ross, "Friends," and *pivot*. "Listen to what she has to say. Just the two of you. No Thalia."

"Yeah," he grunts, drops his side, and steps back to assess the situation. This shouldn't be so difficult, but here we are facing a dilemma worthy of two toddlers in front of a shape-sorting cube attempting to fit a rhombus in a heart-shaped hole. "I'll think about it."

"While you think about that, take a second to think about getting your wife pregnant. You've been together for two years. You're married. What the fuck are you waiting for? Some kind of an invitation? I'll print one out if you want. Maybe Mom would be happier with Thalia if you'd start the grandchildren production already."

Theo barks a laugh, gesturing for me to stand the couch vertically. Shit... where the hell is Nico when you need him?

"You sound like Shawn and Jack. You know they ask us to babysit Josh at least twice a month? They think taking care of the little devil will get Thalia's maternal instinct going again." He steadies the couch when it wobbles, threatening to fall on top of his head. I doubt he'd come out of that without at least a snapped spine. "So far, all it does is make me want to get a vasectomy."

The Duracell Bunny has nothing on Josh. He stirs hell everywhere all at once, even when he's not actually in the room. Our eldest brother, Shawn, adopted the little man with his husband, Jack, shortly after Theo and Thalia's half-assed wedding ceremony at the highly reputable *Viva Las Vegas Wedding Chapel*.

What a fucking joke.

I was ready to kick his ass when he sent a photo of him

and his bride standing outside said reputable establishment to the Hayes brothers' group chat.

Josh was fifteen months old at the time. Last week, he turned three, and he's got more energy in his index finger than a bucketful of Red Bull.

It might be the reason why I love the kid so much. I'm the favorite uncle, closely followed by Cody—my youngest brother and one-third of The Holy Trinity, as I like to call the triplets. Cody, who lets Josh get away with murder.

The other two, Colt and Conor, steer clear, busy chasing pussy as they should. They're nineteen, sophomores in college, and living their best lives.

"We could do with another baby in the family," I say, maneuvering the couch back to a horizontal position. It's too tall to fit through the door upright. "You're not getting any younger. Get to work and aim for a girl, alright?"

"Says you?" Theo smirks. "You're older than me, Logan. You're thirty. And I don't want a daughter. Shit, imagine raising a girl in this day and age. I'd need to dig a basement and lock her in there until she turns eighteen."

A burst of laughter saws past my lips. "You're delusional. She's got six uncles ready to gut any asshole who dares to disrespect her. Don't worry, we've got her."

"I'm delusional? You're talking like she's just behind the wall, sleeping in a crib. She doesn't fucking exist, bro. You've got *nothing!*"

With a grunt and a heave, he braces against the opposite wall, forcing the couch inside the guest bedroom. We both freeze at the sound of the fabric ripping. A sound that foretells marital trouble. No sex for a week if I'm to venture a guess.

I don't want to be here when Thalia sees the tear. And I

don't want to be here when the time comes to drag the sofa back out, so my phone will be switched off tomorrow.

Theo spins on the soles of his shoes, heading back to the living room. "My reproduction schedule is none of your goddamn business. If you want a baby girl in the family, go and fucking make one."

"With my hand? Highly unlikely."

"Too much information." He cringes but amusement tugs at his vocal cords. Even though he's all grown up and domesticated, there's still an immature side to him that likes to rear its head every so often. "It's about time to replace your hand with a girl, don't you think? You want me to set you up? Thalia's got plenty of friends. You could pick and choose."

I *do* pick and choose.

Well, not *I*, as such. Theo, Nico, and our two buddies, Toby and Adrian, choose for me. They're too creative for their own good trying to find a woman who'll say *no* to me. They've been at it every Saturday for two months, choosing girls from each end of the spectrum. I've wooed them all: tall, short, plump and thin; older, younger, loose and conservative. Despite having to buy me a watch of choice each time they lose the bet, they aren't giving up. Not the brightest bulbs in the box.

Enough women have moaned my name, and enough women have ogled me as if I'm sex on a stick to make their words ring true: I am, as most of them put it... *irresistible*. As dumb as that sounds. It doesn't matter how uptight the woman is. I can charm the panties of a nun if I put my head to it.

At first, the guys chose between pretty, feisty teens and pretty, naïve twenty-something year-olds. The bets spiraled downhill from there when they started choosing the not-so-pretty ones.

I should probably stop this nonsense.

I'm *thirty* and have been for a couple of months now, but damn. I don't have anything better to do with my life.

Is it my fault all the best girls are taken? I should've settled down a few years ago when the easy-going, pretty, and smart girls were still available, but back then, I thought with my cock, not my brain. Although considering the bets, I guess I still think mostly with my cock.

"It'll happen when it happens," I say, not keen on discussing the subject. "I'm fine as I am for now."

We continue to clear out the living room. For some reason, it seems smaller without the furniture, which isn't usually the case while I oversee the builds at work. Maybe because I've not seen most of those spaces furnished, so I've got no comparison.

Last year, Theo traded his cozy condo for a four-bedroom house with a big garden and a pool. He should really put a few kids in those spare bedrooms.

The catering company arrives half an hour later, wheeling in trolleys brimming with food. Some set camp in the kitchen; others move outside where the BBQ is ready and waiting. The logo on their aprons is that of Nico's restaurant, *The Olive Tree*, which he owns in part with Adrian. It used to be Nico and Jared's, but since shit hit the fan over a year ago, Nico paid Jared off and appointed Adrian as his business partner.

He then appointed Thalia as head chef. And what a good choice that was. The restaurant quickly became the must-go-to place in Newport Beach thanks to the Greek specialties she introduced. She's a fantastic cook. Useless with cakes, though.

"Right, I need your opinion because I kind of lost the battle." Theo leads me outside so he can grab a smoke. If you ask him, he doesn't smoke. At least not in front of his wife. "Thalia invited Cassidy. You think I should give Nico a heads up?"

"Why? Because she's friends with Kaya?"

Theo cringes at the sound of the unspeakable name, and I see red, too, when I recall *that* night.

I still remember the murderous rage flashing across Nico's face as he stormed out of the employee changing room at the Country Club, where he caught his best friend of twenty years nailing his *girlfriend* of seven months.

Deep down, Nico knew Jared did him a favor by taking the crazy bitch off his hands, but she was the first and, so far, the only woman he has ever dated.

All my brothers think Kaya's betrayal impacted Nico the most, but I know losing his best friend hurt him more. That's not to say he took Kaya's cheating lightly. He cared about her on some level. He had to, or else he wouldn't have lasted seven months.

No sane person would.

I've never met a woman so toxic. So manipulative. So fucking persuasive. She wrapped Nico around her long, manicured finger making him dance to every tune she played. And she played a lot of tunes to fuel, and nurture his flaws, compulsive overprotectiveness, jealousy, and rowdy temper. He always had a short fuse, but Kaya turned it to eleven.

Even though it's been over a year since they broke up, he has never returned to pre-Kaya Nico. Thankfully, he didn't linger in the rage-filled during-Kaya phase. Now he's just... on edge. Wary. Fire, brimstone, and fucking death. He snaps faster than the naked eye can see.

"Obviously," Theo drawls. "Thalia and Cassidy are close, and with Cass being Kaya's bestie, I don't know what to expect from Nico. Thalia doesn't spend time with Kaya, I swear, but

Nico might come to that conclusion."

"Yeah, a heads up might not be a bad idea."

Theo grinds his teeth, taking the phone out to dial the number. "Here goes nothing." His spine straightens, suddenly taut like a bowstring when Nico answers. He's not even here, but his commanding personality works over long distance just as well. "Hey, bro, listen—"

I leave him to it, entering the house to steal a few appetizers while the catering company gets ready. Thanks to Thalia's excellent culinary skills that she passed down to the other cooks at the restaurant, the food tastes just like the heaven she serves when she invites us for dinner every now and then.

Even the Holy Trinity joins in more often now that they've finally hit the age where all seven of us can sit in one room and talk like equals. They've matured a lot since graduating high school and moving out of our parent's house to live with Nico.

"What's the verdict?" I ask when Theo strolls back inside, his face sullen. "Don't tell me he's not coming."

"Oh, he's coming. It took him a minute to mull it over," he snaps and follows it with a heavy sigh. "I hate choosing between any of you or Thalia."

"You're not choosing. It's not like you invited Kaya. Chill. There'll be fifty people here, but if it makes you feel better, I'll make sure Cass and Nico don't cross paths, alright?"

"Yeah? You sure? I know you're not a fan of hers either."

That's not entirely true...

Three years ago, Cass and I went out a few times for drinks. I even took her to dinner before we sealed the deal in bed. Newport Beach is small, though. My brothers found out the very next day that we spent the evening at my favorite restaurant.

Less than twelve hours after I claimed Cassidy's beautiful,

toned body, Theo informed me he got there first.

"I don't mind her." I rummage through the fridge on the hunt for a bottle of beer. "I've not talked to her since—" I apply the brakes before the end of that sentence slips out.

Theo and I both know when I talked to Cass last, and the subject is widely avoided: the night Nico caught Jared nailing Kaya. Cassidy was the one who randomly texted me a cryptic message that day after a year and a half of relative silence.

Cass: Nico should know something. Get him to the Country Club tonight at ten. Employee changing rooms. Delete this message. You don't know this from me.

I took the bait. Cass failed to arm me with specifics; she hadn't mentioned Kaya or Jared, but she mentioned Nico, and deciphering the cryptic message proved all too easy. I wasn't keen on Kaya from the start. I had a gnawing feeling she was cheating on my brother long before Cass sent that text.

What I never would've guessed is that Cruella DeMon was cheating with Nico's best friend. God, it felt good to nail Jared's stupid face. I never liked the prick. Nico steered out the first punch, but *I* broke Jared's nose, and Theo knocked out his front tooth. As a cop, Shawn stood to the side, turning a blind eye to the obvious violation of the law.

"Thanks. I owe you one," Theo says. "Now help me with the wing chair."

Why the hell did I answer when he called?

TWO

Logan

The party was supposed to start at eight o'clock. I was supposed to be there at half past seven in case Nico or Cassidy decided to arrive early, but as fate would have it, it's after eight, and I'm still at home, not even in my car yet. Not even in my jacket or anywhere near the door.

The reason? Theo's fucking dog.

He asked me to take care of Ares for the duration of the party because little Josh wants to ride him whenever he sees the poor thing.

Thoughtfully, I agreed. Ares is well-behaved, so I don't need to worry about pee stains on the carpet or furniture damage. He ate his fair share of shoes, cushions, and belts as a puppy and got it out of his system.

There's just one issue I overlooked: *Ghost.* An albino Burmese Python I bought a few weeks ago because I was sick and tired of coming home after a long day at work to a silent, empty house. It's not like snakes make much noise or greet you at the door, jumping, barking, and licking your face, but just knowing he's here lifts my mood.

I could've bought a dog, but it seemed cruel to leave him alone for twelve hours a day, so a snake it is. A fifteen-foot-long motherfucker whose vivarium takes a third of my living room. A vivarium he hardly spends time in if I'm home.

He's free to roam the house, which might not be the best idea now that I think about it. He scared me senseless the other day when I found him curled up under the duvet in my bed. I wanted company, but not that kind of company.

Ares appears to have suicidal tendencies because he wants to play with the python that could, without much effort, swallow him whole. Pleading, shouting, and threatening him with no toys and no dinner doesn't help. I'm left with no choice but to lock him in the kitchen.

"Sorry, boy, but I don't trust Ghost not to eat you," I crouch in the doorway to pat his head. "Slim chance he'll open the vivarium, but if you piss him off, he might break the glass, and your mommy will cut off my balls if you get hurt here."

He tilts his head, watching me with big, clever eyes as if he understands every word I say. I wish. If he were still a pup, I'd carry him around all evening to keep him away from Josh, but he's not a pup. He's full-grown, weighs sixty pounds, and, as we've established, lifting isn't my strongest suit.

I leave him with a few treats to compensate for locking him in the kitchen with one shitty chew toy because that's all Thalia packed and return to the living room to quadruple-check that Ghost is locked and secure. He lazily wraps himself around a thick tree branch, giving zero fucks about anything or anyone.

The previous owner said he'll be full for two weeks once

fed, so he shouldn't be hungry for another eight days, but I refuse to take any risks. Not when I have *Thalia's* dog under my doubtfully competent care. She'll rip me apart if one hair falls off her baby's head.

Shit, this is nerve-wracking.

What if Ares chokes on that measly chew toy? What if he opens the cabinet with the cleaning stuff my cleaning lady, Mira, uses and bites through a bottle of bleach? What if—

Stop being stupid, Logan.

I close the living room door as yet another precaution. Snakes can't open doors, right?

Fuck! What about dogs?

Maybe it'd be better to stay home. I pull my phone out and shoot a message to the Hayes brothers' group chat.

Me: Can Ares open doors?

Theo: Not that I'm aware of. Why?

Me: Just checking. I'm having a bit of a logistical nightmare trying to figure out the safest way to store the dog away from the snake.

Nico: Store? You don't store a dog, asshat. See? That's why you should've left the little shit with me, Theo.

Me: Fuck you.

Nico: No, thanks.

Theo: Just get your ass over here. You're late.

"Not helping, bro," I growl, shoving the phone into my pocket.

Whatever. I did my best to ensure the safety of the four-legged, furry creature, so my conscience is clear. Theo can perform open-snake surgery if the fucker eats his dog. And I'll move to Mozambique, far away from Thalia's reach.

I slip into my letterman jacket and hop behind the wheel of my Charger, reversing out of the driveway.

"What the hell took you so long?" Theo complains when he lets me in twenty minutes later. "Lock the dog, lock the snake." He gestures left and right. "Job done."

"If this ends in a bloodbath, don't blame me. Ares is in the kitchen. Ghost is in the living room. Two sets of doors between them. It'll have to do," I huff, taking my jacket off.

"Don't tell Thalia about the dog-eating snake."

The woman in question appears in the hallway, greeting me with a dazzling smile and an expectant head tilt: a non-verbal order to kiss her cheek. God help me if I don't oblige.

She's yet another woman my younger brother snatched up first. I got over my initial crush on Thalia fast, but there's no denying she's beautiful. Long legs, a curvy body, and an exotic face. She's a brunette, so not my type, but she's one of those women you can't walk past without a second glance. And to top it off, she's as lovely inside as she is outside... when she's not angry, that is.

Theo's one lucky bastard.

"Happy birthday, honey." I hand her a gift bag and stamp that obligatory kiss on her cheek, or else I'll get a taste of her disapproval. "You look amazing."

"Thank you." A satisfied smile curves her full, blood-red lips. "You look rather handsome yourself."

"Yeah, yeah," Theo interjects, his tone clipped but eyes playful. "Enough. Let's get you a drink." He grips my shoulders, steering me into the open living area, where people crowd the space in smaller and larger groups, talking and laughing over the eighties hits playing from the sound system.

Mom stands to the side, holding a flute of champagne, her assessing eyes scanning the guests. Her new hairstyle, a short pixie cut, makes her look ten years younger than her fifty-seven. You'd never guess she raised seven boys with how fresh, rested, and beautiful she looks.

Dad's wrinkly thanks to his political career and endless smiling, but he's still a sharp dresser at sixty-one. He's got that boy-next-door vibe that won him the election twice in a row.

They probably hoped to have enough grandkids to start a football team by now, but tough luck. Only Shawn stood up to the task, and now that Josh is more manageable, he and Jack are thinking about adopting another kid.

Theo's slacking for no apparent reason; I don't have a girl, let alone a wife; the triplets are too young, and Nico... I don't think that guy will ever find a woman capable of withstanding his crazy ass. Unless there's another one like Kaya around. One who'll have the guts to hold her ground and tame Nico's temper and overbearing personality.

A girl just like Kaya minus the drinking, cheating, hell-stirring, manipulative, crazy, demonic bitch side, *obviously*.

"How's the situation?" I ask when Theo grabs a beer out of the fridge. "Everyone chill?"

"Surprisingly, yes." He comes closer, lowering his voice. "Cass avoids Nico like the plague."

A loud cheer fills the air, and we both cast a sideways glance to where Shawn scoots Josh off the floor, kissing his head.

TOO WRONG

"You're okay," he coos, messing up his light blonde hair. "You need to watch where you're going."

"And *walk*, not run," Jack adds with a smirk before his eyes lock with mine, and a devilish grin twists his lips. "Look, Josh, Uncle Logan's here."

Josh's big eyes follow Jack's finger. As soon as he sees me, he bounces in Shawn's arms, hands outstretched toward me even though I'm at least thirty feet away.

What can I do?

I cross the room, greeting a few people on the way. I kiss Mom on the cheek and pat Nico's back before I reach my oldest brother and steal his kid. "You and me, buddy," I say, snatching a small toy car off the floor before someone steps on it and goes airborne. "We need to keep an eye on everyone, so they behave themselves. You'll help me, won't you?"

He shakes his head, yanking my baseball cap. "No."

Short, sweet, and to the point. I love this kid.

The triplets chuckle, high-fiving Josh.

"Good call, my man," Cody says, keeping at a distance. He learned his lesson not to come close unless Josh has a toy in his hands. If he doesn't, he finds Cody's man bun fascinating and tries to rip his hair out of his skull. "Don't listen to Uncle Logan. Tell him to do the airplane."

Josh bounces around in my arms, excited by the idea. I hand my beer to Cody, then fly the kid around the perimeter of the room for a few minutes. My arms are on fire from supporting his weight on my forearm and gripping his t-shirt to keep him from really flying away.

That'd be a sight to fucking see.

Not Josh flying.

Me *dying* at the hands of my older brother.

"Okay, enough." I set him back on the floor.

That's when my eyes land on Cassidy.

I've not seen her in a while. We bumped into each other five, maybe six months ago at one of the clubs in town, but I was pretty wasted at the time and vaguely recall a nimble college girl hanging on my arm. I had to change my phone number afterward because she wouldn't stop bombarding me with messages and pictures of her boobs. Perky and pretty boobs, sure, but *been there, done that.*

Now that I'm sober... holy shit.

Either my mind plays tricks on me, or time faded the memories because here she is, looking spellbinding in a fitted, red dress, the fabric not a millimeter under her milky collarbones. I smile internally, scanning her flawless legs. Those were wrapped around my waist one night three years ago. Too bad her legs are all she's showing. And not much of them.

Her dress is only an inch above the knee, flared at the bottom, with a silk ribbon tied around her ribs. The blood-red color is the only extravagance, but a bit of lace here and there proves what I already know about Cassidy Annabelle Roberts. She might be trying to fit in with the upper class; to come across as a mature, sophisticated woman, but she's not as well-behaved as she portrays herself.

No, no, *no*... Cass is a wild cookie.

Blonde hair frames her delicate face, and cornflower-blue eyes surrounded by thick eyelashes stare into mine. Lips to match the dress curl into a barely there, uncertain smile.

She tucks a lock of hair behind her ear, stepping from one foot to another like she's uncomfortable standing in a room full of Hayes.

Good.

She should be.

Not only is she Kaya's best friend, which makes her undesirable in our circle right off the bat, but she fucked Theo, and now she stands in his living room celebrating his wife's birthday as if nothing ever happened.

Not to mention, she fucked *me*, too.

And what a night that was...

"More!" Josh jumps around me, hands in the air. "Again!"

I clear my throat, shifting my gaze from Cass to the little boy. "Find Uncle Cody. It's his turn."

"I'll take over." My father stops beside me, overdressed in a three-piece charcoal suit and in *mayor* mode as usual. He takes Josh's hand, beaming. "Come on. I hear Daddy bought you a new car. Can I see?"

Involuntarily and against better judgment, my eyes cut back to Cassidy. She's no longer watching me, engrossed in a conversation with one of Thalia's friends from work.

Was she always this pretty?

She trimmed the too-long hair that used to fall to her ass all the way back to shoulder length. Her sense of style has improved, too. Her dress isn't as modest as I initially thought, but it doesn't reveal much. She used to dress as if to mimic Kaya, showing more ass and boobs than appropriate.

Not anymore. Tonight, she's sexy but classy. No cleavage at the front, but her entire back is on display, revealing sun-kissed complexion.

I travel back to the night we spent together, reliving my own fascination with the dimples of Venus marking her lower back—the sexiest thing I ever saw on a woman.

My cock stirs when the images of her naked body riding me in a sensual rhythm resurface. The way she nibbled my lips and then dug her nails into my scalp when she came on my tongue, and how she smelled so fresh like lemons and ginger.

The porn clip in my head stops abruptly.

"You good?" Nico asks, and I jerk my head to him so fast I hear a crack in my neck. Guilt sprouts in the pit of my stomach as two vertical creases mark his forehead. "You good, Logan?" he repeats. "You look lost."

He hands me a bottle of Bud Light he must've intercepted from Cody, who's flying Josh around the kitchen island. That kid will be a nightmare when he hits his teenage years. Six of his uncles spoil him rotten. It might not be the best strategy, but to hell with that. Shawn's the father. It's his job to raise the kid and our job to make sure Josh knows how to drive his dads up the wall with stupid pranks.

"I'm good." I shove my hands in my pockets to disguise the apparent bulge in the zipper region of my jeans. "I forgot Cass was..." I want to say *coming*, but that's a dangerous play on words in my current state, "...going to be here."

Liar, liar.

Nico's jaw tenses as he inhales a deep breath to cool his jets, and seemingly back in control, he changes the subject. "I'm thinking of renovating the house. You got time this week to draw some plans for me?"

"Sure. Anytime."

As if I could say *no* to the guy who made me a millionaire. It's thanks to him that I could afford the four-bedroom house my company—correction, my *grandfather's* company I work for—built last year.

We spend twenty minutes discussing his idea for remodeling the ground floor before we're interrupted by Theo and a three-tier birthday cake.

TOO WRONG

The conversations die down and are quickly replaced by an off-key, off-sync *Happy Birthday*. Using the few seconds of everyone's inattention, I steal another glance at Cass only to find her looking at me.

THREE

Cassidy

The party ticks away so, *so* slowly. Minutes stretch like bubble gum until I'm sure it must be time to leave, but one glance at my wristwatch proves me wrong.

Thirty-seven minutes.

I've only been here *thirty-seven* minutes.

What the hell am I doing here, anyway?

I'd much rather be at home watching Netflix and stuffing myself with ice cream instead of scrutinizing my every move in a room full of people who, to put it mildly, aren't my biggest fans.

But I'm here.

I'm here because I'm a good friend. That's why.

If not for Thalia being the only Hayes not to treat me like a disease, I would've bailed on the party, but we're friends. *Great* friends. She might be the only person in my life who truly has my back, and we've grown close since we first met two years ago. Sometimes I think it's not Kaya who's my best friend anymore. It's Thalia.

She tries to keep me entertained while the seven Hayes brothers act like I'm thin air. Very foul, smelly air at that. They weren't thrilled with me after the Theo and Logan fuck-fest fiasco, but they were civil.

Not anymore.

Now, I'm a pigeon's crap on their designer clothes. A tangled earphone cord. A stubbed toe. That one customer who waits in line for twenty minutes but doesn't know what to order once he reaches the till. A mosquito buzzing overhead at three in the morning.

Yeah, that's me. The nuisance.

Fraternizing with public enemy number one puts me in the same bag as the girl who drove a knife through Nico's heart.

Although that might be an exaggeration.

I was a first-hand witness to Nico's relationship with Kaya. Truth be told, other than fascination and a sense of higher purpose, he had no feelings for her. No meaningful feelings, at least. More often than not, he forced himself to spend time with her. He forced himself to touch and kiss her. From a bystander's point of view, he looked like someone trying to settle down against better judgment.

And poor judgment is what got him in that mess.

Kaya's a nice friend—caring, helpful, and used to be mostly available when I needed her, but she's no girlfriend or wife material. She's flirtatious and kind of a slut. I'm not judgmental on any level. A girl can sleep around just as much as a guy, but maybe not while she's married...

How can Kaya's husband be so blind? Most of Newport knows she's cheating on Jared almost every weekend. Either the rumors bypass his ears, or he chooses to ignore them.

I didn't expect a *thank you* from Logan after I, in a way, saved his younger brother from a toxic relationship. I also didn't expect the silent treatment that followed or the hateful stares from his brothers whenever we bump into each other.

"This is nice, but I need a night out," Thalia says, stopping beside me. The short black dress she wears struggles to contain her huge boobs. "Do you have time next week? We could invite Mary-Jane and Amy and head over to *Q*."

It's like being stuck between a hammer and a hard place trying to juggle my friendship with Thalia and Kaya. They hate each other on principle, which means planning girls' nights is problematic, at the least.

I always choose between one or the other, but I'd rather split myself in two than ask them to step into one room. I'm sure Kaya would end up in the ER with claw marks across her beautiful face, courtesy of Thalia. She's as fierce as they come and protects her family like a lioness. No one can say one bad word about the Hayes and walk away without tasting her wrath.

"I'll check with them, but I like the idea," I say. "It's been too long. You're too preoccupied with your man."

She smirks, then all-out beams when Theo approaches with a glass of wine. He snakes his free hand around her middle, pressing his lips against her temple, the kiss soft, sweet, and affectionate.

They're adorable together. Two years hasn't diminished how he handles her, as if she's the only woman he sees. I'd never admit it out loud, but Theo and Thalia's relationship is one I'm envious of most. She's his dream come true. Everything he does is with Thalia in mind, and she's the same: in love and being loved. Unconditionally.

Too Wrong

Why can't I find what they have? I'm twenty-five, and I've never been in a long-term relationship.

What is wrong with me?

Why can't I have a man to love me for *me*? A man to come home to. A man to watch TV with and fall asleep next to...

"Time for cake, *omorfiá*," Theo says before he looks at me, nothing more than a polite nod of his chin to acknowledge my existence.

It's more than either of his brothers greeted me with today, but I know he only tolerates my presence because of Thalia.

"I'll be right back," she tells me before hurrying away, her hand in Theo's.

I glance around the room, searching for a familiar face to talk to for a while before I fake a headache, apologize to the birthday girl, and make a swift exit in precisely forty minutes. An hour and a half is enough time among people who despise me. In the crowd of faces celebrating Thalia's twenty-sixth birthday, I spot Logan Hayes.

My body's instantly ablaze as my heart speeds up, hurtling from a steady thumping to a hurried gallop. How long before these foolish feelings run their course?

Three years have passed, but I can't shake him no matter how hard I try. We rarely bump into each other these days, but when we do, it's at the least convenient moment. At the very last second. Just when I think I'm over him, he materializes in front of me as if to say *Nah-ah, princess, I won't let you forget about me* that *easily*.

The feelings flare, throwing me back to my knees.

Back to the state of mind where I obsess over my mistake and wish to find a lamp and summon a Genie to grant my wish: turn back time; let me start over.

I inhale a deep breath through my nose and push it past my lips, forcing the tense muscles in my shoulders and neck to relax.

Here he is... closer than I've had him since Nico caught Kaya in the act a year and a half ago.

Here he is like I knew he would be.

Deep down, I'm honest enough to admit he's the main reason why I showed my face here tonight. Thalia would understand if I asked her to meet me at *Tortugo* for a celebratory drink one evening instead of joining the party, but I couldn't, for the love of that's holy, pass on the chance to see Logan.

All six-foot-one of him, built like the swimmer he used to be in college. Irreverent sense of style, handsome, boyish face despite his thirty years, and eyes I could drown in.

Lord, he's fucking perfect.

The kind of man you swoon over. The kind you stare at for hours and never grow tired of admiring his immaculate hair, high cheekbones, clever eyes, and full lips.

He rushes around the room with Josh resting on his forearm. The little boy laughs, mouth open, hands outstretched, and Logan smiles. And that smile... the glint in his eyes, the curve of his mouth... it does something to me. It brings back an avalanche of unwanted feelings, burying me beneath a thick blanket of intense emotions.

Everyone makes mistakes.

We get drunk at a party and throw up, missing the toilet by an inch. Or don't get to the toilet at all and puke in the living room. We hit the club with friends and make out with the boy our bestie has been crushing on just because she was a bitch earlier and had to learn a lesson. Or worse—we hook up with said guy and consequently ruin the friendship. We spill secrets even though we were told not to utter a word to a living soul.

TOO WRONG

Mistakes. Whether big or small, they're a part of life, a part of growing up, and part of learning how to function in the world and navigate the jungle.

Some we brush off with time. Others live in our heads rent-free for longer... for*ever*. Some teach us a lesson. Others become a bitter-sweet memory of our youth.

Most people make two or three big mistakes. Those we obsess over every now and then regardless of how much time has passed. Those that keep us up at night.

Not many of us make mistakes that destroy our chance at a real, meaningful relationship.

I did.

A mistake that should've never happened to someone like me—a scholar student, a well-behaved, obedient foster daughter, a charity volunteer.

That mistake was none other than *Theo* Hayes.

It was my first day in Newport. I moved in with my friend, Luke, after we graduated college. We were set to work at the Country Club throughout the summer to save enough money to open a photography studio. To celebrate the start of our newfound independence, we headed to town for a few drinks.

Theo was there. Handsome, courtly, funny. One minute I stood by the bar, laughing at a joke he told me, and the next minute I was in his apartment, coming on his dick.

Other than his first name, I knew nothing about him. Not that he was the mayor's son or that he had six brothers. Not even that they were considered Newport's heartbreakers. That last part should've occurred to me when a line of women scowled in my direction while Theo entertained me at the bar.

What I did know was that he didn't want more than sex. Fine by me. I didn't want more, either. Just one night. A spur-of-the-moment kind of thing, my very first one-night-stand. It was fun and satisfying, and the careless joker I met a few hours earlier was still there once we were done. I was sure we wouldn't see each other again after he ordered me a cab.

I should've known better.

A few days later, I spotted him playing golf with three other guys. That's when I met Logan, Nico, and Shawn, but I paid the last two no attention. In hindsight, it might be why—despite their kinship—I didn't realize they were brothers.

One innocent glance at Logan was enough to send endorphins roaring through my bloodstream. The attraction grew throughout the day, unmistakable and more potent than what I've felt thus far. He was polite, charming, and to-die-for handsome. When they finished golfing, he asked for my number and called with a drink invitation two hours later.

I stood in front of the wardrobe for the longest time, trying to decide what to wear, giddy like a teenager that the handsome boy had asked me out. After that, we hung out every evening, and by the weekend, we ended up on a real-life date at one of the most popular restaurants in town. Sparks were flying, the sexual tension hard to ignore.

I caved.

No, I *initiated*, stealing a kiss when the cab driver pulled up outside my studio flat.

Just a week earlier, I was sure no man could top Theo's performance in bed, but it paled as soon as Logan took to the stage. I couldn't get enough of him or close enough to him. I was his, possessed and worshiped at the same time.

His whispers in my ear, the strong but tender touch, his hungry eyes... a fantasy come true.

His undeniable skills were just a cherry on top.

TOO WRONG

I woke up the following day blissfully infatuated, entangled in his muscular arms, and convinced it was just the beginning. The very start of *more*.

The spell broke a few hours later when he sent me a text.

Logan: Congratulations. Two down, five to go. Sorry to burst your bubble but Shawn's gay, Nico won't touch you with a six-foot pole, and the triplets are underaged. Your collection of Hayes brothers stops here.

Never in my life have I felt as humiliated or worthless as that morning when I realized I slept with two brothers just a week apart. Logan ignored my calls and the messages I sent to explain that I didn't know they were brothers. That I didn't know *him* when Theo approached me at the bar.

He didn't reply.

From then on, he ignored my existence every Sunday while he golfed with his brothers.

I should've forced him to listen, but I was embarrassed and hurt. I cowered, avoiding confrontation. As time passed, Logan toned down with the theatrical head-turning and hands-across-chest-folding, but other than *hey* or *Bud Light, please*, we didn't speak. That's until I decided to stop turning a blind eye to my best friend cheating on Nico.

Now, our eyes lock across the room.

My palms turn cold and clammy, nerves rush to the surface, and my heart beats like a stereo. I'm waiting for a smug smirk, teeth grinding, or an ostentatious head turn or eyeroll, but nothing happens. He just stares, his eyes taking in the length of my body in a slow, heated once-over.

I'm held captive under the intensity of his burning gaze for a few long, tense seconds. He turns away, visibly startled by Nico, who stops beside him in all his unapproachable glory.

The Hayes brothers are tall, toned, and warm in complexion with brown or black hair and a few shades of brown eyes. Their unsettling aura makes you wary from afar, but they aren't as intimidating as they seem once you get closer.

At least not six of them.

Shawn's a big, soft teddy. He might be a cop and carry a gun, but he's the gentlest of the Hayes. Theo's the joker, always cheerful, ready to help and relieve the tension. Logan's short-tempered, edgy, and vicious if he wants to be, but he's got a heart of gold and a lighthearted attitude toward life.

I've not spent much time with the triplets, but Cody, Colt, and Conor seem to be upgraded versions of their older brothers, just more reckless. I guess they're still finding themselves growing as men and human beings.

And then there's Nico. In a way, he's a different breed from the other six. Similar looks but tallest with a broad, muscular chest and a tight web of tattoos marking his hands, arms, and neck. Square jaw, jet-black hair, and coal-black eyes. He's the most ominous man I've ever met, and it doesn't change when you get closer. If anything, the unease grows.

I avert my gaze before he catches me staring.

I scan the room again, searching for someone to talk to, but Thalia and Mary-Jane are busy with their other halves. Instead of standing alone by the wall like orphan Annie, I head outside for fresh air while everyone enjoys the cake.

Normally, I would too, but as it contains hazelnuts, I'd need a shot of epinephrine if I tried a piece.

The garden is empty for the moment, but it's decorated for the party with balloons, garlands, and a picture-taking area equipped with an array of props and a colorful backdrop. It's just a matter of time before the party moves outside.

I stop by the pool, where a blow-up flamingo sways with the wind. I'm thankful for a moment of peace. A moment to clear my head that ends too quickly. Mary-Jane joins me with her boyfriend of two weeks, Timothy, and three part-time waiters working with Thalia at Nico's restaurant—*The Olive Tree*.

"Hey, what are you doing here alone?" MJ asks while the three guys strip off their clothes.

Three splashes push me to step back from the edge. "I needed air. It's too hot inside."

"Come on, Mary-Jane!" One of the guys yells. "Get in. The water is great."

She glances at Timothy as if checking what he thinks, and seeing no disapproval, she turns her back to me, flipping her hair to the front. "Unzip me, please."

The bottle-green dress slides down her skinny, tanned legs to reveal black panties and a push-up bra. She's not a shy girl by any definition but considering the guests at the party range in age from nineteen-year-old triplets to their grandparents in their late seventies or maybe even early eighties, I'm surprised she's going along with the swim.

I mean, the freaking *mayor* is in the house.

The guys in the pool howl while Timothy chuckles under his breath, watching MJ sway her hips left and right, blowing him a kiss before she jumps in head-first.

"Come on, Cass! Your turn!"

I stumble back two more steps. "No, I'm okay. Thanks."

One of them, Jax, I think, rests his hands on the tiles, raking his hand through his longish, light hair. The muscles on his arms bulge as he hoists himself out, a gleam in his stormy-blue eyes.

"Loosen up, babe. There's nothing underneath that dress we haven't seen before. Get in the pool."

I wonder if this is what all parties at Theo and Thalia's are like or if the three young boys in the pool mistook the gathering for a frat party. They're in college, after all, working evening shifts at the restaurant to earn money for booze.

For every step Jax takes forward, I step back.

I hold out my hand to keep him at a distance. "I said *no*." My back hits the patio furniture, my pulse roaring the closer he gets.

"Alright, alright. Chill out, girl," he chuckles, raising his hand in defeat. "Suit yourself." He turns around, taking small steps back toward his friends.

I breathe a sigh of relief... all too soon.

Jax spins again, lunging forward to cuff my wrist, and Timothy jumps in to help. Too bad he's helping Jax, not me. The pool party cheers, laughing as the two of them drag me toward the edge despite me trying to free myself from their grasp.

"No!" I yelp, panic rushing through my head and voice. My mind races, and I can't... fuck, my head... I can't breathe already. "I'm not joking! Let me go! I can't swim! Please, I—"

The sentence runs short when they throw me into the water, fully dressed and still holding the glass of wine, its contents spilled all over the tiles.

There's no time for a deep breath. Whatever air was stored in my lungs is ejected when my chest connects with the sheet of water. Fear kicks in the second I go under.

My wet dress drags me down despite my frantic attempts to swim to the surface. Or maybe the uncoordinated hand waving and leg kicking drown me faster.

There's no leverage. Nothing to brace my legs against and

nothing to grab. I don't know; I can't *see* where is up and where is down. My lungs burn, screaming for air, a jab of intense pain coursing through me like a stark-white bolt of lightning, and my ribs feel as if they're being crushed by metal chains.

Oxygen drains from every cell in my body in pure agony. No longer thinking clearly, gasping for air, overcome by the primal need to breathe, I let my lips fall open. I shouldn't. I *know* I shouldn't, but it's a reflex I can't fight.

Water fills my lungs.

A sharp, stabbing pain pierces through my nervous system like thousands of needles, and pain synchs around my heart.

In a daze of terror, my eyes open, and I see the shimmer of sunlight reflecting off the water above as if to mock how vulnerable... how *helpless* I am, silently drowning.

FOUR

Logan

"Come on, MJ!" Someone yells in the garden, and my head involuntary snaps in that direction as I scrutinize the three kids in the pool. "Get in. The water is great," he adds.

Theo shrugs, waving me off when I shoot him a questioning look. "I expected that when Thalia told me to invite everyone from work. They're in college."

That explains their nerve to take a swim while the house is full of more and less sophisticated guests. The mayor is here with his wife. My grandparents are here, too.

Colt joins us with a handful of beers, filling in as our bartender for the evening. "They're alright." He hands me a bottle of Bud Light. "The one on the flamingo is a DJ. He played at our Spring Break party."

"You mean the party that almost had Nico issue the three of you with an eviction notice?" Theo chuckles, glancing sideways at the man in question, who's silently stewing as always.

"You need to learn to control the crowd, boys," I say, then tug a third of my beer. "And next year, make sure to get a few freshmen to do the dirty work."

"Like scraping puke off the pavement?" Conor asks, blowing his longish hair out of his face. "That's not a bad idea. Well done, bro." He smirks, patting my back.

The cocky little prick.

Triplets are still nineteen but just a few months away from turning twenty and getting cockier by the week.

A loud splash reaches my ears when someone—probably Mary-Jane, jumps in the water. Nico cuts her shrieking short, sliding the patio door shut and massaging his temples as if the noise is giving him a migraine.

So delicate, this one. Six-feet-three and benching three hundred and fifty pounds, but at the same time, he's rarely without an AirPod or earphone in his ear, listening to indie alternative rock, pop, or whatever that shit is.

"Top tip," I say, glancing between the triplets. "Hire a few port-a-johns next year and figure out a way to get Nico out of the house for the night."

"Whose side are you on?" Nico clips, resting against the wall. "You saw the state of the house after the party, Logan. Why do you think I want to remodel the ground floor? There's a big splotch on the wall in the guest bathroom after some chick projectile-vomited red wine."

I burst out laughing, recalling the pictures he sent to the group chat the morning after the party two weeks ago. Mayhem doesn't begin to cover it. Broken furniture, red solo cups littering every flat surface, and three bucket-loads of confetti and multi-colored crazy strings.

Oh, and the piano...

I was sure the triplets would pay with their heads for the beer spilled across the top and some asshole napping with his head on the keys. Nico doesn't play anymore, but the instrument in his living room is sacred. No one but our mother is allowed to as much as breathe in its direction.

It took the triplets three days to clean the mess. They replaced the flatscreen that ended up in the pool and re-painted the downstairs toilet but couldn't fix a few broken tiles and a hole some idiot punched in the wall with another idiot's head. Taking pity on the Holy Trinity, I sent my crew of contractors to help. Now I own their asses, and that'll come in handy one day when the time comes to collect the debt.

I pat Nico's back. "Did you forget what we used to get up to when we were their age? Cut them some slack. They'll know better next year. If they don't, you can always cash in their portfolios to cover repairs and a professional clean-up crew."

The triplets shake their heads in sync, positively mortified by the idea. In two years, they'll gain access to the stock portfolios Nico set up for them a few years ago, and I happen to know that each sits in the north six-figure range already.

Mine's on track to hit a million *again* by the end of the year. I already cashed a million last year to buy the house at the developers' price. They sell for north of two million on the market, but I designed and built them. It's only fair I get one cheap.

"I can't swim!" A high-pitched yelp reaches my ears despite the closed patio door. "Please, I—"

I sit up, recognizing Cassidy's distressed voice.

She doesn't finish, cut off by a loud splash. Two guys stand over the pool's edge, two more in the water with Mary-Jane, but Cassidy isn't there. The shriek of her voice has the fine hairs on my neck standing to attention. Anxiety jabs my mind, dragging cold fingernails down my spine while I wait for her to resurface.

Seconds tick by, but there's no sign of her blonde head. The guys stare, smirking under their noses, which is why I'm not moving. They wouldn't stand there ever so casual if she wasn't okay. Fifteen more seconds pass before one elbows the other, pointing at the water, his expression a portrait of restrained confusion. I don't wait for more.

They're glued to their spots as if wondering what their next move should be.

Fucking *jump*!

Fear pierces through me like a steel splinter. Almost half a minute had passed since Cass went under. She should've resurfaced by now. I shove my beer in Colt's chest, jump to my feet and cross the room, eyes on the two guys standing over the pool. Their faces turn more dubious by the second.

Cassidy's *I can't swim!* reverberates in my head on repeat like a broken record, silencing other sounds. I slide the door open and break into a sprint, alert and focused, as I shove aside the two assholes still staring at the pool.

Taking no time to assess the situation, I jump in, aiming for the girl in a red dress who sank to the bottom like an anchor.

She's thrashing as if violently shaken by invisible hands.

I swim closer, my muscles harder than stone. I know why she's thrashing like that. I've seen this back in college during swim practice. One of the guys fainted from exhaustion and toppled over into the pool. He had little air left in his lungs when he hit the water, and it didn't take long before oxygen depleted, and he started violently thrashing about just as Cassidy does now, drowning in my brother's pool.

Dread floods my mind the same way water floods her

lungs. Fear grips my throat. Memories blend with reality, but adrenaline spurs me on, deeper and faster.

Three seconds. That's all it takes to reach her, but it feels like I've been swimming for-*fucking*-ever.

Three seconds that are enough for her to stop moving. She's perfectly still, no longer an ounce of oxygen left in her body. She rests at the bottom of the pool, arms and hair floating around her head, mouth open, eyes shut. I grip her waist, pulling the limp body flush to my side, and plant my feet on the tiles for leverage, mustering all of my strength to shoot up, my vision blurry, eyes stinging from chlorine.

As we break the surface of the water, I suck in a harsh breath, pumping oxygen into my lungs.

But I don't hear the same from Cass.

She's not breathing.

The weight of the inevitable crushes me from the inside out.

My brothers stand by the edge, eyes wide and eyebrows raised. The rest of the party is outside, too, watching as Colt and Conor grip Cass under her arms, hauling her out of the pool.

A second later, I crawl the short distance across the artificial lawn to where she lies, ghastly pale and unmoving. Water drips from my hair, nose, and clothes, and my heart rams in my chest as if it's fucking hollow.

She's *not* breathing.

"Call an ambulance!" I yell, pushing Cassidy onto her back, my ear hovering over her lips.

A sense of impending doom creeps up from the pit of my stomach, seizing my racing mind. I pinch her nose, tilt her head, and open her mouth with trembling hands, then cover her lips with mine, forcing air into her lungs.

Once.

TOO WRONG

Twice.
And again.
And again.
And again.
Nothing.
It's not working.

"Come on, Cass," I mutter, swallowing something hot and bitter stuck to the back of my throat. I find her breastbone with my fingers and place my palm above it, starting chest compressions. "Come on, breathe. Breathe, breathe..." I chant quietly, deaf to the noise around us, focused on the lifeless girl with blueberry-blue lips and cheeks as white as curdled milk. I pump five more breaths into her lungs. "Fucking *breathe*, Cass." My muscles burn every time I press down on her chest.

"The ambulance is two minutes away," Theo says close behind me, his tone laced with a tiny fraction of the terror rushing through me, threatening to turn into a bright white freeze of panic.

This can't be happening.

She can't *die*.

"Don't stop, keep—" he cuts himself off when Cassidy gasps, fighting to inhale a single breath.

Her eyes pop open, mindless animal panic etched in the blue irises. A shudder of relief rattles through me like a picture coming back into focus. She breaks into a coughing fit.

"It's okay, it's okay," I say, repositioning her weak body into the recovery position. "You're okay, Cass. You're okay. Calm down, just breathe."

She jitters on the tiles, gasping for air in between coughing up half of the goddamn pool. She finds my hand and holds on tightly. Jesus, what... fuck! I can't focus on a single thought.

I squeeze her fingers, caressing the line of her spine until she stops spitting water like a loose garden hose, and I get some semblance of sanity while I see that she *is* breathing.

She jerks to a sitting position, breathing erratic, wide eyes staring into mine. Water trickles from her hair and down her nose, cheeks stained with tiny rivers of mascara.

"Don't try to talk," I say. Chlorine must be scorching her throat, and talking won't help. "Just breathe, okay?" I cup her shoulders, inhaling a deep, shaky breath through my mouth, and urge her to do the same. "Good, good," I chant. "Just like that. You're fine. You'll be okay."

She wraps her arms around her frail, trembling frame, teeth clattering from fear more than cold. Blonde hair sticks to her neck as she hugs herself, silent, struggling to contain the panic.

My pulse is still a disorganized gallop, but now that she's breathing, I hear the hushed voices around; I hear Theo still on the phone with the dispatch operator.

"God, you scared the hell out of me." Thalia drops to her knees beside us, wraps Cass in a towel, and hands one to me. She hugs Cassidy to her side, prompting more people to join and check if she's okay.

She almost died. She's *not* okay.

The chatter grows louder when I move away, patting my face dry and raking the towel through my hair; my bones all but evaporated, leaving nothing more than skin to hold me upright.

I stare at the pool, searching for my baseball cap to busy my brain and get a hold of the frantic emotions, but I don't locate it before my eyes come across the fucker who almost drowned Cassidy.

I don't stop to think. I never do.

I jump forward like a spring, grip him by the throat, throw

my hand back, and then send it whooshing across the air at full speed. My fist strikes his jaw. His head turns to the side, and blood bursts out of his mouth. I hit him again, blinded by the tornado of emotions swirling inside my head. It destroys the last of my composure the way the real thing destroys cities.

I can't see straight. I can't grasp a single rational thought as my fist connects with the asshole's face over again. More blood gushes from his nose. He slips out of my grasp at some point, tumbling to his knees, hands clasped over his face.

A few mortified gasps and my mother's outraged and frightened *Logan!* reach my ears as if it's a soundtrack to the unfolding scene, but I don't pay attention.

And I don't stop.

I'm barely able to see past the cloud of red madness.

"What the fuck were you thinking!?" I boom, yanking him by the collar to haul his ass back up. "I heard her scream she can't swim from the fucking living room!"

He pinches the bridge of his nose, head tilted back to increase the distance between us or stop the bleeding. His eyes gleam with fear, and shoulders sag. "I-I thought sh-she was kidding! So-sorry, I-I didn't—"

"Didn't think?!"

Nico grips my shoulder, digging his fingers into the bone hard enough to bruise as he yanks me back a step. "Calm down, Logan," he seethes quietly through clenched teeth so only I can hear him. "She's fine. She'll be okay."

The siren of the ambulance rips through the afternoon air, reminding me about Cassidy. I glance over my shoulder to where she still sits on the ground, pressed firmly against Thalia's side. I grit my teeth, pushing the rage to the background but not before I shove the fucker responsible with all my might.

With one minute of deep breaths, I'm composed when the paramedics, led by my father, enter the garden. His eyes are on me, not a trace of condemnation on his face for my outburst.

On the other hand, Mom's pale face could rival the whiteness of Cassidy's cheeks.

I'm even calmer when the paramedics hook Cass to oxygen and pull her onto a stretcher to take her in for evaluation at the hospital.

"How long was she unconscious?" One of them asks while another covers Cass with a blanket.

She's still shuddering, a harrowed, bleak look on her pretty face, eyes full of fright.

"About two and a half, maybe three minutes," Theo says, approaching the paramedic. "Logan started CPR as soon as he got her out of the water."

I'm only partially focused on helping Theo answer the questions. A, my rendition of the events is tainted by the tremor of panic that sizzled through my veins before Cass started breathing, and B, I'm still too fucking jittery to focus on anything other than her. Most of my attention is on her while she's convincing Thalia not to follow her to the hospital.

Why the fuck not?

Someone should go with her. Someone should keep her distracted. She almost *drowned*. She shouldn't be alone.

"Urgh, fine!" Thalia heaves, her accent flaring, a clear sign she's unhappy. "But call me when you get out of the hospital. And call me if you need anything." She runs inside the house to fetch Cassidy's bag.

Three minutes later, I watch the paramedics carry her out of the garden through the side gate.

Later that night, I lay awake, staring at the ceiling in my bedroom. The moonlight dances on the white canvas, casting shadows which, in a weird, twisted way, remind me of Cass's lifeless body. She could've died today.

Just like that.

A few seconds longer, and who knows if I would've brought her back. What if I were in the bathroom? Or at the front of the house checking out Nico's new car. Or at home, making sure Ghost wouldn't eat Ares.

What if I wasn't there?

No one else paid attention to what was happening in the garden. How long before someone would react and jump in to pull her out of the pool?

Questions and *what-ifs* don't end for hours. The clock on the nightstand reads two a.m. when my phone pings.

Cass: It'll never be enough, but it's all I have... thank you.

I read the message ten times as if it's written in Greek. My fingers hover over the screen for a few minutes before I type a humorous reply in an attempt to break the tension. I feel like I've been trached, but instead of a tube, someone shoved the nozzle of an air compressor in my trachea and flipped the switch, inflating my lungs like balloons.

Me: I think your Guardian Angel has a drug problem.

Cass: He's tired of me now. He's been slacking for a while.

Me: Are you still at the hospital? What did the doctors say?

Cass: That I should take swimming lessons and that I'll be fine. They're releasing me in the morning.

Me: Get some sleep.

Cass: Goodnight.

I type out a reply, then delete it, then type again, and delete that too. After a couple more tries, I toss the phone on the nightstand with a deep groan, forcing my eyes shut.

FIVE

Logan

This is wrong.

If either of my brothers knew I was here, they'd never speak to me again, but I can't stop my legs from moving. I've spent the day talking myself out of coming here, but, as evident by me exiting my Charger outside Cassidy's apartment complex this fine Sunday evening, I failed.

The muscles in my shoulders, arms, and across my chest have been tense since I bolted out of Theo's living room yesterday. A flurry of dreadful emotions is still wrapped tightly around my bones, and I can't shake them.

I need to see her with my own eyes to believe she's okay. To override the image of her ashen face and blue lips flashing on the back of my eyelids whenever I fucking blink.

A text she sent earlier this morning when the doctor released her from the hospital wasn't enough to put my anxiety to rest. It's still there, an unrelenting tightness in my chest.

TOO WRONG

I shouldn't be here.

I shouldn't... but I am.

Against better judgment, I knock on the door three times. Anticipation tingles in my neck and the tips of my fingers, and then my skin prickles everywhere... not in a pleasant way.

Shit. Does she even still live here?

It would've been wiser to think about that before I knocked, wouldn't it? Three years had passed since the last time I was here. What if she moved?

The door flies open, putting my mind at ease for a brief second. It's Cassidy, alright. She still lives here.

And she's fucking naked.

Well, not exactly, but the black night dress is lacey on her stomach and only covers the strategic places. I think that my own blood might give me second-degree burns. My pulse roars inside my head as I take her in, the curve of her hip, the swell of her breasts... Lord, have fucking mercy.

Her eyes grow wider, and her no-longer ashen cheeks pink up before she slams the door in my face, a gust of warm air smelling like her fans my face.

"Hold on!" she yells as soft footsteps retreat further inside the flat.

I wait, my legs nailed to the floor. I wait, even though I itch to kick the door down, run after her and tear the nightdress off that smoking hot body. I wait, even though I want to slam her against the wall, clasp my hand over her mouth, and make her bite my flesh as she comes on my cock.

No.

Hell no.

That's not happening. It can't happen. I'd be as good as dead if Nico or Theo ever found out.

The door opens again, wider this time, and Cassidy gestures with her hand, inviting me inside. In the thirty seconds she was gone, she swapped the black night dress for grey sweatpants and a t-shirt. Too bad she didn't bother with a bra.

Puckered nipples press against the white fabric so thin I make out the exact shape of her areolae. I should leave. I feel like I'm poised on the edge of a cliff, trying to catch my balance and keep my footing. A rush of intense heat fires up in my chest and travels straight to my dick.

"You're the last person I expected to stop by," she admits, resting her back against the kitchen counter, arms crossed under her boobs, making them stand out even more.

Her eyes are higher, asshole. Look up.

I do. Not without struggle. Her eyes shine with uncertainty today. Better that, than the panic I saw yesterday.

Yesterday...

She almost drowned, and here I am, thinking of ways to impale her on my cock. "I wanted to check how you're doing."

A small smile curves her rosebud lips. The same ones that turned a nasty shade of blue yesterday. "I'm better. Do you want a drink?" She opens the fridge. "I've got juice, water, and beer. Not Bud Light, though. Corona."

"Corona's good."

No, it fucking isn't.

Beer is alcohol; alcohol is impaired judgment, and impaired judgment while I'm alone with Cassidy is a big no-no considering my rock-hard cock. Good job that I'm in my jersey, the bulge easily disguisable.

I don't change the answer, watching her pop the caps on two bottles with undeniable ease. The cart girl in her is still alive and kicking even though she quit her job at the Country

Club last year to pursue her dream. She now owns a photography studio in town.

She hands me the beer, eyes on the neck of the bottle instead of my face.

"You didn't sleep much," I say, breaking the uncomfortable silence ringing in my ears.

"How do you know?"

Because you don't look so good might not be the best line to say to a woman. I settle for a less obnoxious option. "You texted me in the middle of the night, then again early this morning."

"I didn't sleep at all. Hospital beds are uncomfortable, and nightmares didn't help." Her cheeks heat again as if she said too much. "You didn't need to come here but thank you."

"Stop thanking me." I take a swig from the bottle, veering the conversation to safe waters. "How is it that you live by the beach in a town where almost every house has a swimming pool, yet you can't swim?"

She moves toward the loveseat on the other side of the room, gesturing for me to follow. Joining her on the loveseat is out of the question. Too close. Too intimate.

I hijack the wing chair tucked in the corner under a row of floating shelves bending under the weight of romance books. The last time I was here, it was dark, and I was too preoccupied with undressing Cassidy to pay attention to the surroundings. The flat is minuscule but functional. The loveseat is pushed against the wall, a few plants stand on the windowsill, and a large floor lamp hangs over the chair I'm in.

Cass tucks her feet under her bum, folding a fluffy blanket and readjusting a few pillows as if she can't sit still. Once she runs out of things to do, she takes her beer from the coffee table, looking at me. "Neither one of my families thought of signing me up for swimming lessons, and none of them had a pool. No beaches, either."

"Families?" I ask, taking off my baseball cap. "Plural?"

"Fourteen of them. I was in foster care for six years before I turned eighteen."

How did I not know that? I know she graduated with a photography degree. I loved the passion in her voice when she spoke about her dream of opening a studio. Her favorite color is blue. Her birthday is in November, she can't stomach seafood, and she's allergic to hazelnuts. I know the answers to all standard first-date questions, but I don't know anything about the shit that matters.

Why do you care?

"Six years and fourteen families? Why were you moving so often? And how did you end up in foster care?"

I prop my ankle on my knee, watching her while she watches me as if wondering whether to brush me off or take a leap of faith and open up about her past.

She wouldn't have hesitated three years ago, but things are different now. The connection we had back then died a sad, immediate death when I learned she slept with my brother a week before we spent the most memorable night of my life together.

To this day, I still recall that intense pull in my gut, that overpowering need to have her close, touch, kiss, and hold her locked in my arms all night. It was, hands down, the most bizarre and fascinating feeling I had ever encountered.

"My dad started drinking when I was three," Cass says, scratching the corner of the beer label with her long, beige fingernail. "Two years later, Mom was drinking too. I was mostly raised by our neighbor, Ms. Jones. She fed me and did a grocery run every morning while I walked to school so she could keep an eye on me. My parents were drunk most days, and once I turned ten, they started disappearing, leaving me alone for days." She blows out a sad, defeated breath down her nose, peering up to meet my eyes, hers dull, lacking the natural glow. "I think Ms. Jones thought she was doing right by me when she called social services."

What kind of parents abandon their child for *days*? I try not to imagine the frightened blonde girl sitting alone in a cold, empty house, hungry and worried, but that's just it… when you try not to think about something, you can't stop.

"She wasn't? You were neglected by your parents, Cass. I'd say she should've called them much sooner."

Knowing this shouldn't affect me the way it does. It shouldn't affect me at all, but I'm not made of stone, and a ball of sadness swells behind my ribs. Cass isn't that little girl anymore, but as she sits on the loveseat, it seems her eyes don't remember how to smile.

Life is unfair. I was cared for, loved, and showered with affection my entire life, living in my parents' mansion, surrounded by my brothers. Cassidy was left to fend for herself. I can't shake the images shuffling in my head. The most bizarre scraps that add to the horrific scene. I don't even know if those are remotely close to what she went through, but I see them nonetheless; teary eyes, dirty clothes, scraped knees.

"My parents weren't the best," she admits with a slight shrug. "But there are worse people out there. Some of the families that took me in…" She shakes her head, dismissing the memories. "I quickly understood hunger and loneliness aren't the worst feelings."

The question lingers on the tip of my tongue. Unasked. I

want to know what the worst feeling is, but at the same time, I don't want to hear it. The scenarios multiplying in my head grow more sinister by the second. I'm already on edge, knowing she wasn't cared for. I don't want her to relive whatever shit she went through.

"Have you ever seen your parents since you were placed in foster care?"

"No. I don't even know if they're still alive." She forces a sad chuckle and suddenly straightens up, cheeks warmer again. "Sorry, I didn't mean this conversation to turn so heavy. It's in the past. I've been okay for years."

Jesus, what the hell is she doing to me? One word, and she almost broke me clean in half. *Okay* instead of *happy*? I can't help but wonder if she's ever been truly happy. She sure doesn't look like she ever was.

"You've been in Newport for a few years now," I say, changing my train of thought again. "You've had plenty of time to learn how to swim."

A soft knock on the door startles us both.

"Sorry, it's probably Kaya."

Every emotion I felt a second ago dissipates and is instantly replaced by pure wrath burning my veins.

Just my fucking luck.

Although, I'm a tiny bit grateful for Cruella's intrusion. Everyone with ties to the bitch is automatically an accessory to Nico's downfall, which means coming here was a dumb idea. Despite my noble and innocent intentions...

I. Shouldn't. Be. *Here.*

Though considering the amount of time I spent gawking at Cass's tits, my intentions might not be all that pure. A phone call would've sufficed, but Logan thinks *after* he acts.

Stupid prick, that guy.

"I'm out." I rise to my feet.

Her pretty face flickers with disappointment, and I clench my teeth, adamant about leaving. She gives me a tight nod, aware there's no way in hell I'll spend one second with Cruella. We cross the room, and Cassidy opens the door to reveal the devil herself, a slim brunette with a strikingly beautiful exterior that doesn't match the strikingly vile interior.

God, she's so fucking beautiful that not one man on earth would resist her charm.

My presence forces a scowl mixed with surprise to twist Kaya's perfect face, and her mouth falls open. "What the fuck are you doing here?" she snaps, arms akimbo.

I shoulder past the bitch, my legs on autopilot.

"Don't be rude," Cassidy hisses. "Just go inside, okay? I'll be right back. Logan, wait. Please."

The door to her apartment closes louder than it should while soft footsteps trail behind me. A small, warm hand cuffs my arm. Or tries, at least. Cass's fingers don't come anywhere near meeting.

"I'm sorry. She was supposed to be here hours ago. I didn't think she'd show up this late." She steps around me, her light, almost platinum-blonde hair flirting with her shoulders. "Thank you for coming. If there's ever anything I can do for you... I'm just saying, I owe you."

"Stop thanking me," I huff, marshalling my expression into indifference, so she won't see how titillating the touch of her hand around my bicep is. "You don't owe me, but if you want to do something, get yourself a new Guardian Angel. I won't be around next time you take a swim, and someone should be."

She smiles an adorable smile that, for the first time, reaches her baby blues surrounded by long, black eyelashes, and the air compressor in my chest fires up again.

What the fuck is that?

Whatever it is, it pushes me a step forward. I crowd her space, towering above her five-foot-five, lean frame, and I *feel* the warmth radiating off her body in waves; the fresh, zesty smell of ginger and lemons; the magnetic pull. She gazes up at me, unmoving, eyes darker, pupils blown. The air around us becomes too thick to inhale when she parts her lips, letting out a long, shaky breath.

The door on my left opens, and one of Cassidy's neighbors stops on the threshold with a black bin bag in hand. I take the opportunity to take a step away from Cass and let the guy pass. Robbed of her proximity, my head clears of the lustful fog, and my hands ball into fists in frustration.

I have no control around this girl. "Good night, Cass."

Another disappointed grimace. "Good night, Logan."

Move... you dumb prick. Fucking *run*.

And I do.

I exit the building because my resolve is slipping, and it's either increasing the distance between us or reducing it until our bodies fuse in her bed.

SIX

Cassidy

The overdoor bell chimes when the last client of the week enters my studio at five to six on Saturday afternoon. Strawberry blonde hair flutters around her gorgeous face as she takes in the place. Craning her long, slim neck right and left, she scans the many portraits hanging on the walls.

"Hey, can I help?" I ask, stopping the tedious task of tidying up the space before we close.

Well, *I* close. My business partner, Luke, took the afternoon off to get ready for a party and left me to ensure the props are safely back in the cabinets and the studio is ready for a commercial photo shoot he has booked on Monday morning with the local jeweler.

"Hey, yes. You're Cassidy, right? I've been told you're the best around here when it comes to portrait photography," She comes closer, eyes still on the pictures for a moment before she extends her hand. "I'm Aisha Harlow."

"Harlow," I repeat, knotting my eyebrows. "Aisha Harlow. Why does that sound familiar?"

She beams, biting on her lip coated with pink lip gloss, clearly pleased I recognize her surname. "Maybe you've read one of my books?"

"Yes!" I exclaim when it clicks. Aisha Harlow, the Queen of smutty romance. "I've read them *all*, girl. God, I *love* your writing." She has a knack for storytelling. From the first words, you're sucked in and can't put the book down.

Just one more chapter... yeah, right. Whenever I get my hands on her new release, I don't start the book until I have six to eight hours free to finish it in one sitting.

"I didn't know you're from around here."

"Not many people do," she admits, circling the room again. "I tend to say I'm from Orange County but don't specify Newport Beach." She spins on her high stiletto heel to face me again. "Anyway, I need a reliable photographer to snap pictures for the covers."

I quickly recall the covers of Aisha's books, wondering what type of photography she has in mind. "So, handsome, half-naked men in sexy, broody poses?"

"Exactly. I'll hire a model I like and send him your way so you can work your magic." She points to Luke's picture that's displayed by the main door. The camera loves him. He's handsome and a touch narcissistic and loves the attention posing in front of a camera provides. In his spare time, he eagerly volunteers to model for me whenever I want to expand my portfolio. "That sort of thing. I know it's getting late, and I've got somewhere to be right now, so how about you tell me when we could talk this through over coffee?"

I pull out my notebook to check the calendar. "I'm free

on Tuesday from noon till three. Does that work?"

"Perfect. Meet me in the café around the corner."

We exchange phone numbers, and Aisha leaves, her step bouncy, hair and hips swaying. A tall, ripped, bald man waits outside, resting against a black motorcycle. He's an incarnation of one of the male characters in her books, and I wonder if he's her boyfriend or just a research case.

I finish cleaning and locking the studio and then text Luke, my excitement palpable in the air.

Me: You'll never believe WHO just came by the studio!

Luke: Jesus.

I chuckle, open the door to my car, and place my bag on the passenger seat.

Me: Almost. Aisha Harlow. Remember the book I gave you last month? She wrote that. She wants me to take pictures for her covers. We're meeting next week to talk over the details!

Luke: Holy shit! You lucky duck. You better recommend me as the model for one of them.

Me: She saw your picture. I think you have a shot.

We text back and forth for a while, and once again, he tries to convince me to join the party tonight. As much as I love Luke and his boyfriend, I'm not keen on their crowd. Too much alcohol and coke-snorting for my liking.

I toss the phone on the passenger seat and start my beloved

yellow Fiat, reversing out of a parking space. "Mickey" by Toni Basil seeps from the speakers, but it's not the radio. It's my phone and the ringtone I set for MJ.

"Hello?"

"Babe! Please tell me you're free tonight!" She cries. "Amy stood me up, and I need a wingman!"

"A wingman? Isn't it wingwoman?" No, that doesn't sound right. Winglady? "I don't have plans, but—"

"Thank God! Amy's got a stomach bug and—" She gasps theatrically. "Holy cow! Maybe she's pregnant?! I mean, who the hell starts puking out of the blue? She's been moody as fuck lately, too."

"Babe, you're veering off-topic. People do get sick out of the blue, you know?" I check the rearview mirror when someone beeps while I'm waiting for the red light to change. Shit. It's already changed. "It's not like you get a postcard a week in advance as a heads-up."

"Yeah, yeah," she mumbles. I think she's eating. Knowing MJ, it's probably a glazed donut. I wish I had her metabolism. She can eat whatever she wants and never gains weight, while I kill myself at the gym to stay in shape. "But if she *is* expecting, remember I guessed it first."

"I'll make a note of that. Now get to the point."

"Oh, right, yeah, so please, please, *please* come with me tonight! It'll be so much fun, I promise!"

"Come with you *where*?"

"Express Dates! I booked two spots, but as Amy may or may not be with child, she can't come. *Please, please*—"

"Alright!" I cut the pleading short. She will mutter *please* on repeat for as long as it takes me to say yes. I groan, flipping the indicator. "That sounds dreadful. Why would you even want to go there?"

"To meet guys. Why else?" She huffs down the line. "Come on, you could use a guy, too. When was the last time you had a date?"

Three months ago. I went out with a guy I met online. His name was Mathew, and he made it a point of honor to ensure I knew it was spelt with just *one* t. He's the reason why I signed out of dating apps. A young God in the pictures turned out to be a scrawny, scruffy man with a Napoleon complex. Worst date of my life. At least at the Express Dates, I won't be buying a basket of crap.

"Fine. Where and what time?"

"*Well...* it's at that new bar not far from *Q. Amaretto* or *Argento*. We need to be there at seven. I'll pick you up quarter to."

"Seven?! It's ten past six, and I'm not even home yet."

"Love you!" She giggles before disconnecting the call.

Great. I've got half an hour to get home, take a shower, get dressed, and do my make-up. Who the hell does she think I am? Sonic the Hedgehog?

SEVEN

Logan

Thirty people.

Fifteen women, fifteen men. Five minutes per date.

Not how I imagined Saturday evening, but Nico, Adrian, and Toby are getting too creative. Well, I guess in this case, it's Nico's messed-up brain at work. It was his stupid idea to take part in Express Dates.

"Tonight is the night!" Toby booms, entering the modern cocktail bar, a spring in his step. "You're going down, Logan. Down, d-d-down, *down*!"

Fuck if I will.

Adrian grips my shoulders, swaying me from left to right, his excitement reflected in an ear-to-ear grin, teeth showing. They might be onto something. Express dates are the perfect setting to find a girl who'll tell me to beat it. It's not a place for people wanting to have a bit of fun. No, express dates are designed for those searching for a soul mate and getting pretty desperate.

I'm not worried, though. In fact, I couldn't care less.

The bets started out fun, but after a few weekends, they got just as boring as anything. Too bad my pride won't let me wave a white flag. I've won eight watches thanks to those bets, and I'll win the ninth.

The hostess at the door writes our names on white labels and sticks them to our chests. She's plausible—blonde, decent rack, and nice hips, but like most women in Newport Beach and Orange County—forgettable.

"Feel free to grab a drink and then take a seat at a table of your choice once the first bell sounds." She gestures toward the double door.

Adrian walks in first, turning his head left and right. He's openly staring, on a hunt for someone to stick his cock in tonight. Anyone will do. Adrian's not picky.

With five minutes to order a drink before the torture begins, I rest my elbows on the counter, waiting for the bartender to approach. I've not been here yet, even though the place has been open for six months. Newport is the mecca for people loaded with cash. New bars like this pop up all over the place while young entrepreneurs try to capitalize on the wealthy.

The room is dimly lit, fifteen small booths scattered around to form a semi-circle, each equipped with a table and a small bouquet of lilies of the valley. Their aroma hangs thickly in the air, overpowering fifteen brands of perfume and fifteen brands of cologne. Most booths are already occupied by women waiting for the dates to start.

Thankfully, I don't recognize any of them, and not one catches my attention for longer than a quick glance.

Toby gestures for the bartender while I scan the room,

wondering which woman my friends will choose to be my target tonight. Not one stands out of the crowd, and not one looks particularly prone to fun.

Not one looks particularly prone to say *no* to me, either.

"Hell yes!" Adrian whisper-shouts, craning his neck to see over my shoulder.

I do a one-eighty just as two men move away with their drinks, revealing a slim, sharp-featured woman in a *suit*—a white shirt, red blazer and trousers to match. She's in desperate need of a little procedure I like to call a *stickectomy*. Definition: she has a stick up her ass, and someone should remove it immediately.

I doubt I'll be the one to accomplish the task, though. She's Nico's type. Dark, straight hair in a high ponytail, features sharp enough to cut glass, and a no-bullshit look on her stunning face. I turn to my brother, but he's not interested in the brunette, eyeing something on the other side of the room.

I follow his line of sight and curse inwardly.

Mary-Jane crosses the room, closely followed by none other than *Cassidy*. A navy dress with short sleeves hugs her hips and waist, accentuating the not-too-big boobs.

"I'm out," Nico says, draining the glass of whiskey the bartender slid his way less than thirty seconds ago. "Call me when you're done here."

"No way." I grip his forearm before he wanders away. "Chill, it's just Cassidy and Mary-Jane. No Kaya."

"Yeah, and whatever happens tonight will be promptly reported back to Kaya. Thanks, but no thanks."

"Why do you care if she knows what you're doing?" *Please, dear God, please* don't let my brother still have feelings for Cruella, or I'll have to knock rational thinking back into his brain with a baseball bat. "To hell with the bitch, Nico.

And to hell with Jared, too."

He grinds his teeth, glaring at Cassidy as if she were the one cheating on him. A minute goes by while he's deciding Nico-style—overthinking and overanalyzing. "Fine." He turns back to the bar to order another drink. "But you're taking over my dates with Cass. I have nothing to talk to her about."

Dumb idea.

Really fucking dumb idea. My mind has been occupied by Cassidy for two weeks now. I shouldn't spend another minute in her presence, but it's either that or Nico will storm out without a backward glance.

"Yeah, whatever. She doesn't bite, bro. Don't forget it's thanks to her that—"

"Zip it," he snaps, his tone implying he'll bite my head off if I don't drop the subject.

There's no talking to him about the night he saw Kaya with Jared in a compromising yet creative position.

The girl Adrian chose as my game tonight stilettoes across the room, her steps small but confident, shoulders back and head high. Her long ponytail swings to the sides before she takes a seat, crossing one leg over the other. She's unapproachable in a sexy way. Her every move is punctuated by an aura of superiority, making men do a double take. I almost hear the thoughts screaming in their heads.

She closes her blood-red lips on a straw, cheeks purposely hollow when she sucks in a sip of a pink cocktail as if to subtly admit she's a freak in bed.

It does the job. She'll be hit on by every asshole here. Me included, apparently.

"Maybe that's not the best idea." Toby pulls a face, eyeing the sex bomb with a glint of awe and timidity shining in his blue eyes. "I think she might chop Logan's dick off if he steps out the wrong way. I don't want to have that on my conscience."

"I agree," I say, genuinely relieved. I sure don't do well with overconfident, standoffish women. "She's way out of my league. Let Nico have her. If anyone can tame Queen Bee, it's you." I elbow his ribs to cheer him up a bit, but the smirk I want in return fails to arrive.

Figures. The day that asshole actually smiles, I'll probably be so taken aback I'll have a goddamn aneurysm.

He glances over his shoulder to check her out, moderately interested. I don't think there's a woman walking this earth that'd make Nico fall over his feet.

"Game on," he says.

Adrian huffs, unamused. "Fine, you can have her, Nico. And you," he grips my shoulder, checking the women out again, "take the one at table six."

The girl in question can't be older than a senior at college and has been ogling us since we walked through the door.

"At least try to make this a challenge."

"Look at her!" he cries loudly, and a few heads snap in our direction. "I bet she's a preacher's daughter." A preacher's daughter in need of some serious fucking. "She won't fall for your bullshit. And if she will," he glances between Nico and Toby, "I'll buy him that watch myself. I'll even get your face tattooed on my ass if she gives you her number, man."

I don't always want to punch Adrian, just most of the time. He's such an animal.

"So I don't have to kiss her this time?"

"No, but you only have two dates to work your magic."

"I really don't want to tattoo Logan's face on your butt, Adrian," Toby says. "I don't want to touch your butt!"

TOO WRONG

"Good evening, and welcome to Express Dates." A man at the front of the room booms into a microphone, stopping our conversation. What a *pity*. "The rules are simple. Please affix the label with your name to your chest and sit at a table of your choice. Once the bell sounds, gentlemen move to the next table, clockwise. We'll have a fifteen-minute break after round one, and you can call out a waitress anytime if you need a refill. Enjoy."

Most men rush to take a seat, but the four of us have all the time in the world. Maybe if I were supposed to sit at table six and start the show, I'd rush, but there's already some asshole there. Once most men choose a table, I sit by number twelve where a trust-fund, spoiled bimbo with Botox almost seeping out of her pores toys with a lock of pink hair.

Cass is on the other side of the semi-circle, and I have a clear view of her pretty face. I still don't know what the hell changed that made her beauty pop, but she draws attention like a loud bang on a silent night.

From time to time, I glance toward my target's table, hoping to learn something about her before our date. I like to have an ace up my sleeve, but she gives me nothing to go by. Her body language is reserved, hands on the glass, a slight hunch to her shoulders. I turn to her more often because that's about all that stops me from openly staring at Cassidy when she laughs with different men at her table.

They wouldn't know where to start to make her scream.

The label on the girl at table six reads *Sofie*. Her wineglass has been empty for at least two dates, but neither of the jackasses before me noticed. I call over a waitress and order another beer for myself and wine for her. That's my usual strategy: charm the girl with drinks.

"I don't drink wine," Carmen, the woman before me, points to her tall glass of beer.

If the fact she gulps lager like a dude isn't repulsive enough, the large, black goop of mascara in the corner of her right eye sure is. I don't mind women drinking beer, but Carmen isn't drinking. She pours the golden liquid down her throat without swallowing as if it's a party trick that's supposed to impress me.

"I noticed."

The bell rings again. It's my turn to sit in front of Cassidy, but I walk past her, holding up my index finger to let her know I'll be right back. I stop at table six, placing the wine beside Sofie's empty glass. Her eyes roam down my body, lips pursed, and a satisfied gleam shining in her eyes. She's pretty, and I can picture myself trailing a line of kisses up the column of her throat, but then she opens her mouth, and the bubble bursts.

"Am I supposed to drop my panties now?" she asks, a hint of playfulness layering her voice.

The line hits me all wrong. Instead of being excited by the possibility, I have an eye-roll kind of moment. "You're supposed to say *thank you*, honey."

A faint blush creeps onto her cheeks, marking her neck and cleavage along the way. "Thank you ..." She looks down at my chest. "...*Logan*. I don't think it's your turn at my table just yet."

No, it's not, and the impatient man on my left thinks so too, his arms folded across his chest, eyes pinning me down with a forceful stare.

"I'll be back in five," I add before I hit reverse and sit by Cassidy's table.

She toys with ice cubes in her half-empty glass, looking out of place, unsure what to expect from our date. Neither do I. An aura of imminent danger settles around us as the ginger and lemon scent of her body lotion or hair shampoo targets my nose, and my dick stirs hell in my jeans.

Down, boy.

"Have you signed up for swimming lessons?" I ask, lacking a better idea. My mind blanks around her.

A light, casual chat is what I'm aiming for. Nothing inappropriate. Nothing to suggest I have the urge to spread her wide open on the tiny table between us, lick her sweet pussy until she comes, and then drive my cock deep inside to feel her come around my length.

"No, and I won't," she admits, unease fading, a smile taking its place. That's better. "Maybe my angel will stop using."

"Don't rely on that guy." *Aaaand...* blank. I've no idea how to proceed. I've not been this awkward around a woman since *ever*. Cass and I spent a few evenings together three years ago, so I know about the shit that's usually discussed on first dates. It's not like I can ask about her favorite color again. "So..." Crickets. All-round *crickets*. What the fuck do I say now? My pulse riots before a last-resort, not-too-bright idea pops into my head. "What brings you here of all places? What kind of guy are you looking for?"

"Amy's not well, and MJ needed a chaperone."

"You didn't answer my question." I drink from the bottle of Bud Light. "What kind of a man are you looking for, Cass?"

"What about you?" She side-steps again, combing back those alluring blonde strands that tangle in the long earrings she wears.

I want to reach out, untangle her hair, then nuzzle my face in the crook of her neck and *inhale*.

Why didn't she answer? Is she embarrassed? Undecided? Maybe she's taken. Maybe there's a boyfriend at her tiny studio flat, waiting patiently until she comes home.

Unlikely.

No sane man would let his girl get hit on by fifteen men.

"I see you're still betting the guys they won't find a girl who'll resist your charm." She casts an inconspicuous glance over her shoulder, checking out my target for tonight. "She's cute. I can't see you losing tonight."

I already forgot about the preacher's daughter, too preoccupied with Cassidy. I've not realized I've been leaning further and further across the table until she rests her elbows on the tabletop, mirroring my stance. The pleasant scent of her body intensifies, summoning the memories again.

Sweet, breathless gasps in my ear when I drove into her, my head in a state of utter confusion because that night, we weren't fucking. I can't say we were making love, but it was more than what I've experienced thus far and ever since.

"Adrian thinks she's too good of a girl to fall for my shit."

Cassidy casts another glance over her shoulder. Goosebumps dot the delicate skin of her neck, stealing my attention, and I need to fight my instincts not to lean over the table and kiss them away.

"Adrian might be a poor judge of character. You won't have to try too hard."

I know. Sofie's been gawking over here twice a minute, seductively licking her lips. She'd let me have my way with her at the back of this bar without giving it much thought.

The bell rings, ending the date, and I check Nico's location to make sure I'll switch with him at the right time. He's three tables away, about to sit in front of Queen Bee.

"Good luck," Cass whispers when I rise to my feet.

"I don't need luck, princess."

TOO WRONG

Her lips part into an inaudible *oh* at the endearment, eyes widen, and pupils dilate. She probably recalls the last time I called her that. Three years ago... *come for me, princess.*

Sofie beams when I arrive at her table, readjusting my jeans as I take a seat. I've lost interest in pursuing this girl, but even without wooing or engaging in conversation, Sofie twirls her hair around her finger, batting her eyelashes.

You're trying too hard, honey.

I'm still within earshot of Cassidy's table, my back to hers, so I can't see, but the tone of the man's voice paints a vivid picture of what Cass must look like right now—arms crossed, eyes narrowed, lips pursed.

"You're impossible," he says louder than necessary. "What was wrong with our date? We had a nice meal, you laughed, we talked—"

"Do you think you can coerce another date out of me?" Cass asks. "Have some dignity."

"You need to grow up and fast, sweetheart. You think you'll find your Prince charming here?! Look around! I'm the best shot you have."

"I don't want a Prince charming, and I sure don't want a misbehaving puppy."

I bite my tongue to stop myself from laughing. The waitress stops by the booth to see if we need a refill. Acting on an impulse, I order a beer for myself and a daiquiri for Cass, instructing the waitress to deliver it to her table.

Sofie's talking my ear off for two more minutes before the bell rings. If held at gunpoint, asked to quote one sentence that came out of her mouth during our date, I'd end up with a through-and-through gunshot wound to my head.

She's so dull she'd put an insomniac to sleep.

Once I reach my next date, I no longer bother to even fake interest. I'm chasing my own thoughts, trying to make sense of my sudden obsession with Cassidy.

Her lifeless body flashes before my eyes as if to answer the incessant questions. Is that why I can't stop thinking about her? Because I saved her life?

That's *infuriating*.

I can't fucking drown her to fix the problem.

And it is a problem. Going after her would equal going against my family, and that can't happen. They come first.

Always. No matter what.

The woman in front of me seems mildly annoyed, and rightly so. I'm vague, disinterested, and gawking over my shoulder too often, checking on Cass instead of Sofie.

Some guy in a white polo shirt sits in front of her, his demeanor laid-back, careless even. Cass brushes a few strands of hair away from her face just as the bell rings, and it's once again my turn to entertain her for five minutes when Nico trades with me, taking table nine.

The polo-shirt guy meets my gaze as he rises to his feet with an annoyed scowl. "Don't bother with this one. All you'll get here are blue balls."

"I bet yours already are. Move, or I'll give you a black eye to pair with the set."

He scoffs, shaking his head as if he feels sorry for me.

Kids are taught algebra, mitosis, and where Mongolia is, but no one teaches them that pissing off a guy twice their size is a bad idea. Someone really should include that in the curriculum. Maybe if the polo shirt got the memo, he'd think twice before disregarding me. That's strike one. One more, and he'll bleed.

He moves to the next table, his attitude changing to gigolo

when he spots Sofie, the eye candy.

Cass clears her throat, drawing my attention.

"What?" I ask, taking a seat. "Would you rather have Nico here?"

"No," she mouths, alarmed by the idea. My brother has that effect on women—scares them without saying a single word. "Thank you for trading with him."

"He threatened to leave when he saw you, so I didn't have much choice."

Her smile slips immediately. "If you'd rather stand by the bar for the next five minutes, I won't mind."

My eyes drop to her lips for a brief second before I look back up in time to see her cheeks heating. "I'll stay."

EIGHT

Cassidy

MJ closes her hand around my arm and drags me down a narrow corridor. She pushes the door to the toilet open, her eyes glassy from wine, excitement, or because she's horny.

I can't tell.

"I'm in love!" she squeals.

Horny. Definitely horny.

"Already? Doesn't take you long, does it?" I turn toward the mirror to check the state of my make-up and hair. "Who's the lucky guy?"

She grips my forearm tighter, stepping from foot to foot like an impatient, ecstatic child. "Adrian, the guy who's always with Nico and Toby. We used to text a bit, but he lost interest, and now..." she squeals again. "I think he's ready to start over! What am I supposed to do? I want him. I really, really want him! I want him for longer. Maybe forever."

That's not a first. MJ falls in love three times a month on

average. Her affection dies as fast as it comes to life like a cheap firework. Timothy is a prime example; *I love him!* fast forward two weeks, and *I hate him!* She's a challenge to please.

I rack my brain, combing through the dates, trying to recall Adrian and my general impression of the guy, but since Logan sat at my table, I've been watching him through a single-point focus lens, and every other man became a blur.

MJ snaps her fingers in front of my face. "Earth to Cass. What's up? Who are the dreamy eyes for?"

"No one worth my time," I say aloud as a reminder of the dreaded fact that keeps eluding me. "About Adrian... I have no idea what you're supposed to do. Wrong person to ask. I've not been out on a decent date in a long time."

"But guys keep coming back to you regardless! Take James. He's been staring at you all night! He wants you even though you cut him loose an hour into your date."

"James wants to get in my pants. I assume Adrian already was in yours. Maybe try and make him work for it this time?"

She kisses my cheeks as if I've unraveled an ancient secret. As soon as we're back in the dimly lit room, James blocks my path. MJ flees, winking at me out of his view, her heart and mind set on playing cupid.

"Hey, babe," he drawls with a cocky grin. "How about you give me another chance? Let's ditch this place and grab dinner, hmm? What do you say, babe?"

I want to say *don't call me babe; it sounds cheap*, but I have an unclear feeling it might spur him on. He touches his hand to my face, caressing my cheek, and stares into my eyes in a way he considers seductive but comes off creepy.

"You're not stupid, so I don't know which part of *I'm not interested* you don't get." I step back so he can't touch me.

"There won't be another date."

His jaw tics, and his patience wears off just like during our first date. He cuffs my wrist, forcing me to follow him into the corner of the room. He pushes me against the wall, looming over me, still holding my wrist. My heart thumps faster. His hot breath fans my face, making me break out in chills.

"What the hell is your problem, Cass? Take that stick out of your ass and let's go have fun. You'll love what I'll do with you."

A small smile blossoms on my lips when Logan materializes behind him and grips his shoulder, knuckles white the harder he squeezes, yanking James back, a stormy glare aimed at the back of his skull. "I can't say you'll love what I'll do with you if you don't let her go. It doesn't take me much to snap, so I suggest you back the fuck off."

James rolls his eyes, not anticipating what he'll find behind him. "You got a problem?" He turns around, shrinking in on himself when he's forced to tilt his head back to meet Logan's stare. "This doesn't concern you, man. Cassidy is here with me."

What? Who does he think he is?

"I'm not," I clip, pushing away from the wall.

Logan's eyes dart to me, sliding down my body briefly before he focuses his attention back on James. "As I said, I don't take long to snap, *man*. You're on borrowed time already. Keep that in mind while you decide what your next move should be."

James's hands ball into tight fists at his sides, and for a short moment, I think he'll throw care to the wind, take a leap of faith in his questionable abilities, and hit Logan, but a heartbeat later, he shrugs out of his grasp and storms away.

"Thank you. He's very frustrating." I step closer, drawn to Logan, the safety he offers, and the intoxicating smell of his toned body.

"Yeah, I can see that. Get back to your table. We're about to start the next round." He gently pushes me in the right direction, heat pooling in my stomach when his big hand connects with the small of my back. "I'll see you in half an hour."

Half an hour that couldn't have passed any slower. I try my best not to glance in Logan's general direction, not to watch him entertain the women who stare at him as if they can telepathically force him to fuck them right here. The few times I cave and steal a glance, his eyes are on me, and a shiver slides down my spine, my pulse racing.

Adrian sits at my table not long later. He mostly talks and asks about MJ which is a nice change of topic from the standard date questions: favorite everything. I finish my drink when Logan comes back with a glass of daiquiri in hand, his face unreadable.

He slides the drink across the table, eyeing my lips for a fraction of a second before he averts his gaze. "Are you staying for the afterparty?"

"Afterparty?" I echo. No one mentioned that before.

"Yeah, Toby said that once the dates are over, people stay behind to get to know each other better."

"Is that before or after I'm supposed to hand out my phone number?"

"After. How many guys will get it, Cass?"

Zero.

"I'm not sure yet."

His eyes narrow, and he grits his teeth, I think. He composes himself so fast I'm not sure if I really saw a shadow of annoyance flicker across his face or if I made that up. "Adrian, Nico and Toby won't get your number. Neither will that idiot... James, was it? You're down to eleven."

"The man in the polo shirt won't get it, either. Ten."

He leans back in the chair. "The guy at table seven is picking his nose. Nine."

"Table thirteen; he's a gynecologist and lectured me about the tell-tale symptoms of ovarian cancer."

We narrow the list of possible candidates down to three, and with each one we eliminate, the reasons get sillier.

"Table one," Logan says in a hushed voice, hands resting on the table, our faces inches away while we whisper not to be overheard by the men we're ruling out. "He's got something stuck in his teeth. Two."

A shadow of a smile, barely a suggestion of one, plays across his full lips. He's so damn handsome. The smell of his cologne wraps around me, nuzzling me into a false sense of security. All I want is to curve myself into his body and fall asleep with my face buried in the crook of his neck. I want his arms around me. I want his lips on my temple. I want him to *want* me.

To care about *me*.

"Cass?" He nudges my hand with his finger. "What are you thinking about?"

"Sorry." I quickly glance around the room. "I'm not sure who's left, but whoever the second to last guy is, he's too *something*, so that leaves one."

"I think you're stuck with me, princess."

I hope to God he can't see how much that endearment affects me. Memories hit me square in the jaw as the night we spent together replays in my mind. "Aren't you spoken for by the cute blonde at the next table?" I say, forcing my vocal cords to work as I inhale an inconspicuous, calming breath. "Besides, you already have my number."

His face falls, a muscle feathering his jaw, and he draws his eyebrows together when the bell rings as if he forgot during the last five minutes that I'm the enemy and the girl who slept with his brother.

I arrange my mouth into a believable smile, despite feeling like a kicked puppy.

One chance. That's all I want. One chance to start over and show him how much I could love him. I never had anyone in my life who I truly loved. The feelings stir within me, waiting for an outlet. Logan would be happy with me. I'd make sure of it if he'd only let me in.

He bobs his head in agreement, his lips sealed, and with one last look at me, he walks away to take care of the pretty little blonde sitting behind me.

I steal a quick glance, watching the man I can't get out of my head flirt with someone else.

***

"And?" MJ asks when we exit the cocktail bar after the Express Dates end. To my surprise, she didn't want to stay behind for the afterparty and cling to Adrian. She decided we should hit the club, and if Adrian wants to find her, he has her number. "How many guys got your number?!"

"Two." I look left and right before crossing the street.

"Two?! What the hell, Cassidy? Why just two? There were so many hot guys there tonight! And I'm sure every one of them would give an arm and a leg to take you out. Well, apart from Adrian, obviously. Who are the lucky two?"

I wouldn't consider them lucky. I'll probably ditch their calls if they decide to get in touch. There's no point in accepting a date invitation while Logan's so deep under my skin.

"Mathias and Wes. How many got *your* number?"

"Six!" she huffs, hooking her elbow with mine. "You know, in case Adrian doesn't call. If he does, though... God, I'm so nervous! I think I'm in love with him!"

Ever so dramatic.

"He'll call. He'd be an idiot not to. Come on. I'll buy you a drink." I hook my elbow with hers, starting us on a stroll down the main street.

We arrive in front of *Q*, the hottest club in Newport, but we don't get through the door before MJ freezes mid-step and drops her bag on the ground. She falls to her knees, frantically searching for her phone. The way her hands tremble and lips stretch into a wide grin, I know she hopes it's Adrian.

"Hello?" Cue an even bigger smile. "Oh, okay. Yeah, sure. We're about to get into *Q*." Her face falls a bit. "Oh... well, I..." She glances at me with a pained frown.

I don't need an explanation for her sudden stuttering. It's Adrian on the other side of the line, and he wants to see her, but he doesn't want *me* to come along. Although it's probably Nico who threatened to leave if I join them.

He has no reason to avoid me. He must think I'll tell Kaya about his every move, but I don't spend as much time with his ex as I used to. She's on a downward spiral, unwilling to fight the alcohol addiction and gaining another in the form of drugs.

Or maybe it's Logan who doesn't want me there.

"It's fine," I mouth. "Go."

She covers the microphone with her hand. "Are you sure? I don't want to ditch you!"

Yes, she does, but I'm used to that by now. At least she has a reason I can get on board with. Many before her didn't.

I've been expendable to most people, and at some point, I got used to being left behind.

"I'm sure. I'll take a cab home."

She kisses my cheek, pressing the phone back to her ear. "I'll be there soon."

In the meantime, I wonder if texting Thalia at ten in the evening and asking her to meet me in town for a drink is pushing my luck with Theo. It probably is.

"I'm so sorry, babe," Mary-Jane sighs, a stray-dog look twisting her features. "I know I asked you to come, but—"

"Don't be sorry, just promise you won't end up in bed with him tonight, okay? Make him work for it."

She nods vigorously, hugs me again, and walks away back in the direction of the cocktail bar, leaving me alone on the curb. Instead of annoying another Hayes brother by demanding his wife's presence, I haul a cab and head home.

Even though I understand MJ, my stomach still churns, a ball of sadness swelling behind my ribs.

Back in my flat, I kick off my heels, open a bottle of Corona and plop down in front of the TV, curled under a soft blanket. An episode and a half of *YOU* later, my phone pings on the table. A text message from the one person I never expected to hear from waits on the screen. My blood turns hot and sticky at the sight of his name and five words.

Logan: I think we should fuck.

My heart picks up rhythm, beating out of my chest when an array of enticing, highly erotic images play on the backs of my eyelids. Goosebumps dot my skin, and I feel the fine hairs on the nape of my neck stand on end.

He wants me?

After all that happened?

Why? What am I missing? What changed?

I swear under my breath, furious at him for texting and at myself for pondering the idea. We can't do this. All he wants is sex, and while I know it would be amazing, I also know that come morning, my feelings would flare, and forgetting him would be that much harder.

My fingers hover over the screen. Hundreds of answers to that text form in my head. Some snarky, some rude, some very inappropriate, but he did save my life recently, so I settle for a less aggravating reply.

Me: If this is a joke, it's not funny.

I can act unaffected over a text, but the truth is, the cat is out of the bag, and all I can focus on is that night three years ago when we had sex. The way his full lips grazed my skin, teeth nipping the soft flesh. The rushed, demanding pace of his thrusts. His soft whispers in my ear; strong hands on my hips; the warmth of his skin...

I squirm on the loveseat, squeezing my thighs together, already worked up like the entire line outside a whore house on a nickel night. After a minute of silence on his part, I toss the phone aside and head for the bathroom.

I need a shower. A cold shower to calm down because there's no way I'll give in to the ache and make myself come with Logan on my mind. Not again.

Ice-cold water doesn't cool the fire blazing inside my head and between my legs. If anything, I'm even hotter when I exit the bathroom wrapped in a white, fluffy towel.

TOO WRONG

My phone pings again.

Logan: Three words. Two fingers. One night.

A wave of heat travels from my head down my abdomen and caresses the backs of my thighs. I remember those three words. I remember Logan pushing two fingers inside me, his hot lips on my neck as he whispered *come for me*.

And I did. So many times during that night. I was exhausted when we collapsed next to each other, panting, breathless and sweaty. Logan's a pleaser. He gets a kick out of seeing a woman come thanks to his efforts. Not that it takes him much work to trigger an orgasm. He's not simply good with his lips, cock, and fingers. He knows how to take care of the mind.

I don't reply to the text. I won't give him the satisfaction. He's with Nico, and it must be their idea of entertainment.

Let's see if Cass is still hot for your dick, bro.

Urgh! To hell with integrity. I need to come, and I'll come thinking about Logan. I reach into the nightstand drawer to pull out my trusted silicone friend. He's long and thick, just like Logan's dick, but as good as it feels buried deep inside me, it's no match for the real thing.

NINE

Logan

Three years.

Three. Fucking. Years.

And poof.

I'm back thinking about Cassidy every day, imagining what it'd be like to pin her to the mattress again after all this time.

Thinking? Hah! Try *obsessing*.

I've slept with many women since I had her, but not one made me feel the way Cassidy did that night—like I was floating. An out-of-body experience can't compare to sex with her. The world could've literally ended while we were in bed, and I wouldn't have noticed.

I.

Shouldn't.

Be.

Here.

But I'm not thinking with my brain tonight. I'm thinking

with my dick, and it doesn't know any better, so once again, I knock at the door to her flat. It takes a while before it swings open, but I struggle to stay in place once it does. All I want is to grip her waist, yank her to me, and close her mouth with mine.

She's flustered, a little breathless, and once again in a skimpy night dress. The look painting her face betrays what she was doing moments ago.

I know that look.

I remember.

The glow in her glossy eyes is unmistakable.

She scowls at me, cheeks a radiant shade of pink, pupils blown. "What are you doing here?"

Her lips part ever so slightly with each shallow breath, eyes shimmer with pleasure, and face glows, making her beauty pop even more.

Naughty girl.

Caught in the act.

Well, *almost*.

"Were you thinking about me?" I lean closer, pulled by an invisible rope. She knots her eyebrows together, acting stupid even though we both know that won't work. I can almost smell her arousal. "When you made yourself come just now... were you thinking about *me*, princess?"

Her scowl deepens, and she grips her waist with both hands, her eyes darkening to stormy blue. The pink of her cheeks morphs to scarlet, spilling down the porcelain column of her neck and lower to her cleavage.

Don't be embarrassed, baby. It's hot.

"Two words, one finger," she clips, flipping me off, and lifts her chin to come across as confident. "Fuck you."

"I'd rather fuck *you*." I step forward, leaving enough space so she can slam the door in my face if she wants, while I beg whoever watches over me not to let that happen. "You don't have a boyfriend."

"No, but that doesn't—"

I catch her wrist and tug until her boobs press against my chest. The candy-hard nipples stand out, almost peeking through the fabric like a non-verbal invitation to take one in my mouth. An electric current zaps my nerve endings at the touch of her hot body, and my chest tightens the same way it did three years ago. There's something about Cassidy Annabelle Roberts that renders me bewildered.

Her eyes darken, the arousal surfacing despite the recent orgasm she gave herself. I take her face in my hands, and my lips come down on hers for a deep, urgent kiss.

Three *years*, but her body's reaction to my touch is still the same. She gives in without hesitation, trembling in my arms, her anger obliterated when our tongues tangle, exploring, tasting... Jesus. Christ. She tastes so good.

"Your mouth says no, but your body says yes," I whisper, caressing her puckered nipple with the pad of my thumb. I move the other arm across her shoulder blades, pressing her to my chest. Still not close enough. I want her closer. "One night, baby. Just sex. I'll make you feel much better than whatever toy you used just now, and I'll be gone before your legs stop shaking." I squeeze her butt, waiting for a *yes*, but instead, a sweet, sharp gasp slips past her lips. That's all the green light I need.

I lift her up, entering the small studio apartment.

"One night," she breathes in the shell of my ear as the door slams shut. The wetness between her legs rubs against my t-shirt, soaking the fabric on my stomach. "You better deliver."

"Your memory fails you." I cross the familiar living room, a spring in my step as I reach her bedroom in five long strides. "Last time you begged me to stop making you come." I throw her on the bed, yanking my jersey over my head. "Tonight, I won't."

"You won't make me come?"

I sink to my knees, my cock throbbing, straining against my zipper, but there's something I need more than my own release.

I grip her thighs and jerk her to the edge of the bed like a fucking savage. "I won't stop. Now... open, baby, show me how wet you are." Again, no hesitation. She lets her legs fall apart when I trace my fingers up her thigh, locked in some alternate dimension as I watch her skin break out in goosebumps. "Two fingers," I whisper, pushing them inside the slick warmth of her perfect pussy. "Three words... come for me."

My head spins. I have no restraint left as I dip my head, inhale her scent and let myself go wild.

I suck and lick her clit, feeling her walls tighten around my fingers within seconds. It's a skill apparently, that few men possess. Most can make a girl come on their lips or fingers, but not many can do it this fast.

If I put my head into it, I can have Cassidy panting inside of a minute, and tonight, I'm all in. Focused, determined, starved for every sound she makes when she comes.

Three years didn't fade the memories of the night we spent together. It took a while before I accepted we wouldn't happen the way I wanted back then.

I'm painfully aware we shouldn't be happening right now. Not even on such a primal, physical level, but breaking the unwritten rules fuels my hunger. Something about those erotic, breathless moans of hers gives me a headrush.

I pump faster, curling my fingers to stroke her G spot when her body vibrates, and her tight pussy pulsates as she comes, squeezing my head with her thighs and panting my name.

I'm high on her taste.

High on this moment and nowhere near done. We've got one night, and I'll make the most of every second. She's still riding the tidal wave when I start from the top, curling my fingers to tear another orgasm out of her as fast as possible.

Cassidy squirms, jerking her hips, pressing herself to my lips as I suck and pinch the hypersensitive, swollen bundle of nerves on the apex of her thighs.

"Again, princess," I rasp, increasing the tempo of my fingers sliding in and out of her. "You need to come again."

And again, and then some... because if there's one thing I couldn't get enough of last time, feeling her come is it. I bring my other hand to her pussy, covering my thumb in her wetness, and move it lower, circling her back entrance as I apply enough pressure, so she lets me in.

I want all she can give me tonight.

Cass stills, her spine rigid as she raises the top half of her body on her elbows. "Logan, I—"

"Easy," I cut in, peppering her bare stomach with soft kisses. "I've got you. It'll feel so fucking good, baby." I climb higher, catching her lips in mine. "Do you trust me?"

She bites her lip, inhaling a sharp breath, her face a rictus of doubt. "I—" She stops, releasing all air out of her lungs, her shoulders relaxing. "Take what you want," she whispers and falls back, those cornflower-blue eyes shut tight.

I will. I'll show her highs she never knew existed.

It takes a few minutes before she melts into the mattress again, but once the tip of my thumb disappears, Cass is coming again, but once the tip of my thumb disappears, Cass is coming hard, my name on her lips among an array of faltering moans.

"I want your pussy first," I say, angling my head to watch her slowly calming down, her swollen lips parted as she inhales sweet, sharp breaths. "When your mellow, satisfied, and comfortable, I'm claiming your ass, too."

Her eyes pop open, nothing but a fulfilled gleam in them this time. She weaves her fingers through my hair, urging me higher until she can reach my mouth and slip her tongue inside, the kiss slow but hot enough to set my lungs on fire.

"Don't hurt me," she utters, pinching my bottom lip with her teeth. A soft sigh escapes her as she leans back and drops her hands on the pillow, hinting at submission.

Fuck, *yes*.

I loved it when she did that three years ago—a clear sign she was ready for whatever I had in store. Tonight will be the best night of her life, I swear.

"I won't hurt you. Tell me you're on birth control," I strip off my clothes and pull her night dress off.

"Yes, but—"

"But nothing." I climb back on the bed, the mattress dipping under my weight. Heat radiates off her toned body, and I feel how hot she is even before I lean over her, chest to chest. "You think I'd gamble your health, Cass? Never. I'm clean, baby." I wouldn't risk unprotected sex if I wasn't sure I was good to go. In fact, I've *never* had unprotected sex, but tonight, I'll be damned if I let anything spoil the moment. I guide my cock to her entrance, holding her wrists in both hands. "I don't want anything between us. I want to feel you, so either kiss me or tell me to get out of here if that's not okay."

She bites her lip, scrutinizing my face like she's trying to judge whether she can trust me. "It's okay, and you don't have to worry about anything on my side, either," she says quietly, her cheeks heating. "It's been a long time since I was with—"

Nope.

I push my hips forward, burying myself inside her in one urgent thrust to shut her up.

We won't discuss her sex life right now.

We won't ever talk about the men who had her before me. If she says she's good, I believe her. Cass is a lot of things, but a liar isn't one of them. A satisfied moan reverberates in the tiny bedroom when I take a second to savor the moment.

"Fuck," I growl, lace our fingers, and push our hands far above her head. "I missed you."

I'm not moving, buried to the hilt. My heart is ramming in my chest, and hers matches the rhythm, slamming against her ribs so hard I can feel it everywhere.

A small smile curls the corners of her lips a second before she yanks me down for another deep kiss, her tongue rediscovering my mouth with such urgency you'd think she was starving.

"I missed you, too." She arches her spine as I pull back, and we fall into a rhythm.

My brakes give out, each thrust deeper, harder. I'm losing my fucking sanity here, focused solely on how good she feels, how warm she is, how her smell soothes my senses.

She moves her hips, meeting my hurried strokes, and digs her nails into my hands that still hold hers. "Yes, just like this, Logan, don't stop."

I grip her waist, using her body as leverage and an anchor. "Do I look..." I retreat and drive back inside, tearing a needy whimper out of her, "...like I need pointers?"

I most certainly do *not*.

TOO WRONG

We only had sex once before, but that was enough to learn her body. I know where to press and bite to get a reaction; to bring her to the edge and keep her there until I'm ready to tip her over. To make her scream and spasm.

And tonight, I live for those moments.

"Don't hold back," I whisper, upping the tempo when I feel her body shudder with a promise of another release. I tend to one nipple, kneading the other breast while she knots her fingers in my hair. "One more, one more," I chant, locked on her face. "One more, baby. "

"Logan," she whimpers, forcing my forehead to rest on hers as she clings to me, clawing, drawing long, angry lines down my shoulder blades as the orgasm hits her hard. "Enough. Please, I... I... I can't—"

"Yeah, you can." I press my lips to her forehead, keeping them there for a moment before I lean back on my calves. "I'm not done with you yet." I flip her onto her tummy once she calms down. "Face down, ass up for me."

I tie her hair in a ponytail with my fingers, tugging until she dents her spine, showing a sexy line. Satisfied, I slide the head of my cock between her swollen, soaked folds, stroking up and down a few times, then move higher, pressing against the back entrance. She tenses, stills, and stops breathing all at once.

"It's okay, princess, relax," I lean over her back, increasing pressure on her virgin hole. "It'll be good, I promise. You'll love feeling me there."

I slide my hand down her stomach, finding her clit with two fingers. I rub small circles while I slip inside her ass inch by inch, slowly, so fucking slowly, letting her adjust.

Cass lets out a quiet, satisfied cry, gripping the sheets with both hands. I kiss her back, shoulders, and neck, pulling out and pushing back inside at a steady, unrushed pace, slipping in deeper every time. Careful, slow strokes at first gain pace with each satisfied sound she makes.

"Oh, *oh*," she squeals, her thighs quivering. "Just like that."

Damn this girl.

"If you don't stop telling me what I'm supposed to do, I won't let you come again." I release her hair, pressing my palm to the side of her face to force her cheek on the pillow.

She's so beautiful when her lips part and moans come out disjointed every time I push back into her, focused on how she trembles when I hit a sensitive spot. She lifts her toned ass higher, silently asking for more.

Perfect. So *fucking* perfect...

I knot our fingers again, locking her in a purposely built cage of my arms, my chest to her back, a mist of sweat covering our bodies as I move my hips back and forth, the angle letting me in so deep I struggle to keep my orgasm in check.

That never happens. I can go on for hours, but I'm already on edge with Cass, barely holding off.

She squeezes her thighs together, making the tight space between them even tighter. "Oh, God!"

"I told you you'd love this," I say in her ear, my muscles on fire, chest rising and falling faster. I hit the same spot over again, losing my grip on reality. "One more, baby. Just one more, okay?" I need to feel her choking my cock in her ass.

She starts pulsating around me, the intense pleasure coursing through her body different from what she's used to, I'm sure. A few more deep thrusts and all air leaves my lungs in a sharp burst when I come, too, feeling fucking weightless.

TEN

Cassidy

The air around the room smells of lust, Logan's strong cologne, and my perfume, hinting at what the four walls around me witnessed just moments ago.

My knees are weak and won't hold my weight for a long time, but my breathing steadies along with the thumping of my heart. Erratic while Logan wrung... I'm not sure how many orgasms out of me, and slower now that I lay on my bed, my eyes still closed. The green, satin bedsheets only cover the left side of my exhausted, sticky body. My hair is fanned around me, a few damp strands sticking to my neck and forehead. It's a mess, and I assume so is my make-up, but I don't care.

It doesn't matter.

Logan matters.

How he makes me lose any inhibitions, how he makes me feel important and cherished for the first time in my life... how he makes me believe that nothing bad can happen if he's around—that matters.

Years have passed since we were this close. Years I spent remembering every tender touch of his hands gliding down my body. Years I spent craving his lips and his attention, longing for his dark, brown eyes to look at me and *see* me.

And tonight, he saw me. He saw right through me.

For a brief time, while he strived to please me in ten different ways, he saw me, but now, he doesn't even look at me as he shoves his t-shirt back on, tugging until it falls down his muscular abdomen. The man is made of sin. I'm sure God put him on Earth to make women swoon. He slides a pair of black jeans up his long legs, then buckles up his belt.

Neither of us speak. The lustful daze gives way to awkward tension. It hangs thickly in the air. It feels like a hand gripping the back of my neck and shoving me down.

I lived through a fantasy that plagued me since our first night. A fantasy that can't compare to reality. Logan knows where to touch, kiss and stroke me to elicit a soul-shattering orgasm. I'm sure the feelings webbing inside my head are to blame, but orgasms with Logan are something else. Not one guy I let in my bed over the years could compare.

He's the most extraordinary man I've ever met. Tender, demanding, and affectionate in bed; cold, arrogant, and distant as soon as the curtain drops. Disappointment shouldn't infest my mind while he's getting dressed. I knew the score before anything went down tonight.

Three words.

Two fingers.

One night.

I agreed because I'm physically incapable of saying *no* to Logan while his hands and lips worship my body. I'm not sure

I'd say *no* even if he didn't touch me. His fascinated, almost possessive eyes roving down me would've been enough for, *yes*.

Logan pulls his cap on, backward as always, and turns to me, resting his fists on the bed. "This stays between us," he says, his voice just a touch above whisper. He dips his head, his face hovering above mine. "No one can know."

Nodding, I pull the sheets higher to cover more skin. I knew how this would end, but tears prickle my eyes, and my stomach drops to my feet. It's a blessing the room is bathed in darkness, the only light coming from the outside streetlamps, sneaking in through a gap in the curtains.

"I know," I whisper, too afraid to speak up in case my voice breaks. "I'm the dirty secret."

He dips his head lower again, pressing a soft, delicate kiss to my lips. "I'll see you around. Sleep, princess."

The door to the flat closes behind him moments later.

I inhale a deep breath, fanning my face with both hands to stop the tears. With a deep, calming breath, I flip onto my side, hoping to God that come morning, I'll bury the feelings he evokes once more.

***

When noon strikes on Tuesday, I drop what I'm doing, and grab my bag, ready to leave the studio and head to a café nearby to meet Aisha. Luke has been talking my ear off all morning, almost on his knees, begging to join us for coffee.

"You'll meet her when she comes over for the first photoshoot. I can't take you with me today. You're not a people photographer, so there's no reason for you to be there other than your disturbing fascination with men in her books."

Luke focuses on commercial photography but loves taking his camera out into the wild to snap pictures of wild animals. Although that's more of a hobby than his source of income.

"Disturbing? Girl, if those men were real, I'd never snap a picture of jewelry again. I'd just photograph their cocks until the end of time." He hands me my portfolio, blowing a few loose, blond strands of hair away from his face. "Fine. But don't stay out too long. I'll die of curiosity." He sends me an air kiss as I leave and closes the door behind me.

Aisha's already in the café, sitting by one of the tables, chatting over coffee with a stunning young girl that looks like she teleported here from the 1950s. She's in a white A-line swing dress with blue and red flowers printed on the fabric. A matching headband pushes her long, dirty-blonde hair away from her doll-like face. I imagine a hundred different photos of this girl I could take. The camera would love her flawless skin, big eyes, and outrageously full, plump lips.

I'm underdressed in boyfriend jeans and a white t-shirt. Aisha's sporting a tiny, spaghetti strap number with a low-cut cleavage and enough jewelry to put Luke's clients to shame.

"Hey, sorry if I'm late."

"No, no, no, you're not. Sit down." She moves her bag off the chair and summons the waiter. "We bumped into each other outside." She gestures to her friend. "But she's leaving now, aren't you?"

The blonde shoots her a doe-eyed look. Although her eyes are so big and round, it might as well be a normal look for her. "Yes, I'll leave you to it," she says, rising to her feet dressed in cute heels. She grabs the take-out coffee and flings a crossbody purse over her shoulder.

"It was nice meeting you," I say on autopilot, too late to

bite my tongue. We've not technically met. I don't even know the girl's name, but the atmosphere between her and Aisha suddenly grew heavy, and I had to loosen the tension somehow.

The girl blushes bright pink faster than I can blink, either embarrassed or uncomfortable. She offers an awkward smile and walks away, her heels clicking happily when she exits the café in a whirlwind of wavy hair and a flowery dress.

"Shit, I'm sorry." I glance at Aisha. "Did I upset her?"

She waves me off, rolling her eyes. "Don't worry about it. She's not upset, just socially awkward."

The waiter approaches to take our order while I show Aisha my portfolio and the portraits and full body shots I took over the years that suit her book covers' aesthetic.

"He's the guy I want for the next cover." She takes out her phone, showing me pictures of a toned, tattooed, broody model with deep brown eyes and dark hair. "In the book, he's an ex-convict, straight out of jail where he spent three years for aiding and abetting manslaughter."

She explains her vision for the photoshoot, and we set a date when the model is available for a few hours in the morning. I catch myself thinking that Aisha reminds me a bit of Thalia. They're both chatty, spirited, and beautiful.

"We should celebrate," she says an hour later. My latte is cold, and my notebook is filled with notes, instructions, and ideas based on her monologue. "How about a girl's night out? Are you free on Friday? You could grab your friends, I'll grab mine, and we'll meet at *Q*."

I'm surprised by the offer, but only a little bit. Aisha's a people person, open, confident, and a touch intimidating with that no-bullshit attitude. "Sounds good. I've not been out in ages, and my friend mentioned a girl's night not long ago, so it'll work perfectly."

We part ways, and I spend the rest of the afternoon answering too many of Luke's questions. The positive side of his nosiness is that it takes my mind off Logan. Unfortunately, not for long. As soon as I'm back in the empty studio flat, my mind wanders on its own accord, replaying the images of Saturday night that are permanently etched into my brain.

Every touch of his fingers, every kiss, and every thrust comes back to torture me and intensify unwanted feelings.

***

Day and night.

Night and day.

My mind is hostage to the thoughts of Logan. Regardless of how often I try to convince myself that I have no feelings for him, deep down, I know it's a lie. It has been for three years. How many times will I crawl out of the ditch? How many times will I try to stop loving him before it finally works?

He's a disease affecting my mind. Schizophrenia or paraphrenia—either-or. I'm delusional in one way or another considering a tiny, anemic part of me dreams of having Logan to myself. I picture holding hands with him; feeling his kisses on the tip of my nose; hearing him laugh while we watch a movie.

I'm definitely crazy. I just don't have the papers.

Logan's an itch I can't scratch. A parasite feasting on my brain and heart.

I chuckle under my breath... he's a heartworm.

"You're not listening," Thalia clips, touching my hand to snap me out of daydreaming while we sit outside a small cafe by the pier enjoying iced lattes before we head to town and spend the rest of Friday shopping. "What's going on?"

"It's nothing." I shake my head, dismissing the HD image of Logan's face from the forefront of my imagination. "Sorry, I've got a lot on my mind."

She narrows her eyes and purses her lips, clearly unhappy with the answer. Of course, she sees right through me. We've grown closer over the last two years, and lying through my teeth no longer works on her. She knows me too well to be easily dismissed. And she cares enough to dig deeper.

It's no longer Kaya whom I call for advice or a casual chat. It's Thalia. We meet for lunch at least once a week, touch base over the phone, and go out drinking whenever we can get our schedules lined up.

Kaya used to be there for me if I needed her, but since Nico caught her cheating, she dived head-first into her addiction as if drinking numbs her pain somehow. She's too busy chasing men and living her best life to remember about me most of the time.

I huff, rubbing frustration away from my face. "Fine. I might as well tell you..." I drop my hands back on the table as Thalia leans closer, her ears perking up. "I met a guy."

Your brother-in-law.

I can't add that part. As much as I love and trust her, I'd never put Logan at risk.

Excitement blossoms on Thalia's face, her cheeks flush pink, and she grabs my hand, giving it a light squeeze. "Finally! I'm so happy for you! Who is he? Where did you meet?"

"Tone down with the smiles." I tuck my hair behind my ears, doing my best to look her in the eyes. "It was just a one-night thing. I knew before it happened that it'd just be this once, but I can't stop thinking about him."

The ear-to-ear grin slips from her face, but her eyes still sparkle. "Okay, you completely ignored my questions. Who is this guy? Where did you meet?!"

Logan's words ring in my head like a church bell. *This stays between us. No one can know.*

I hate lying to Thalia, but what choice do I have? "Just someone I met at the Express Dates last week."

"Ahh, right! MJ said you gave your number to two guys. Why don't you tell him you're open for another night? Maybe if you hook up again, he'll realize he wants more than just sex."

"No, he won't. He made it very clear. Besides, I don't want a relationship, but sex…" Bullshit. I want Logan. All of him, but I know it would never work thanks to my history with Theo, and all of the Hayes thinking of me as the enemy. "He's so freaking good," I continue, absentmindedly tapping my nails against the tabletop. "I'd keep him for a bit, have fun, you know? But he just wanted one night, so that's that."

She scoffs, cocking one eyebrow like she can't believe my naivety. "Oh please, do you really think he'll pass on casual sex if you offer? He's a guy, Cass. Tell him he can take what he wants and never call you again, and he *will* take."

It's true with most men, but not with Logan. At least not in this scenario when I'm the secret no one can know about. Hooking up again is risky. Someone could see him entering my apartment building or spot his car outside.

I mean, it's a small chance. The Hayes have no reason to be around the part of town I live in, but no matter how small, it is a risk, and Logan's too loyal to his brothers to throw caution to the wind.

"Do you know where he lives?" she asks, covering the

froth in her cup with two spoons of sugar.

"No, why?"

She shrugs but winks at me, her lips curling again. "Too bad. You could show up at his house wearing something sexy. No way he'd turn you down."

No, that's... shit. That's actually not a bad idea. Logan enjoys sex, and he enjoys my body. If I could surprise him, maybe he wouldn't say no. After all, I saw the desire burning in his eyes when he looked at me last week.

"What if he shuts the door in my face?"

"What if he doesn't?"

Yeah... what if he doesn't?

ELEVEN

Cassidy

Stupid, silly, reckless.

That's me. God, what was I *thinking* coming here?

I've never been to this part of Newport. The estate has been under construction for two years, but judging by the cars dotted around the driveways, all the houses are now occupied.

Logan has been overseeing this project since the beginning. He's the Architectural Director at Stone & Oak Residential Construction Company, owned by his grandfather. If the rumors are true, he's one of the most visionary architects the company has seen in fifty years. I knew he was working on this, but I didn't know that one of the beautiful, two-story houses with a pristine front lawn and white and gray cladding was his.

Obtaining his address wasn't easy. I couldn't ask Thalia without piquing her interest and risking questions I wouldn't know how to answer, so instead of putting myself on the spot, I settled for a much creepier, disturbing option.

I followed him home yesterday... in an Uber. My car is too noticeable. He would've seen me coming from a mile away, so I called a driver I use whenever I hit the club with Thalia or Kaya. He's a cool kid, earning money to pay for college tuition. He didn't mind playing detective, but the look on his face when I asked him to follow Logan's car was priceless.

I'm not proud of myself, but now that I stand in front of the door, dressed like a hooker, I can't bring myself to regret playing stalker. If there's one thing about Logan I know for sure, it's that he enjoys sex too much to send me home once he sees what hides underneath the long, gray cardigan I wear.

His car sits in the driveway, and the lights shine inside, so he must be home. I just don't know if he's alone. It'll be difficult to explain my visit if one of his brothers is with him and decides to open the door instead of Logan. It's not like I have a believable lie at the ready. Or any lie for the matter.

It'll be heartbreaking if he's got a woman there, ready to get naked and hop into his bed. Or worse, ready to cuddle into his muscular chest on the sofa and watch a lame TV show.

Hopefully, choosing Wednesday to pay him a visit will save me from heartache and humiliation. It's unlikely he'll have company at eight in the evening on a weekday, right?

One deep breath filters through my lungs, calming my mind and keeping my courage intact. This is what I want, need, and can't stop thinking about.

Replay.

Passion, lust, desire.

I want to feel it again. His big, strong hands on my body, soft lips on my skin, breathless whispers in my ear as he goes above and beyond to make me come any way he can. A rush of heat hits me at the thought, the anticipation sky-high already.

Emotions are absent, locked in a bulletproof container, and buried deep under the ocean where no one—except for me tomorrow—will ever find them.

Tonight is about being physical.

Just sex.

Nothing more.

That's all I came here for: to feel my body relax in his arms and then tense when a sudden wave of pleasure hits me like a freight train, stripping my mind of the firewall and sending me rushing into a state where nothing bad can touch me.

The second deep breath is to clear my head and focus on what lies ahead. The man I crave with my entire being. The man I've fantasized about non-stop for almost two weeks. The man that makes my heart skip a beat.

With a trembling hand, I knock three times, shaking my head slightly to fan out my hair, letting it flirt with my shoulders. I untie the belt of my cardigan, revealing a set of red, lacey lingerie I bought especially for Logan. I spent the afternoon at Victoria's Secret, looking for something that visually enhances my small boobs and accentuates my toned ass.

I kill myself at the gym five times a week to keep that ass toned. It's only fair I use my best feature to convince Logan to sleep with me again.

Lord, I think I've got this backward. Aren't men usually the ones who trick women into sleeping with them?

My heart skips a beat when the handle moves, the lock clicks, and the door opens inward. A soft glow of LED lights attached to the wall an inch above the floor illuminates Logan, casting shadows across his bare chest and handsome face.

He's not wearing his signature baseball cap tonight. His dark, haphazardly styled hair is short at the sides and longer at the top, with a few stray locks kissing his forehead. A towel hangs over his neck as if he's ready to work out.

He doesn't say a word, looking me over, feasting on the luxuriously expensive lingerie. A muscle ticks in his jaw, and his eyes darken with every inch of my body he discovers.

A subtle change happens before my eyes when desire takes control of his mind. The grip he has on the door tightens, teeth grind. He rifles me down with a piercing stare, a wave of heat passing between us.

The smell of his cologne makes me feel at home: safe and calm, but I push those thoughts aside. *Physical.* This is supposed to be physical.

No emotions, no feelings, no longing.

Just crazy, wild sex.

I step forward before I change my mind and run with my tail between my legs. I rise on my tiptoes and press my lips to his, bracing against his chest to keep my balance.

He doesn't react.

He's not moving, not returning the kiss, stiff as a board.

An anticlimax of shame burns my cheeks, kicking the rhythm of my heart into a disorganized beat. I break the kiss, settling back on my heels, and inch away, but Logan doesn't let me take one step. He grips my jaw with one hand, wraps the other around me, and catches my lips with his, dragging us inside his house.

It's the sweetest torture when his tongue teases my lip, begging for more. I part my mouth, letting him deepen the kiss, adding gasoline to the fire raging in every cell of my body. I'm the opening of a volcano, ready to erupt when the door slams shut with a bang.

Logan shoves me against it, devouring my lips as if this is

the first time he has ever kissed me. As if he waited to taste me for years. His big body presses into me so hard I feel his erection jut against my tummy.

He skims his hand from my jaw, down the side of my body, and grips my thigh, lifting my right knee up to rest on his hip bone. I keep it there while he touches the inside of my leg, getting closer to the most sensitive spot.

"I knew you'd come for more," he says, his voice heavy as he rests his forehead against mine, touching the damp fabric between my legs. "So ready for me..."

"Always," I utter, breathless and shamefully aroused.

A torrent of pleasant shivers zips down my spine when he moves my panties aside and slowly pushes two fingers inside me as if he's savoring the moment.

"Oh... shit, I—" Words die on my tongue. He's had his fingers inside me for ten seconds, but the orgasm is right there already. And just as it's about to hit, he pulls his fingers out. "Logan, *please*..."

"Shh, princess, it's okay. It's coming. I promise."

He wraps his arms around my waist, lifting me into his arms, and crosses the hallway, aiming for the stairs. I kiss and nibble the heavenly-smelling flesh in the crook of his neck, drunk on endorphins. It's a stupid, immature thought, but I want to give him a hickey. Mark him so no other woman will sleep with him for a while. I don't go ahead with the idea, too afraid he'll throw me out of here before he makes me come.

And I *need* to come.

I've been aching for his touch for two weeks, which might be why he got me to the edge at the speed of light. The long, silicone cock in my nightstand doesn't do the job half as well as Logan.

TOO WRONG

The world doesn't exist when he carries me up a flight of stairs. I knot my fingers in his hair, tugging gently when we're halfway down the landing, and he stops, pushing me against the wall to kiss me again. There's no longer any blood in my veins, replaced by lust mixed with adrenaline.

Pictures fall off the hooks when he starts walking again, his lips not leaving mine. I doubt he sees where he's going, but I don't care. As long as his arms are around me, I don't care about anything. Cold satin gives me goosebumps when he throws me on the bed.

"Fingers, lips, or cock?" he asks, sliding the straps of my bra down my arms. He unbuckles the clasp and throws the scrap of red lace on the floor. My panties fly across the room next, a second before Logan dips his head to suck one of my nipples.

"All three, please," I breathe, drowning in the moment.

He pushes two fingers back inside, his touch like an electric shock to my nervous system. I'm so worked up from two weeks of imagining this moment that Logan has me on edge again within half a minute. I close my eyes, spasms running through me, the incoming orgasm something to behold.

"Nah-ah," he whispers. "Look at me, baby. Don't lock yourself in your head. You need to watch me fuck you. You need to see how perfect you are when you take me. You need to memorize every second so you can make yourself come thinking about me from now on because this is the last time we're doing this."

Any other time that would hurt, but I refuse to let his words get to me. According to our previous deal, tonight shouldn't be happening. I'm grateful he made an exception and didn't tell me to get the hell out of his house.

Holding his gaze isn't easy with the waves of pleasure

rumbling through me. I want to close my eyes, throw my head back and surrender to the thrill, but I don't. His hooded eyes are glued to my face, his pupils blown as he brings me higher.

"Now," he says, curling his fingers to graze the most tender spot. "Come for me, princess."

And as if it's an order, my body vibrates, and the orgasm hits. The sound of blood sings in my ears, dark spots blur my vision, but I don't look away. I hold his eyes hostage, coming apart at the seams. A wave of fire floods my body, intense and all-consuming to the point it makes my eyes prickle.

"You're so fucking hot when you come," he says, easing his fingers out to caress my pussy. "I want one more."

He dives between my thighs, licking, sucking, and getting what he wants in two minutes flat. I'm not done trembling when he kicks his sweatpants off, watching me as I eye his dick. I have no idea how he fits that inside me.

He climbs back on the bed, resting his back against the headboard, and cuffs my wrist, helping me up. "Ride me. Show me what you've got."

"You should've asked before my legs became jelly." I kiss his lips, then tug his arm, forcing him lower until he's no longer sitting but lying on his back, head propped on the pillows.

I ease myself down on top of him, loving the control and dominance of having Logan at my mercy, dependent on my touch and pace. He grips my waist when I rest my hands on his chest and kiss his lips, letting my hips do the hardest work.

It's like twerking, just faster, naked, on my knees, and with his cock sliding in and out of me.

"Fuck." He gauges his fingers into my flesh hard enough to bruise. I think he realizes that because a second later, he eases off a little. "Baby, you need to slow down, or this will end much sooner than I'd like."

I bite his lip, keeping the excruciating pace intact despite how weak my legs feel. "You said *show me what you've got*, so shut up and take it."

I should've listened...

If I did, we would've been in bed for much longer than the few intense minutes, but I can't bring myself to regret it when his teeth sink into his lower lip in a display of pure, unrestrained pleasure. He holds my hips, pinning me down, eyes on mine as he spills deep inside me with a low, stony growl.

A minute. That's all the time he gives us to catch our breath before he pats my hip, urging me to get off him.

"Last time, Cass," he says, moving to sit on the edge of the bed. "Don't show up here again."

I bob my head, falling back on the pillow, eyes closed, body weak and warm. I feel him get up and hear the bathroom door close. The shower starts running while I lay there, ghosting my fingers over my swollen lips. The thought of Logan naked under the stream of hot water gets me worked up all over again.

Last time echoes in my head, a pang of disappointment coursing through my veins. A part of me understands why he doesn't want to continue casual sex regardless of how good we are together. He cares about his brothers. He'd never jeopardize their relationship for the sake of fucking me every now and then. There are hundreds of women in Newport he can screw with no consequences.

He has no reason to keep this up.

Unlike me.

I've been suppressing my feelings, but it's like fighting the wind.

Don't show up here again.

It'll be safer for my sanity to oblige. Safer for my heart because the fire rekindles every time his hands touch my skin. I want to stay here just a bit longer; watch Logan when he emerges from the bathroom; study and memorize the contour of his face, high cheekbones, and full raspberry lips that skillfully worked my body.

My heart skips a beat when he turns the water off, and the shower door slides with a characteristic sound. I sit up, holding the sheets close to my chest. Maybe he'll be up for another round if this is the last time? I'm weak and exhausted, but I'll muster some strength if it means holding onto him for longer, but first, I need to clean up.

The bathroom door opens, and Logan casts a sideways glance at the bed. His step falters, features pinch. "What are you still doing here?" he snaps. "You know where the door is, Cass. We're done here. Off you go."

Blood drains from my face. My blissful smile vanishes without a trace. I didn't expect to cuddle but being thrown out like a cheap hooker ten minutes after he fucked me and before I could wipe his cum dripping down my thighs cuts me deep.

"Get moving," he clips again, throwing my cardigan at the bed without another look my way.

His attention doesn't deviate from his phone as I get dressed quickly, the insides of my thighs wet and sticky, making a mess out of the expensive, red panties. I thought I had reached the limit of humiliation three years ago.

I was wrong. This is worse.

Tears sting my eyes when I shove my hands into the sleeves of my cardigan and tie the belt around my waist, careful not to look directly at Logan. Two weeks ago he kissed me before he left my flat. I expected the same today. A kiss and *I'll see you around*, but I must've overstepped an invisible line when I showed up at his doorstep.

In true Logan fashion, he took what I offered, and once satisfied, he let his true colors shine.

I retreat out of the room as if a pack of vicious dogs is hot on my tail. I almost trip over my feet dressed in heels when I fly down the stairs, taking two at a time.

How can a person feel so blissfully satisfied and fulfilled one minute, then balance on the verge of bursting into tears the next?

I don't even know why I'm so emotional. It's *Logan*, for Christ's sake. What the hell did I expect? That he'll fetch a warm washcloth? My eyes prickle with tears, my vision blurry as I reach for the doorknob.

Heavy footsteps resonate behind me. Logan's not rushing, casually strolling down the stairs. I feel his burning gaze on my back as if he's holding me at gunpoint. "You got a car around here?" he asks, no trace of annoyance from two minutes ago.

I don't answer. My voice would betray the upcoming tears, and no way I'll give him the satisfaction.

I fling the door open, my chin quivering harder with every step. Warm, salty drops fall free, trickling down my cheeks before the door fully closes behind me. I feel so... *used*.

Worthless, dirty, and stupid for coming here in the first place.

My car is parked two streets away because *I* am considerate and didn't want to leave my yellow Fiat in front of Logan's house in case someone decided to pay him a visit. I pull the visor down, check the state of myself in the mirror, and wipe away wet traces of mascara off my cheeks, inhaling three deep, calming breaths.

This is *nothing*.

I'm used to being treated like a leech. I've survived worse than Logan Hayes. My life has been filled with people who didn't give a damn about me and to whom I've been a nuisance since the day I was born. My alcoholic parents only cared about a few hundred dollars they received from state benefits. It was all about money for the foster families that took me in, too.

I survived neglect, hunger, and loneliness.

Pain and fear.

Humiliation.

Heartache.

Logan won't be the one to break me.

I turn the key in the ignition and shift into gear but fall short of pulling away when a set of knuckles taps against the window. Logan stands by the car wearing sweatpants and a white shirt, hot as sin A-grade douchebag.

"What?!" I snap, pressing the button to roll down the window, eyes on the road, foot on the brake.

He bends down until we're at eye level and rests his elbows on the door. "Why are you upset?"

I scoff. The humiliation tearing me apart morphs into anger. "I'm not upset." My nails whiten more the harder I grip the steering wheel, but I curl my lips into a mocking smile. "I'm always super happy when I'm treated like a hooker."

"A hooker?" He cocks an eyebrow, his lips forming a thin line as he tries to hold a smile in check. "What did you expect? You came over to fuck, right? Did I not deliver? Or did you think you could stay the night?"

"Of course not!" I might be living in la-la land, dreaming of Logan being mine, but I'm not stupid. It's just sex, and I agreed, but... "I just didn't expect you to kick me out before I could wipe your cum off my thighs, asshole. *Move* before I drive over your legs."

Recognition flickers across his face as if a bulb lit up over his head. "Shit." He carelessly scratches the back of his neck. "I didn't think, alright? I thought you wanted to cuddle, and that's not happening. You should've told me you wanted to grab a shower instead of storming out like a fucking drama queen. I don't read minds, Cass."

"It's basic courtesy," I snap, my chest so tight it feels as if my bones have cinched around my lungs. He has no idea how uncomfortable and demeaning it feels to pull on a pair of panties while I'm wet with *him*. "Next time you touch yourself, come in your pants and take a walk. See how you like it." I press the button to close the window and release the break, forcing him to step aside or the back wheel of my car will mark his shoes.

TWELVE

Logan

An all-black Audi R8 sits parked outside of the four-car garage next to the triplets' Mustangs, Shawn's Ranger, and Theo's Camaro. No space for my Charger.

If they'd park closer together, I'd fit my car beside the shiny Audi, but no. No way I'll fit in there with how Colt parked his Mustang as if he's ninety and blind in one eye. I block the driveway altogether, parking sideways in the narrow spot a few yards from the electric gate.

No one's going home tonight.

The warm evening air stings with BBQ smoke and ocean breeze, soft wind rustling the leaves of an old oak tree nearby. I lock the car, shoving the keys deep into the back pocket of my jeans. With a bottle of Mom's favorite wine in hand, I knock on the door of the masterpiece of an estate that's my parents' house. Floor-to-ceiling windows surround the nine-bedroom three-story house I spent twenty-one years in.

TOO WRONG

Growing up, my room was on the top floor overlooking the garden equipped with a full-sized tennis court, spa, and a pool. I used to climb in and out of there, using the railing of a wraparound balcony to lower myself to the balcony below, then jump onto the deck, and off I went, partying into the early morning hours. Mom and Dad found out about my escapades when I was in my sophomore year of college. I snuck a girl into my room, and later on, I tried to sneak her out again the same way she came: through the balcony.

Unfortunately, she was tipsy and broke her ankle, landing on the deck at three o'clock in the morning.

I got an earful from Mom and permission from Dad to bring the girls in through the front door and let them out the same way. He's as laid back as they come. I guess it's a must-have quality when you're raising seven boys.

As per family tradition, I arrive fashionably late for the monthly get-together my mother insisted on hosting once the triplets moved out to live with Nico.

"We need to spend more time together."

While I don't mind, I am worried. Mom's growing more insecure by the week. She fights to feel needed and craves the attention of her sons to the point where I'm scared she might blackmail Dad into having another baby. I shudder, pushing away the images of my parents trying to conceive at their age. It'd be quite the accomplishment for Mom at fifty-seven to endure pregnancy and labor.

Theo opens the left wing of the large double door, distracting my messed-up head from picturing my parents having sex.

"I'm glad you're late," he says, waving a hundred in my face. "Nico was certain you'd be on time today."

That guy has too much cash if he's willing to bet on me

arriving on time. "Does he know me at all?" I shoulder past Theo and his wide grin, shedding my jacket in the foyer.

I hang it over the grand-staircase railing and smile when an acoustic piano version of "Imagine" by John Lennon reaches my ears. The house smells like freshly baked apple pie, which means grandma is here.

I move to one of the three living rooms where my mother sits in front of a 1904 Steinway grand piano, hands on the keys, head swinging to the music.

As expected, Nico's on the armrest of the white chesterfield sofa, eyes glued to our mother. I'd bet a hundred dollars he was the one who asked her to play. And that's the kind of bet that wouldn't lose me any money. Nico rarely relaxes, but whenever he listens to Mom play, the anger that usually surrounds him like a stormy cloud is absent.

Mom lets the last note linger in the air when the song ends. I remember her spending every evening in front of the piano when I was a little boy, but I failed to appreciate her talent and sheer love for the instrument until later in life.

A smile spreads across her face as she spins on the stool. "Logan!" she cheers, rushing toward me in a light, flowy dress.

Not many fifty-seven-year-old women could pull off a dress like this—flared at the bottom, tight at the waist—but my mother is naturally beautiful; Miss California thirty-odd years ago. Lean figure with a wasp waist and the face of an angel. If I had a sister who'd inherit most of Mom's features mixed with just a sprinkle of Grandma, she'd be the most stunning girl on this side of the Atlantic.

And seven of her brothers would kick ass left, right, and center to keep unworthy pricks away.

"Everyone's outside already," she says, taking the wine and

pressing a soft kiss to my cheek. She rubs the spot, probably wiping off a cherry-red lipstick mark. "I think your Dad might need a hand with the BBQ."

The weather improved over the last couple of weeks. May brought a heatwave worthy of the hottest summers, so we can enjoy a barbecue outside instead of spending time at the long table in the dining room.

"We've invited the Maroons, too," she adds, sparkles dancing in her molten-steel gray eyes. It's baffling that neither one of my brothers inherited the unusual color. We're all shades of brown, from Cody's caramel to Nico's almost as black as his fucking soul. "They moved back here a couple of weeks ago."

"Who?" I ask, drawing my eyebrows together.

"The Maroons!" she repeats as if she thinks I didn't hear her the first time.

"Mom, I'm asking *who* the Maroons are."

Theo tsks in the corner, shaking his head, a scowl of disapproval tainting his features and enhancing the scar marking his cheek. "That's low, Logan."

"It's fucking *appalling*," Nico adds, equally outraged, although it comes across more genuine on him than Theo. "Shame on you. How could you forget your fiancée's surname?"

A shit-eating grin twists Theo's lips, and a short laugh follows. "She still has the fucking ring you gave her!"

"Language, Theo," Mom clips, shooting him her signature *I-take-no-prisoners* look.

He throws his hands in the air. "Really, Mom? *Really*? I'm thirty soon. And you didn't scold Nico when he said the *f* word. That's not fair."

"Nico, language, baby. Please," she says, but her tone is soft, eyes playful. That bastard could get away with murder.

"Back to the subject at hand. What fu—" I sidestep the landmine, catching a scowl on Mom's face in time to correct myself. "*Effing* ring?"

"The engagement ring you made out of copper wire and glue," Nico explains. "It's the first time I've seen it today, bro, and honestly? Nice work."

Shit. A wire ring with a small white pebble glued to the top with super glue. I glued my fingers together while making the engagement ring for the girl next door and cried for an hour before Mom came home and helped me.

Annalisa Maroon.

Gorgeous blonde with big eyes half-covered by an awkward fringe. Annalisa, the little bully. A pretty bully with cute pigtails. The love of my life for a month or so back in kindergarten. How, on God's green earth, did I forget the girl I wanted to marry when I was four?!

Baffling.

It's not like she didn't move across the world to live in Australia before middle school started and never came back to Newport until, apparently, now.

"She's still just as pretty as she was when she was a kid." Mom beams, the fond glow back in her eyes.

I can't keep up with this woman. On the one hand, she's jealous of Thalia and annoyed she stole her son. On the other hand, she wants another son to settle down. Either she can't add two and two together, or she has more against Thalia than she and Dad are willing to admit.

There's the issue with Thalia being accused of murdering her husband when she lived back home in Greece, but I don't think my parents are aware of that. And even if they know, the charges were dropped, and Thalia was ruled innocent, so

Mom has no reason to be so pissy.

It's not like she killed the guy, anyway. At least that's the official, united front of Mr. and Mrs. Theo Hayes.

"Go say *hi*." Mom pushes me gently toward the patio door. "She's outside."

"Yeah, Logan, go say *hi*," Theo emphasizes. "She hasn't stopped talking about you two since she got here."

I don't want to say *hi*, but what choice do I have? I head outside, followed by my brothers. Annalisa sits by the pool with Thalia, laughing at something my sister-in-law must've said. She's still pretty, alright. A halo of platinum blonde hair falls to the middle of her back, her legs are long and smooth, and she's as skinny as they get.

Too skinny.

Collarbones and shoulder bones protrude, and the cleavage of her dress hides a flat chest. Cassidy is skinny, too, but she has a bit of fat on the bones to grab and enough tits to fill my hand.

This will be a long day if I keep comparing one blonde to another. Why am I even thinking about Cass? It's been a week and a half since she stormed out of my house, close to tears. At first, I was beyond annoyed at the dramatic exit. I went upstairs into my bedroom, ready to crash, but guilt gnawed at my brain like a woodworm.

Maybe I was too harsh in telling her to get going, but in my defense, I didn't expect her to still be in my bed when I got out of the shower. None of the women ever stay that long. It's an unwritten rule everyone around Newport Beach seems to know, understand, and abide by, so Cass breaking said rule took me by surprise.

Didn't she get the memo?

Regardless of her blatant overstay, instead of crashing for the night, I pulled a t-shirt out of the wardrobe and followed Cass to her car. I'm not a knight in shining armor. Not by any definition, but I'm not a teenager. Letting a girl leave when she's distressed, without at least trying to find out the reason, is a play you can expect from arrogant, careless kids.

Now, knowing why she left in a hurry, I wish I was still a self-centered teenager just that once. That way, I'd keep thinking she was upset because I hurt her feelings.

Turns out, I jumped to conclusions way too fast. She didn't do anything wrong. *I* messed up sending her on her way before offering a washcloth. I've never been in a similar situation. I've never spilled inside a girl before Cass. The notion of my cum making a mess, dripping from her sweet pussy and down her thighs, didn't cross my mind.

Nothing does when I've got Cassidy naked and breathless. My mind fucking blanks, focusing solely on her. She's addictive. The way she comes, parts her lips, and moans taking me in...

I'd kneel on glass to fuck her again.

Which is why I can't.

While in the heat of the moment, it's easy to forget that if my brothers were to find out about my dalliance with the public enemy's bestie, I'd lose them. Maybe they wouldn't point-blank cut me out of their lives, but we wouldn't spend time together as we do now. They'd boot me out of the chat, stop calling and stop coming over. We'd only see each other on special occasions like birthdays and weddings.

There's a reason why the seven of us are so close: rules. We started creating those once we hit our teenage years, and the testosterone spilling out of our ears got in the way of us appreciating one another.

Brothers come first.
No dibs on chicks.
Never touch your brother's girl.

There are more, and there are exceptions, but what I have with Cassidy doesn't fit into any exception. She fucked my brother. She's best friends with the girl who hurt Nico. That's enough to deem her off-limits to all Hayes, but the list of sins doesn't end there. Over the years, Cass has been talking behind our backs, warning girls away. She even warned Thalia when Theo first met her. She's been getting in our way for a long time.

"Look who's here," Annalisa beams, rising to her feet, flinging the blonde hair over one shoulder. Someone should feed that girl. Her legs resemble two thin sticks. "I was starting to worry you wouldn't show up." She crowds my space to kiss my cheek as if we're long-time friends.

I've not seen her in twenty-five years. She's a stranger, and the gesture is not appreciated.

"Hey, Ann. Good to see you," I say, hoping the short, clipped line will be enough to paint a picture—Logan, out. Not interested. I veer off to the right, lean over Thalia's lounger and kiss her cheek, or else I'll hear about it later. She's the most spirited woman I've ever met. "Hey, honey, please tell me you made the Greek salad and the dip."

A BBQ just isn't the same without the tzatziki dip since Thalia became a part of the family.

"And the skewers," she admits, reaching for a tall glass of iced tea.

Her inquisitive eyes jump from me to Annalisa, who must still be standing a few feet behind. If only Thalia knew how much she has in common with my mother. They're both trying to play cupid every now and then as if I'm incapable of finding a woman by myself. The track record of my relationships confirms the statement, I guess.

Funny that neither of them gets on Nico's case.

"What did you make?" she asks in a normal tone, then mouths, "she's *cute!*"

I answer the statement with a firm shake of my head, begging her to put down the bow and arrows with heart-shaped heads she's undoubtedly aiming at my ass, and then I tackle the question. "I made an appearance."

"You made that last time. It's getting old."

I ruffle the mass of her curly hair, turning back toward the blonde stick woman. It hurts just thinking about fucking her. I'd bruise my thighs, ramming into her from behind.

Grandma saves me from entertaining my long-lost love by walking out of the house with a plate of apple pie slices. At seventy-nine, she's the most elegant woman I know. Always dressed to impress.

Now, her low heels click on the decking as she strolls toward the table in a cream, over-the-knee dress, pearls adorning her neck and dangling from her ears, white hair cut short and styled back. Grandad stands by the BBQ equally as elegant in a smart yellow shirt tucked into a pair of gray chinos.

Thankfully, apart from the older generation, no one made much effort. I don't stand out in my distressed black jeans, a Los Angeles Dodgers jersey, and a white cap on my head as per usual.

"Logan," Grandad calls me over, his tone hinting that this will be about business, and I see my mother frowning. "Just five minutes, sweetheart," he tells her, drapes his arm across my shoulders, and leads me away from prying ears. "I wanted to tell you the news first before I make the announcement at the board meeting later this week." He rests his back on the fence surrounding the tennis court.

I narrow my eyes, trying to read the news from the look on his face, but William Hayes has a killer poker face. An aura of authority surrounds him regardless of where he is or what he does. I stand straight in his presence like a soldier at attention, my spine like a metal pole. He exudes ruthless confidence and makes you feel like you're in danger.

Both Nico and Colt inherited the quality. Colt's more mellow, though, while Nico took Grandad's genes and cranked them up to fucking infinity.

"I've decided to retire at the end of the summer," Grandad says, each word punctuated. "Your grandma..." He clears his throat, loosening the collar of his shirt. "*I believe it's time for me to enjoy the silver of life I have left.*"

Yeah right. It wasn't his call. Grandma made him do it, I'm sure. She's been busting his ass for years, asking him to retire, and it looks like she finally wore him down. At eighty, you'd expect he'd be retired for at least ten years, but I could never picture him willingly handing over the company he built from the ground up. I thought he'd die at his desk, working until he drew his last breath.

A sense of dread washes over me at the thought of Stone & Oak being sold to the highest bidder.

"I'm happy for you," I say and surprise myself when it comes out genuine. "You deserve the rest."

He bobs his head, peeking over my shoulder with unseeing eyes. "I want you to take my place, Logan."

There's a moment of silence as if someone muted the whole goddamn world with his words. I stare at him, wondering if I heard him correctly. There is no denying I work my ass off at the company, and without sounding arrogant, I *am* a fine architect, but I've only been there for six years. Not in my wildest dreams would I have expected to receive an offer like this one.

"That's very generous, but I'm not sure I'm the right person for the job. I don't have the knowledge or experience—"

He shushes me with a dismissive wave of his hand. "It's not that hard or complicated. I'm not retiring tomorrow. We have time to get you settled into your new duties. I know this is sudden, and you need to sleep on it, so let's not dwell on the subject today and enjoy the BBQ instead. We can talk more tomorrow." He pats my shoulder, gracing me with a rare smile. "If I didn't believe you have what it takes to lead my company, I wouldn't have chosen you."

Way to boost my ego.

I'm on cloud nine for the rest of the day, joking with my brothers, dodging Annalisa's flirting, and stuffing myself with food and beer. Cody ends up moving my car to let everyone out close to nine in the evening, but I don't leave. I crash in my old room, wondering what my life will be like in a few months when I take over Stone & Oak.

THIRTEEN

Cassidy

Aisha sits on the loveseat in my studio, nervously tapping her foot on the floor and glancing at the clock every ten seconds. The model she hired for the photoshoot should've been here half an hour ago.

Thankfully, I had no idea what working with Aisha would be like or how demanding or picky she is, so I hadn't booked any other photoshoots for today. I don't mind the wait.

"Maybe he's stuck in traffic?" I ask, emerging from the kitchenette with coffees. "He's coming from Los Angeles, right?"

She bobs her head, lips in a thin line, and glances at the clock again, eyes narrowed.

"Do you have his number?"

"I tried calling, but it goes straight to voicemail." She pulls the phone out, tapping on the screen. "I'll call his agent. Maybe he knows what's going on."

I sip the coffee, watching the street, while Aisha paces the room, a phone to her ear. She huffs, one hand propped on her hip, eyes spewing fire as she glares at my camera and the photoshoot set-up to capture the perfect image.

I've studied the covers of her books and browsed Amazon for hours over the past few days, trying to spot the trends and judge what sells. Aisha's covers feature broody, sexy, ripped men. As appealing as that is, I can't shake the vision that hit me when she told me a bit more about the plot and the heroine—a young girl with long blonde hair. She's the daughter of a police officer who jailed Aisha's male character.

Obviously, they fall in love. The heroine gets in trouble, but even though it jeopardizes the hero's freedom, he puts her on a pedestal, going against his principles and beliefs to protect her.

She's the most significant part of the story, and I see her on the cover with the hero.

Aisha growls, shoving the phone back into her tiny bag. "He's not coming. His agent double-booked the day, and he's off to shoot elsewhere because it pays better." She stomps her foot. "You'd think they'd have the decency to call and let me know!" She collapses onto the loveseat, hiding her pretty face in her hands. "God, what am I going to do now? The cover designer needs the shots by the end of the week. The cover reveal is two weeks from today!"

"Hey, don't worry. If you can hire another model, I'll juggle my appointments, and we'll get the shots done. I don't mind working after hours."

She peers up, clearly distressed. "That's the problem. I can't get another model. I'd called ten different agencies before I booked Killian, and we'd been waiting so long for today! No one has any availability."

That's an issue. I can shoot in the middle of the night, but it's no use if we don't have a model. Luke would gladly stand in, but he doesn't fit the hero's description in the slightest. He's more suited for the villain of the story.

"What about that biker guy?" I ask, remembering he was tall, ripped, and could pass for the hero.

Aisha cringes, clutching the cup of coffee with both hands. "No, we're not exactly on speaking terms anymore. Urgh! I really need to start planning ahead of time." She glares at the door as if willing some hottie to arrive and save the day. "What about you? You know anyone who fits the character and would be willing to do the photoshoot? I'll pay double Killian's rate, and that guy charges a bomb."

Do I know any tall, dark-haired, broody, handsome, ripped men? If one. I can think of three right off the bat, but I doubt either will agree to help. Not if I'm the one asking.

Aisha's face lights up as if she can read my mind. "You do know someone, right? Oh, please, please, *please* call him," she's almost on her knees, hands together as if she's praying. "Please."

I push the air through my nose, the hairs on my neck standing to attention at the thought of reaching out to Logan after he threw me out of his house three weeks ago. I grind my teeth, chewing the words, my tongue slick with bile rising to my throat. I don't want to do this. A lead weight pulls at my chest, my fingers numb from clenching the cup I'm holding too hard.

Under normal circumstances, I wouldn't dream of asking him for help, but... *always* a fucking but.

This is my job.

Aisha is my client, and my client's happiness always comes first. Furthermore, I like the girl, and I love her books. If we don't find a model, she'll have to change her publishing schedule, and I know for a fact it'll piss off a lot of readers.

"I can ask, but don't get your hopes up," I force the words past clenched teeth, bracing to lose a bit more self-respect. "He's not the most easy-going person."

"Okay, okay! I'm not getting my hopes up," she beams, contradicting her words. "Please ask him."

I'm too chicken shit to dial Logan's number, so I shoot him a text, typing and re-typing the message three times before the words make sense.

Me: Hey. This is unusual, but I'm out of ideas and options, and my client is losing her mind. A model booked for a book cover photoshoot today didn't show. I need a substitute: tall, toned, dark hair, dark eyes. Rings a bell? I'm too scared of Nico and Theo to ask, and the triplets are too young.

My heartbeat pulsates in my fingertips when I hit send, watching the screen. Logan reads the text within a few seconds as if he held the phone when my message arrived. Three dots start dancing, and a cold sweat makes my skin feel clammy.

Logan: If you want me, you need to ask nicely.

The nerve of him.

He didn't bother to nicely ask me to leave his house. Jerk. I type out, *forget it* but catch a glimpse of puss-in-boots-eyed Aisha watching me as if I'm a Genie about to make her wish come true. I take a deep breath, shepherding the anger soaring through my veins, delete the line, and stuff my pride in my back pocket for now.

Me: Can you please take your shirt off in front of my camera today? You'll need to sign release forms so the pictures can be used for the cover and marketing. Aisha's paying good money for the shoot.

That's probably not the way to convince Logan. He's not short of cash by any definition.

Logan: What time do you want me there?

He'll do it? Just like that? No questions?
A smug smile stretches my lips. I think I'm winning for the first time since I met him. He must feel at least a little bad about what happened if he's ready to help.

Me: As soon as possible. I'm ready whenever.

Logan: I know you are, princess.

My stomach tightens in sync with a rush of heat prickling my cheeks. What the hell is he playing at? He said we're done. He told me to memorize what it feels like when we're in bed and use my imagination whenever I need to come—which I've done a shameful number of times during the past three weeks—because we won't fuck again, but now his text reads like an innuendo.

Has he changed his mind?
I hope not. There's no way I'll give in to the asshole again after how worthless he made me feel.
Nope, that's a lie.
I'm too weak, too defenseless in his presence to say *no* if he'd like to pick up where we left off.

"What's the verdict?" Aisha asks, squirming in her seat. The tiny blue dress she wears struggles to keep her boobs in place.

"We've got a model. He'll be here soon."

She claps like a child, then lunges forward and wraps her arms around me, kissing my cheeks. "I owe you *big* time!"

Yes, she does, and one day I'll knock on her door to collect the debt—thirty-six of her books, *signed*.

We spend forty minutes talking over the details for the nth time, but I can't shake the idea I have in my head.

"Have you ever thought of including a couple on your covers?" I flip through the pages of one of the albums to show her what I have in mind. "I had an idea when you told me about the heroine." I point at a picture of Luke, shirtless and glaring into the camera, his hand across the shoulders of a woman standing a foot to his left, facing him.

"Ooh, I like this," she says. "We can think about it with the next book. Unless you have a friend who fits the heroine?"

"No, but you do. The cute blonde from the café."

"Mia?!" She cocks a questioning eyebrow, then bursts out laughing when I nod. "No way. I mean, you're right, she fits the heroine to an extent, but she'd never agree to be featured on the cover. She's too shy for that."

"No one would know it's her. You can't see the girl's face in the picture." I tap the photo again. "Just her back and hair."

Aisha leans over the album, thinking for a moment before she shrugs. "Won't hurt to ask, I guess." She dials the number, sipping her coffee. "Hey, a question. I'm doing the cover shoot today. How would you feel about posing with the guy?" She pauses, listens to Mia, and rolls her eyes. "No one would know it's you. Hold on." She snaps a picture of the one in my album. "Check the message I sent. This is what we're thinking."

Another pause, longer this time. Long enough that Aisha starts tapping her foot against the floor. "Please, I'll drive you to Austin in September if you do this for me."

It takes a bit of back and forth, but when Aisha bounces in her seat, smiling from ear to ear, I know Mia said *yes*. Before they finish talking, the door to the studio opens, and Logan walks in, no baseball cap on his head, hair damp. A gush of warm breeze breaches the studio, carrying the smell of his cologne across the room.

My knees turn weak, and every muscle in my body seizes. It's so unfair that I melt into a puddle at his feet whenever I see him, yet he's utterly unaffected by me.

Aisha cuts the call, eyes on the masterpiece of a man shedding his brown leather jacket. No jersey underneath, just a plain white t-shirt, damp around the collar where beads of water dripped from his hair, marking the fabric.

"Who would've guessed?" Aisha chuckles, but the sound is laced with a flirty undertone. "Welcome, Mr. Hayes."

One eyebrow crooked higher than the other, he eyes her up. By the look of him, he's having a hard time placing Aisha. "Yeah, sorry, honey, but you'll have to remind me who you are."

Aisha swats at the air, her smile intact. "You don't know me, Logan, but this town is too small for anyone not to know the Hayes. I've seen you around. I'm Aisha Harlow." She gets up on her four-inch heels and extends her hand, scrutinizing Logan like he's a pair of shoes she wants to break in.

They shake hands, and finally, he looks at me. The pressure of his eyes roving over my body, the rich complexities of brown and gold flecks, and the way he holds a smile at bay has my heart singing. I'm not as sexy in a pair of jeans and an oversized t-shirt as Aisha in the tiny dress, but his attention is on me, not her and damn if that doesn't stroke my ego.

"Shit. I bet you don't have a hairdresser on call, do you?" Aisha huffs, running her fingers through Logan's hair. "That needs styling before the shoot."

A pang of envy, like the swift kick of whiskey, burns my insides. *Hands off, girl.*

"I got you a model," I say, careful not to let my voice betray that I want to remove her hand. "He can do his own hair."

"Yeah, I bet, but I'll take care of it myself today. I need to pick up Mia from college, so I'll drop in at the store and get some products." She grabs her bag and rushes out of the studio, showing me thumbs-up behind Logan's back.

Why did I call him in here? Aisha's beautiful, blonde, confident, and not an enemy of the Hayes clan. She'll probably end up in Logan's bed tonight.

I tip my head to one side, closing my eyes briefly to get the irrational emotions under control. If he wants to fuck her, there's nothing I can do about it.

The atmosphere shifts the second Logan and I are alone, as if Aisha took most of the oxygen with her, and now the air is too thick to inhale. "Thank you for agreeing to help," I say. *I wish you wouldn't.* I point at the loveseat. "Sit down. We need to wait for the girl to arrive before we can start."

He sits, the fresh, showered smell of his body now much closer and messing with my head.

"A girl?" he questions.

"Last minute addition," I point at the album on the coffee table. "This is what we're trying to recreate."

He leans closer, studying the picture while I gather the cups and move to make coffee. Anything to busy my hands.

Logan follows. His tall frame crowds the small space when

he leans against the doorframe, watching my every move like a hawk stalking his prey. The coffeemaker works at a snail's pace, filling a tall cup with black coffee. On the flip side, the bitter aroma blocks the scent of Logan's shower gel.

I shift from one foot to the other, aware of the dampness between my legs. I hate that my body betrays my mind. I hate that despite how deep Logan can cut, I'm turned on whenever I see him.

He pushes away from the wall and stands behind me, gripping the countertop on both sides of my waist. I feel the heat rolling off him, his chest hovering over my back. "Are you still mad, princess?" He dips his head, his warm breath on my neck.

"I wasn't mad."

I'm overcome with a sudden, hot rush—a sensation only Logan ignites. The vibration of his voice travels from his chest to mine when he moves closer, leaning into me, and I feel the outline of his erection pressing against my butt.

"Are you upset?"

"I... I don't know why I expected you to be less of an asshole in the first place." My voice is weak, the words almost a whisper when he places one hand on my stomach, spreading his fingers in a possessive manner. "You need to let me go, Logan."

"Why?" he hums, his lips brushing against the soft spot where my shoulder and neck meet. "You don't want me to let you go, Cass. Admit it."

I shake my head *no,* but my eyes flutter closed when he traces open-mouthed kisses up to my ear, grazing the skin with his teeth. "We're done," I whisper, but tilt my head to the side, giving him better access. "Remember? You said it."

"We never began, baby." He moves the other hand to grip my hip, pressing himself into me harder. "We'll never begin, but you've been good at keeping your mouth shut, and I can't seem to shake you out of my system... I think I need to *fuck* you out."

I'm not in control of my body when he's this close. The cards are in his hands. *He* calls the shots. I'm a puppet, reacting to his touch and bending to his will, but I am, at least for a little while longer, in control of my mind.

"You think I'll be your booty call after how you treated me last time?"

He moves one hand to my breast, kneading gently, tearing a soft gasp out of my lips before I can swallow it. My head falls back, resting against his shoulder.

"Yeah, I think you will," he says, sounding pleased. The smug bastard. "What have you got to lose?"

My sanity.

Integrity.

Pride.

My *heart*.

My eyes roll back into my head when he pinches my nipple, building on the anticipation tingling between my legs.

"Say *yes*." He spins me around, dark eyes on mine, one hand under my chin, fingers tilting my head, so I'll look up. The other hand touches the button that fastens my jeans. He flips it open, slides the zipper, and shoves his hand under the fabric, touching my soaked panties. Applying just the right amount of pressure, he rubs small, perfect circles. "*Always* so ready for me," he says, reminding me of what I told him three weeks ago. "You want to come, baby? Tell me to make you come."

And once again, I'm unarmed. Helpless against the need thrumming around my entire body. "Yes." I buckle against him, pressing myself into his fingers. "Make me come."

His lips crash onto mine, and he retreats his hand fast, yanking my jeans down to my mid-thighs. "We don't have much time before Aisha comes back, so *I* choose." He spins me back to face the coffeemaker, placing my hands on the counter. "Cock. You'll come on my cock."

The fabric of his jeans ruffles as he pushes his pants down and grips my hip with one hand, yanking my soaked panties to the side. He bends his knees, guiding his erection to my entrance. I expect a quick thrust, but Logan rubs the swollen head of his cock between my folds, the slick wetness aiding his work.

"Hold on," he grinds out, wrapping one hand under my breasts, the other still on my hip as he fills me in one swift move. "Fuck, you feel amazing."

He feels amazing. Whenever he's around, I'm calmer than I've ever been before. At ease. Composed. *Happy* despite our relationship being purely physical. The pent-up pressure that's been building inside me since I last had him this close, gives way. I love when his hands wander my body while he slides in and out of me in a heated, unforgiving pace, lips on my neck or shoulder, his chest flush against my back.

I shouldn't feel safe with Logan. I should run, hide, and not let him touch me because that man will be my death. He already owns my heart and body. It won't take long before he claims my mind. Once I lose that, there'll be no saving myself from the pain.

Logan Hayes will chew me up and spit me back out when he gets his fill.

And I can't do a damn thing to stop him.

FOURTEEN

Logan

Having learned a lesson from my mistake, I grab a roll of paper towels when I pull out of Cassidy, spin her around and *kneel*.

"I can do it myself." She reaches to snatch the towels out of my hand, but I swat her away, my heart thumping faster.

I'm riveted, watching the pearly trickle of my cum drip from the pink of her pussy and down the pale, milky skin of her thighs. It's undeniably hot that she let me come inside her; that she trusts me this much.

"Not this time, but don't get used to this." I clean her up gently, best I can with dry paper towels. "I'm not doing a good job down here, princess."

"Thank you," she says when I rise to my feet.

She fastens the button of her light, baggy jeans and turns away to face the coffee machine, the skin in the crook of her neck flared thanks to my teeth. I'm only half aware of what my lips and hands are doing when I'm with Cass. Every time

I slip inside her, the Earth stops spinning.

It's just us, locked in an alternate dimension.

Not unlike the first time, the world could go to hell while I'm buried in her pussy, and I wouldn't notice. Her scent drives me fucking incoherent, and the cute whimpers fuel my hunger. I push through the sting of my muscles burning with the effort, driving into her like an animal in heat, starved for the way she soaks my cock and clenches around me when she comes.

"How long will this take?" I ask, snatching a cup of black coffee from the counter.

Cass starts the machine again, picking a caramel latte on the touch panel. "That depends on how well you and Mia work together and with the camera."

An overdoor bell chimes, informing us of Aisha's arrival.

Perfect timing. Not a minute too early.

I stroll out of the kitchenette, curious about the girl I'll be posing with. Aisha stops by the loveseat and flings a large bag off her shoulder, heaving with the effort. Partially hidden behind her back, wearing a pink pinafore dress, a white, long-sleeved blouse, and a pair of white sneakers, stands a tiny girl.

Honest to God, I've never seen a girl this dainty. About five-foot-nothing, she resembles a fine porcelain doll. Long, dirty-blonde hair is braided into a crown, cheeks a deep shade of pink, and big, green, cute eyes.

"Hi," she says in a sweet, melodic voice, a shadow of a smile twisting her full, pouty lips. "You must be Logan."

"Yeah, and you must be Mia."

She bobs her head, glancing at Aisha, who empties her bag, littering the coffee table with hair products before hurling a pair of jeans and a white tank top at Mia. "Put this on."

Where?

Other than the doorless kitchenette, there's nowhere for this girl to change, and I don't think she'll casually strip in the middle of the studio without bursting into flames. She's so fucking timid I feel like a big bad wolf when I move to grab a tall room divider, and she takes a step back even though she's not in my way.

The room divider is probably an expensive prop, but it'll serve its purpose. I block the kitchenette doorway, gesturing for Mia to get in once Cassidy emerges with a cup of coffee.

"How old is she?" I whisper to Cass, my eyebrows drawn together. No way I'll touch her if she's not legal.

"Eighteen," Aisha chirps, not at all quiet. "Sit down, Logan." She points to the director's chair by the window, a comb in hand. "Don't look so mortified. I've done this before."

I'm only mortified about touching Mia in case she shatters to pieces at the touch of my hand.

While my hair is subjected to all kinds of pulling, spraying, and modeling, Cassidy works on the set-up, muttering a string of incoherent gibberish under her breath. I catch actual words like *lighting, exposure,* and *lens,* but other than that, she's not making much sense.

Mia comes out of the canteen in light jeans and a tank top, hiding the two inches of bare skin under the collarbones with her arm, cheeks still scarlet.

It's good that she's not supposed to face the camera. She's so shy I dread the upcoming hours, but I also keep stealing sideways glances at her round, absolutely flawless face. It's almost unnatural. She's not wearing make-up but looks photoshopped.

I bet one of the triplets would lose his shit for this chick. She's gorgeous. Probably not their type due to sheer insecurity radiating off her, but Conor could make it work. He acts tough, but he's the most caring of the seven of us.

Stop playing matchmaker, idiot. They're all kids.

"Are you in college, Mia?"

"Yes. OCC."

"Then I bet you know my brothers. There's three of them, Cody, Colt, and Conor."

"Yes, they're impossible to miss," she admits, tugging on her bracelets as if talking to me is too stressful. "We've been in the same schools since kindergarten."

"Are they behaving themselves?"

"I wouldn't know." She accepts a cup of coffee from Cass, relaxing a little and no longer covering her chest. "They're a year above me. We don't have any classes together."

"What about the parties?" I ask, and wince when Aisha pulls my hair too hard. "Watch it," I tell her.

She just scoffs. "Does she strike you like a party girl?"

Mia's face falls at the comment, eyes no longer glowing as she sinks into herself, abashed.

Wow. How can anyone be so timid?

"Right, I think that's perfect," Aisha adds. "Now, shirt off, stud. Let's see those pecks."

I cock an eyebrow, smirking when I pull the t-shirt over my head, taking zero care not to mess up the hairstyle she worked on for ten minutes. Her eyes roam my chest, head tilted to the side as if I'm a dress she considers buying. Cass spins around, blue eyes on me, and she swallows hard, desire clogging her throat. It'd be safer if she'd stop gawking at me like she's ready for my cock again.

"Let's start with just you. I'll need a few shots for promotional material," Aisha says.

I. A. DICE

Judging by Cassidy's glaring and the twitch of her lips, Aisha might be stepping on thin ice, trying to take the reins. I take my place in front of the camera, and during the next thirty minutes, I discover that posing isn't as easy as it seems. Cass keeps repositioning my head or arms, scolding how I *look* at the camera.

Lose the grin
Smile.
Shoulders back.
Don't frown.
Frown.
Look at the door.
Look at me.
Scowl.

Jesus Christ. All the while, she jumps around the set, readjusting the lighting after every picture, changing the camera angle, or replacing lenses. She's in her element, confidence and passion written all over her face, and a major turn-on at that. She's talented, too. She plays with lights and shadows, creating the most engaging shots.

I flick through the pictures while she swaps the backdrop. Aisha peeks over my shoulder, which isn't easy at her height, but she makes it work without resting her chin on my shoulder.

"Mia, are you ready?" Cass asks.

She peels those big eyes from a copy of "Around the World in Eighty Days" by Jules Verne and tucks the book in her bag. She crosses the room, shoulders tense, steps small.

"Let your hair down, sis," Aisha says, and Cass's and my heads snap over to her. "What?"

"You didn't say she's your sister."

"I thought it's kind of obvious. We do look alike. What

does it matter, anyway?"

Okay, that's it. I don't like Aisha. Her attitude toward Mia is obnoxious. She barks orders at her like a dog, and Mia obliges without hesitation. I have no idea where the need to fight her battles comes from, but it floods my system, and I want to tear Aisha's head off.

"Where do you want me?" Mia lets down her long, wavy hair, stopping a foot away from me. "Is this okay?"

"Logan first." Cass positions me to stand with my back to the backdrop, glaring at the camera, then shows Mia what her stance should be.

"Stand straight!" Aisha snaps, barging onto the set to push Mia a step forward. "He won't bite, you know?"

Mia bounces off my chest. She braces her palms against the muscles on my stomach, then immediately backs away. "Sorry."

"Either sit down and, shut up find someone else to do the shoot." I stare Aisha down. We won't get much done if Miss Big Shot Author doesn't shut up. "Or better yet... it's almost lunchtime. Go and grab us something from *The Olive Tree*." I take a few hundred's out of my wallet and shove the money in her hand. "Tell them to let the chef know I sent you."

"The Olive Tree?" she asks, her tone sweet like sugar, my outburst completely ignored. "Why? That's on the other side of town."

Which means we'll have an hour to work in peace. "My sister-in-law is the head chef there. She knows what I like." I'm sure if Aisha weren't desperate to have the pictures done today, she'd tell me to leave, but she needs me too much to argue.

"Why did you send her to Nico's restaurant?" Cass asks once Aisha leaves. "What if—"

"She's stressing Mia out," I say, staring at the little bundle of nerves toying with her gold rings. "You should tell her to fuck off every now and then."

Another barely-there smile lifts the corners of her lips, and her cheeks heat as if in sync. "It's easier to nod along."

"You can't let her walk all over you like that."

She doesn't reply, glancing at Cassidy and awaiting instructions. The shoot takes all but half an hour without Aisha's comments and commandeering the entire session.

The first time I wrap my hand around Mia's back, she shakes like a leaf on the wind, but after a few of my not-too-funny jokes, she calms down and lets me pull her in close.

FIFTEEN

Logan

Weeks pass me by since I accepted Grandad's offer to take over the company. May turned to June before I noticed. And now, June is almost over, too. The last few weeks are a blur of meetings stretching into late evening hours and mind-blowing sex with Cassidy.

At first, I capped the visits to two a week, but halfway through week two, I couldn't wait until Saturday and arrived at her flat sooner.

Now, I'm there every other day and still want more. I want to be there twice a *day*, make her come on my fingers and cock before work, then again after, but I draw a line at every other day. It's too much, anyway. And somehow wrong that after two months of regular sex, we're still going at it like bunnies.

Cass opens the door when I come over on Wednesday, a whirlwind of cute annoyance: angry and irritated, cheeks pink, hair gathered into a messy bun on the top of her head. She looks like she spent the afternoon on a treadmill, running at twenty miles an hour.

"Tonight isn't the best time. I meant to text you, but I forgot. Sorry. Can you come back tomorrow?" she asks but pulls the door open wider. "I'm in the middle of making a mess and hurting myself." She lifts her finger to her mouth, sucking off blood seeping from a scraped knuckle.

My cock should not grow painfully hard at the sight, but it does. Every move Cassidy makes is ridiculously titillating.

There's no furniture in the flat. At least not in the living slash kitchen slash dining area. The door to the small bedroom stands open, blocked by the loveseat, the room packed beyond capacity. I doubt even Josh would find a way to crawl in there.

"My landlord decided to change the floor," she says while I take in the scene. "But the contractor only had enough time to dismantle the old one today."

"And you decided to lay the new one down by yourself and without any tools." I shed my jacket, rolling the sleeves of my long-sleeved jersey. "You're right. All you're doing is making a mess." I point at the chipped hardwood panel in the corner. "Wait for the guy to come back."

She folds her arms, pushing her boobs out, making it painfully obvious she's not wearing a bra under the black t-shirt. She's ridiculously sexy, even when dressed like a slob. Sweatpants hang low on her hip bones, hair spills from the bun, dancing across her shoulders, her t-shirt is stained with glue, and a smudge of blood marks her forehead.

"That's the problem," she huffs, opening the fridge to grab two beers. "The landlord called an hour ago to say the guy won't come back for two weeks! He's trying to find a replacement, but no one will get here tomorrow." She hands me a bottle of Bud Light, hauls herself onto the counter, and starts nervously peeling off the label from her Corona. "I don't mind sleeping on the floor for a few nights, but I can't get to my clothes or the bathroom, and I haven't peed in six hours."

Beer won't help with that.

I assess the space, counting the packs of flooring by the wall to make sure there's enough, then check what tools are available—a tiny hammer, three screwdrivers, a big-ass kitchen knife, and a tape measure.

Not enough. Was she hoping to cut the panels to size with scissors?

I didn't come over here to lay the floor down. I came to lay Cass down and eat her out, but there's nowhere to lay her down.

Shit. I guess DIY it is.

I set the beer aside, marching out of the flat to fetch a toolbox from the trunk of my car. It's an old habit to have it stashed in there. I enjoy the occasional handyman work and became the go-to guy in the family whenever anything needed fixing, but for the past year, I've been locked in my office and hardly had time to play with tools.

Now that I'm taking over Stone & Oak, I won't be getting my hands dirty at all.

"I thought you left," Cassidy says when I return, dropping the toolbox in the middle of the room that's no bigger than my master bathroom. "I can do this by myself, Logan."

"Say *thank you* and get your pretty butt here to help." I dismantle the three panels she laid down, then open a roll of floor insulation. "This goes first."

"I thought it was to cover the parts of the floor that are done while I work on the rest," she admits, helping me roll out the insulation and cut it to size. "Okay, what's next?" She's excited now, sitting cross-legged on the floor with a smile.

Her face lights up with that smile, and I can't catch my breath for a second. That stupid compressor fires up in my chest, inflating my lungs to the point they synch around my heart.

"Now, we lay the floor," I say, clearing my throat. "No glue, though. It clicks in place."

I show her how it's done and when she gets the hang of it, I let her work while I cut the panels to size to fill in the gaps by the walls. Half an hour later, half of the room is done, and the bottle of Bud Light beside me sits empty.

"We need more beer, baby."

I swear internally, assembling my face into stock indifference while avoiding her eyes, focused on the task. No biggie.

Yeah, right.

Things are getting out of hand if I can't keep the endearments in check outside the bedroom.

Cass either doesn't notice or chooses not to make a big deal out of it, for which I'm eternally grateful. Fucking her out of my system isn't working. I thought I'd be over the attraction by now. We've had sex in every position imaginable and on every surface in her flat, but I can't get my fill of this girl no matter what. She's Xanax, and by the look of it, I have severe anxiety.

I'm stepping on thin ice coming over here every other day. At some point, someone will notice. Someone will spot me leaving her flat, and the news will reach my brothers, and then... I don't even want to go there.

"I signed up for swimming lessons," she says, handing me another beer. "I had my first lesson yesterday."

"Oh yeah? How did that turn out?"

"Not too well." She yanks her t-shirt up to reveal a red

and purple bruise on her back. A spike of anger jabs me in the ribs. Her instructor, whoever he is, should get a kicking for letting this happen to her. "I slipped on the ladder while getting into the pool and went under."

Cold shivers chase up my back, and my stomach feels hollow when the image of her lifeless body flickers in front of my eyes as vividly as if it's happening in real time. I don't think I'll ever forget the fear rising in my chest when I pumped air into her lungs, trying to bring her back.

"I get that you can't swim, but there's more to it, right? You're afraid of water."

"It's not as odd as it sounds," she insists, cinching her shoulder blades together. She stops clipping the floor in place, suddenly as rigid as a taxidermy animal. "I don't mind water in the tap. Only when it's deep enough to submerge my head."

I swallow around the hot lump lodged in my throat. The look in those cornflower-blue eyes of hers makes my skin itch. It's not sadness. No, this is more sinister: vulnerability laced with fear. Her aquaphobia isn't without reason. Something happened to trigger the response.

"Did you drown as a kid?" I ask, trying and failing to keep my tone light. I'm ticking inside, remembering what she told me about foster care.

Let's say I quickly understood that hunger and loneliness aren't the worst feelings.

Cass turns the other way, gritting her teeth to stop the memories from overwhelming her. She resumes clipping the next panel in place but tosses it aside ten seconds later. "I was five…" Sitting with her back to me, she stares at the balcony door as if she can't look me in the eye while telling the story. "It was the only holiday my parents organized. Nothing fancy, just a few nights at a cheap motel in Laguna Beach. There was a pool there," she sighs quietly. "I remember how excited I was because I've never been in a pool before. I hadn't even seen one at that point, so I spent most of the first day in the water while my parents sunbathed, drinking on the loungers."

I don't like where this is heading. A heavy, ominous aura settles around us. An airless mounting sense of unease that makes my skin crawl. I'm glad she trusts me enough to speak, but I dread what she'll say next when she tucks loose strands of hair behind her ears, hanging her head low.

"My dad was nodding on and off, and Mom yelled at him to go back to our room. She wasn't drinking heavily in public back then, but she was far from sober. I remember Dad swaying on his feet, too drunk to see straight. He toppled over into the pool, and the cool water sobered him up a bit. Enough to realize he had to get out."

My hands ball into tight fists, anger rising in my mind, chest, and heart. This is worse than I could've anticipated.

Worse than I imagined.

"He used me as leverage to keep his head above the water, pushing me under over and over again," she continues, her voice void of emotions. Her words are distant, as if she's reading a script instead of reliving the hell she went through. "Mom ran inside to get help. I was only five, but I remember it so clearly... the bubbles rushing to the surface around me, the pain screaming in my lungs filling with water, how Dad fought in a frenzy, afraid to drown, but not afraid to drown me." She straightens her spine, exhaling a defeated breath. "The pool wasn't that deep. Water wouldn't reach higher than his neck if he stood, but he was too drunk to realize."

Words fail me. I'm shaking inside so hard my bones feel

like bobbleheads. What do I say to a girl who was almost killed by her father? I've heard my fair share of gore stories like this one from Shawn, but they were always about strangers. No one I knew or even met, so it never hit me this hard.

"What happened next?" I ask, my voice rough, throat dry. "Shit, Cass... tell me he paid for hurting you."

She shakes her head softly. "I don't know what happened later. I woke up at the hospital the next morning and spent three days in the ICU. When I came home, Dad was there, drunk." She lifts her head and slowly turns around.

No tears stain her cheeks. Not one glistens in her eyes. It's like another stab straight through my neck. She should cry. She should *feel*, but she seems numb and hollow inside.

I cuff her wrist and pull her in, cradling her in my lap, forcing her to cuddle into my chest.

We're not a couple.

Our relationship doesn't include hugging.

I doubt she considers me a friend, but my reaction is an involuntary reflex. I don't know if she feels safe with me, but I sure fucking hope so. She lifts her hand slowly, carefully as if unsure if she's allowed, but ends up weaving her fingers in the hair at the back of my head.

"In one of the foster homes when I was fifteen, there was a boy my age," she says, her warm breath fanning my neck. "He hated the whole world on principle. I'm sure he was hurt as a child, and it was his way of dealing with the issues, but..." She inhales deeply, nuzzling her face further into me. "He quickly learned that I'm afraid of water and shoved my head in the bathtub almost every day so he could see me kick and scream as if my fear gave him some sick pleasure."

I have the urge to find and gut the fucker. Him and Cass's

dad, too. We might only be sleeping around on paper, but she's been a part of my life in one way or another for years. I can't stand on the sideline, unaffected by what she said.

"I'm sorry you had to go through that, princess."

"It's okay. In a way, you overrode the bad memories when you pulled me out of the pool at Theo's. You were so gentle with me and determined to calm me down. Zack laughed when I coughed up water on the bathroom floor. Seeing you try to help... I don't know. It lessened the fear somehow."

My chest fills with a sense of pride, and my hold on her tightens on its own accord. She starts to relax against me. Her muscles have more give in them, but I can feel how hard her heart pounds against her ribs.

Only then do I realize I've been stroking her hair, combing it back behind her ear over and over again. It seems to have a soothing effect on her, so I don't stop.

I should, but I won't.

"Two years later, I was taken in by an older couple who couldn't have their own kids. They were lovely people, and I learned to trust them after months of help and affection. They paid for my therapy. I healed as much as I could. I don't let what happened in my past define me, but..." she chuckles weakly, inching away to look at me. "I don't like water, and I don't think it'll ever change." She moves away, sliding off my lap to continue the job.

I can't help the disappointment settling over me. Having her close when it wasn't leading to sex, when it was just a moment of affection... fuck. It felt *right*.

Everything about us is wrong. Too wrong, but that moment just now was so fucking right.

I want to reassure her somehow, put a smile back on her

face, but I doubt she wants pity.

Within the hour, the floor is done, and her bedroom is decluttered. We spend the next hour in the shower and in bed, but sex is different tonight. I don't want things to change, but I can't do shit about how I feel. My touch on her body is more tender, my kisses deeper, and it means *more*.

It's not just another physical endeavor.

It's still hot and demanding, but the warmth filling my chest and how affected I am by her touch is new.

SIXTEEN

Cassidy

Logan: An Uber will pick you up at 7 p.m. and take you to my house.

I stare at the text, two lines marking my forehead. I've not been over there since my unannounced visit.

We fuck in *my* bed.

My kitchen.

My couch.

My shower.

Nothing has changed in the schedule since my impulsive confession two weeks ago about being drowned by my father. Logan still comes over every other day and hasn't mentioned the subject again.

I'm glad. I shouldn't have told him any of that. Letting my guard down was stupid and irresponsible at best. Not even Kaya knows about the shit I lived through at the hands of my parents and foster families. Zack was the only one to feast on my phobia, but a few others took pride in turning my life into an even bigger hell than it already was.

The landlord wired a few hundred dollars into my account when I told him the floor was done. Logan's too proud to accept money for helping with the job, but he's not big enough of an idiot to refuse a gift.

Or so I hope.

I've been on the lookout for something meaningful but not personal for a while and finally had an epiphany this morning.

I take a long bath and pamper myself with scrubs and face masks before slipping into one of the three matching lingerie sets I own. I throw a light dress on top, and with time to spare, I make an effort with my make-up. Not enough effort that it's blatantly obvious I tried harder to impress him, though. Logan's not stupid. He'd see through the ploy from a mile away, and I'm not about to jeopardize what we have.

I know he only wants sex, but after three months in his arms, feeling his kisses on my skin, and seeing the determination on his face every time he goes out of his way to elicit the most intense pleasure, I'd lie if I said I'm not hoping for more.

And I let hope consume me bit by bit because lately, it's not *just* sex. Since he helped me with the floor, we've been texting back and forth. Nothing important, nothing meaningful, but it feels like a step forward.

He sent me a picture of a baseball cap he bought one day; a question about flowers for his mother's birthday last week; *you'll need an umbrella* yesterday before I even woke up.

My romantic side clings to the notion of *us* the way children cling to their security blankets. I'm daydreaming like an infatuated teenager of me and Logan *dating*, kissing in front of his brothers, eating dinner at Nico's restaurant, and falling asleep next to each other.

Silly, *delusional* me.

Dreams don't hurt, though; we all have some that have very unfavorable odds of coming true. Winning the lottery would be a prime example. Logan is a winning lottery ticket, but I won't be the one cashing him in. I only have him for safekeeping.

At seven o'clock sharp, I take the backseat of an Uber Logan ordered. Twenty minutes later, hidden behind a pair of oversized sunglasses and under a white, wide-brim straw hat, I knock on his door.

It flies open, revealing the man of my normal and wet dreams whose eyes skim down my frame, a smug smirk curling his mouth at the corner. "You look like you're about to cheat on your husband with the pool boy."

I tear the shades off, step inside, and smack him with the rim of my trendy hat. "I thought you'd appreciate the effort considering this," I point between us when the door clicks closed, "is a big secret, right?"

Amusement fades from his features, and he narrows his eyes at me. "I should've told you not to wear make-up. There are baby wipes in the bathroom down the hall. Take it off."

I spent half an hour drawing and redrawing so the eyeliner would look even on both eyes, and now I'm supposed to wipe the effort off? Yeah, no. "Why?"

"I want to replace another bad memory with a good one."

"You're making no sense, Logan. Try again."

He scratches his neck and huffs, clearly uncomfortable. "I want you to get in the pool with me."

I step back as if we're already outside, standing over the edge. During the failed swimming lesson, my heart tried to claw its way out of my chest, my throat turned dry, and my eyes prickled with unshed tears. I bit my tongue so hard I tasted blood even before I put my foot in the pool, and the panic got the better of me after ascending two steps down the ladder.

I told Logan I slipped. The truth is my legs were so weak it felt like I was walking across a narrow plank stretching fifty floors above the ground in a gusting wind.

I didn't slip.

I blacked out.

Thankfully, only for a few seconds. And those few seconds lasted long enough so that I was no longer in the water when I opened my eyes. I lay on the tiles, soaking wet.

"That's not a good idea. I tried and failed, and—"

"Hey," he says, stepping closer to take my face in his hands and force my eyes on him. "I won't throw you in, Cass. No pressure, just try, alright? I got you a few bottles of Corona to relax. I won't drink, and I'll stay on top of the situation if need be."

This isn't what I expected when I got in the Uber. We were supposed to have sex like always, but *this?* I'm overcome with sudden, irresponsible happiness that he wants to help, but at the same time, I'm a pig about to be slaughtered.

Still, there isn't much I'll refuse Logan.

"I don't need to take my makeup off. There's no way I'll willingly dip my head underwater."

"Okay, leave the makeup."

Something touches the back of my leg, and a jab of spine-chilling fear has me lunging forward, headbutting Logan in the chin, lip, and nose, and screeching like a five-year-old.

"Shit. What the fuck?" Logan mumbles, massaging his jaw. "I think you broke my tooth."

His words barely register as I watch a massive white and yellow snake attempt to climb up my leg. I shriek again, climbing Logan like a tree. I wrap my arms and legs around him and grasp his shoulders, digging my nails into his neck. The snake is only partially in the hallway. Two-thirds of its at least fifteen-foot-long body is still in the living room.

"You're afraid of snakes, too?" Logan mutters, amusement lacing his voice. "Relax."

He readjusts his hands to support my butt, giving it a light squeeze. No need to hold me. I won't slide down while the snake is under his feet. I'll gauge my nails into Logan's flesh, holding on like ivy before I give up.

"His name is Ghost. Say hi."

"Hi?!" I squeak, arching back to look at him. A stubborn splinter of guilt assaults my conscience when I see his lip swelling, but it's not enough to distract me from the main issue. "It has a name?! What is *wrong* with you?!"

Logan chuckles, squeezing my ass tighter. "He's not venomous, and he's pretty slow. You can outrun him. Unless you prefer to hang onto my neck, then that's cool, too, but you'll find he won't have any trouble climbing up here."

I move higher, my boobs pressing against Logan's face.

He plants open-mouthed kisses on the soft spot in-between. "I'm enjoying this," he breathes, his voice heavy with lust. "I'll bring him over when I come by next time."

"No, you won't!" I bounce in his arms. "Move, Logan. Move! Get me out of here!"

He laughs again, kissing up the column of my neck before he takes a wide step over the snake. He carries me into the kitchen to sit me on the oversized island.

"He won't hurt you. He's as mellow as they come. In fact,

he likes to cuddle."

"Cuddle? He's not *cuddling* you!" I shove a finger into his chest. "He's checking if you'll fit inside him!"

He's not chuckling anymore. He's all out laughing in my face. As the mature woman I am, I fold my arms.

"He'd have to be twice as big as he is to eat me. I did my research before I bought him. If I don't let him wrap himself around me and keep him in his pen at night, I'll be fine."

The snake enters the kitchen. He must smell my fear because his red eyes are on me, and I pull my legs up, paying no attention to my stance—cross-legged in a dress on the island. So very lady-like of me.

"Can you please put him in his pen for now?"

Logan grips the counter leaning closer to get eye level with me. "Will you get in the pool?"

"That's blackmail!" My eyes are glued to the monstrous snake gliding across the marble floor with undeniable grace. "Forget it. I'm going home."

"No, you're not. We're not done here." He moves away to fetch me a bottle of Corona, then scoots Ghost off the floor and half carries, half drags him out of the room. "There," he says a moment later. "Safe and secure."

"You're not normal," I huff, taking a large swig of beer. "He'll kill you. Mark my words."

"I've had him for four months, and he hasn't hurt me once. You, on the other hand..." He gestures to his face and the swollen lip, leaving the rest of the sentence unspoken. "Come on, you can sit by the pool while I take a swim."

I glance at the floor again, expecting the snake to materialize in my path.

"You want me to show you he's locked?"

"Yes."

He lifts me into his arms and carries me to the living room, where the snake is, in fact, locked in a vivarium the size of my bathroom. I think my entire flat would fit in this living room.

"Okay, you can put me down now."

He doesn't. He takes me out to the back garden and sits me on a comfy couch two feet away from the edge of the pool. I openly stare as he shimmies out of his pants and yanks the t-shirt over his head, exposing his toned body.

The Hayes are all handsome, taking the finest genes from their parents and grandparents to create God-like specimens with an array of sexy features, but Logan is *my* kind of hot: toned but without bulky muscle; broad shoulders, well-defined abs, triceps, and lats. With a splash, he's in the pool, swimming the length under the sheet of clear water to resurface at the end.

"Show-off," I mutter sipping from the bottle. "You make it look so damn easy."

He swims closer, resting his elbows on the tiles surrounding the pool, and rakes his fingers through his dark hair. "It is easy. How about you dip your legs first?" He supports his body with one hand, takes my sandals off with the other, and then points to the tiles. "Sit here."

"It's wet." I'm grasping at straws, searching for excuses not to get too close to the water. "I'll ruin the dress."

"Take it off. No one can see you here."

"What about your neighbors?" I glance around the houses nearby, but all face Logan's garden at an angle, and not one window overlooks it. With a huff, I slide the straps of my dress down my shoulders. "I think you like what you see," I tease to break the tension when his eyes rove my body dressed in a set of black lingerie.

"What's not to like?" He pats the space between his elbows and holds his hand out. "Sit. Legs on my shoulders."

Determination in his eyes helps me keep my fear in check. I sit, gritting my teeth when the cold water soaks my panties. Logan dips lower so I can rest my legs on his shoulders, my knees on both sides of his neck, feet in the air, a safe distance from the calm sheet of water.

It's both soothing and unnerving because Logan's in control right now. He can dip lower and submerge my legs, which won't be half bad if he stops there, but his hands are cupping my hips, and he can easily drag me into the pool.

My heart races at the thought.

"Drink," he says, his fingertips caressing my flesh.

I arch to grab the bottle, and he uses the opportunity to yank me closer to the edge.

"Relax, I said I won't throw you in. You need to get in on your own terms, but," he reaches between my legs, hooking his finger in my panties and moving them aside to expose my pussy. "You smell so good I need a taste."

He dives between my legs, not waiting for the green light, and he teases the taut bundle of nerves at the apex of my thighs with the tip of his tongue. Sitting so close to the water, I'm tense, but Logan does a great job relaxing my body and mind.

An unhealthy thrill jolts my senses. We're in the garden, in plain view. It's still daylight, and he's eating me out like he's been starving for days. A soft moan charges past my lips, and my eyes flutter shut.

"Shh," he tuts against me, his warm breath fanning my skin. "No one can see us, but they will hear if you don't stay quiet."

I arch my back, resting my head against the bottom of the couch. I'm biting my cheek to keep the moans inaudible, picturing us as if I'm watching from above: Logan in the pool, head between my legs resting on his shoulders.

My thighs spasm every time he strokes my G spot, bringing me closer. It takes longer than usual, but once the orgasm arrives, Logan clasps his hand over my lips, muffling my gasps, his fingers pumping in and out to prolong the high. My eyes dance with white spots, the orgasm so intense I want to rip my hair out.

"Look at me," he says, his hands no longer touching my skin, warm breath no longer on my clit.

My eyes pop open, meeting the feline satisfaction of his stare. He floats five feet away from the edge, prompting me to glance at my legs. They're in the water, submerged up to my knees. I take a deep, calming breath. This isn't so bad. Legs in the water are okay. I've done this before when I stepped into the waves at the beach.

"How's that?" He swims closer, pushing my knees apart so he can stop between my legs. "Scary as hell or bearable?"

I smile, staring down at him. "Bearable."

"Good." He hauls himself out of the pool and disappears inside the house to fetch another bottle of Corona. Instead of jumping back in the water, he shoves the couch away, settling behind me, his thighs boxing mine in. "Lean back."

I rest against his cool, wet chest, too calm and comfortable for my own good. "Why are you doing this? Why are you trying to help me?"

"Why not?" He drapes his arms across my collarbones, pressing me closer. "I'll still slip inside you later." He nips my earlobe. "I have this fantasy of fucking you in the pool, so I'm acting on selfish motives here."

I move my feet slowly, focused on the pleasant sensations

instead of the memories. The water moves around my legs in swirls, creating an odd sense of freedom.

"Will you hold me?" I turn my head, pressing my cheek against his chest. Despite the swim, he smells like his spicy cologne instead of chlorine. I'm taking advantage of the situation, grabbing handfuls of the intimacy, curving myself into his arms, and memorizing the happiness and calmness stuffing my chest when he's this close. "If I go in," I clarify. "Will you hold me, so my head stays above the water?"

"I won't let you go, Cass." He grips my chin and tilts my head back to reach my lips. My body ignites at the kiss. It's unlike any we've shared. Not the usual urgent, demanding make-out sessions designed as part of foreplay. This is different. Intimate, almost affectionate. "You're safe with me." He grazes his nose up my cheek, forcing my heart's rhythm into cardiac arrest range. "I'll go in first."

I'm cold when he jumps in the pool, shooting up a moment later, splashing me with more cold droplets.

"Wrap your hands around my neck," he says, standing between my legs again. Even with the growing feeling of unease in my stomach, I do as I'm told. "Tell me to stop if you don't feel comfortable, okay?"

Words are stuck in my throat, and a single bob of my chin is the only answer he gets. The anticipation of fear might be worse than fear itself.

Logan holds my gaze as he slowly drags me closer by my hips until I no longer feel the tiles under my ass. He supports my weight as he lowers me into the water, and I wrap my legs around his ribs, holding on for dear life.

Slowly, I start sliding down to his waist, focused on the determination shining in his eyes. My body's detached from my mind, trembling like Bambi taking his first steps on ice.

I'm scared, but not *that* scared.

Fear is manageable when Logan's close.

I hold my hands around his shoulders, clinging to his body as if he's my lifeline, eyes shut tight. Water rises from my waist to my boobs before he snakes one hand around my lower back.

"How's that?" he asks, his cheek against mine, his voice barely a whisper. "We're by the edge. I can lift you out in a heartbeat."

I let all air out of my lungs through my nose in one long breath and open my eyes, glancing around and down to where my body is underwater in Logan's arms.

A nerve-shaking, blood-to-soda-turning sort of fear flutters in the pit of my stomach. Ice-cold vapor ripples against my spine, summoning memories too painful to bear.

I cling to Logan, the only person in my life who offers a semblance of peace. I crash my lips to his, fighting my way into his mouth, acting on the intense need to distract my mind and stop the panic from spreading through my body like a vibrating tone.

"Out," I whisper the order. "Please, take me to bed. I need a distraction."

"Don't say *please*, when you want me inside you," he growls, biting my lip. "Close your eyes. We're *not* going out." He pushes my panties aside again and impales me on his long, stiff cock. The sudden intrusion while we're enveloped by the incarnation of my fear elevates the sensation: a mixture of pleasure and dread. "There you go... eyes on me, Cass. Focus on how good it feels when you're with me, baby." He steps closer to the edge, urging me to hold my weight. "Elbows back. I said I won't let go of you, and I won't. I want you to arch your spine."

I nod, getting into position. He thrusts harder, one hand on my hip, the other around my back, acting like a shield to stop me from bruising my flesh on the rough edge of the pool.

I focus on the first rays of orange and pink painting the blue sky above with sunset, deaf to the water splashing around us, numb to everything save for Logan's touch.

The resolve in his hooded eyes, his parted lips, and his muscles tensing with every thrust flip a switch in my brain, morphing fear into bliss. Courage sprouts against all odds like a flower growing in the desert.

Now or never.

"Move back," I say, pushing myself away from the edge until I'm almost lying, only my face above the water. He's still driving into me, but his moves are calmer and slower now. "Don't stop. Don't let go."

He digs his fingers into my hip bones when I take a deep breath and tilt my head back, going under in a fusion of fear and freedom.

The bottom of the bathtub that Zack pushed my head into flashes before my eyes. I see the bubbles of oxygen rushing to the top. I see my hair floating around while I braced my hands against the bottom, fighting to push up, but Zack was stronger.

My mind jams up, closing itself into a knot. Panic squeezes my chest faster than I can blink. I jerk myself out in a flash, thrashing about, clinging to Logan, my mind like the inside of a plane after *we lost an engine* announcement.

Logan's lips come down on mine before I draw in a single breath. I don't need air after three seconds under, but panic tries to choke me—a big, tight fist clenched around my throat.

It eases off as fast as it appeared when my mouth works

in sync with his, the kiss slow, hot and soothing.

"Calm down." He rests his forehead against mine, unmoving, his cock still inside me, arms around my back. "Calm down, princess. You're okay."

I nod, swallowing air and clinging to his chest. "I'm okay. I'm okay, I'm *sorry*. I thought I could do it."

"You can. You *did*. On your own. You want to let go of the fear, but it'll take time. Don't expect to get it over and done with in one evening. You did great tonight. I thought you'd sit this entire time soaking your feet."

I kiss his forehead. "Thank you, I—"

The sound of the doorbell startles us both. We were somewhere else just now, unavailable to the outside world, but reality seeps in, murky, bitter, and unwanted.

Logan tenses under my touch, eyes glaring at the open patio door. "Fuck." He hauls me out of the water. "Shit, it's probably one of my brothers." He jumps out, grabs his phone, tapping the screen a few times, then swears under his breath again, showing me a live feed from the camera above the front door.

Nico's there, his car parked by the curb.

In a hasty confusion, I grab my dress, pulling it over my wet body dotted with goosebumps.

"Just..." Logan's eyes dart from me to the screen of his phone and back. "Shit, you need to hide." He takes my arm, yanks me up, and drags me inside the house. "Grab your bag."

I'm too stunned to utter a word when we rush through the kitchen. I snatch the bag, shades, and my hat from the island, hugging my shoes to my chest, barely keeping up with Logan's long legs.

He yanks the garage door open. "Stay here until I come get you." He shoves me inside, slamming the door shut.

My eyes prick, welling with fresh tears. Who does he think he is to lock me in here? Couldn't he have told me to go upstairs and wait in his bedroom? Or better yet, couldn't he lie to Nico and get rid of him somehow? At the first possibility of being caught with me, the sweet man Logan's been all evening changed back into an asshole.

Why am I surprised?

Why does it hurt that he left me here alone and cold?

Why did I expect something else entirely?

I let the romantic side of me take the reins tonight. Logan's been acting out of character, and I let myself hope that we were heading in the right direction. That regardless of how adamant he is to keep our relationship purely sexual, there's more to it. That he *cares*.

Silly, stupid, *idiot* me.

I plop down on the concrete floor in the pitch-black darkness, shivering from cold and the remnants of fear, searching through my bag to find my phone. A small silver gift bag catches my attention.

I forgot to give it to Logan...

SEVENTEEN

Logan

"You're distracted," Nico points out, tugging from the bottle of Corona. "What's going on?"

He took Ghost out of the vivarium while I jogged upstairs to put on sweatpants and a t-shirt. The snake lazily curls into a donut beside him, surprisingly comfortable around someone he doesn't know. I guess vicious creatures stick together.

I'm not getting out of this conundrum now. For some reason, the whole Hayes clan is coming over. If my phone wasn't set to silent while I was with Cass, I could've avoided their visit, but when Nico rang ten times in a row, I didn't answer, prompting him to come over. Now, Shawn, Theo, and even the triplets are on their way.

Something's up.

It's not unusual for us to invade one's house, but I can feel it in my bones that something is wrong.

My palms grow more damp with each passing second.

I think they know about Cass and me.

I think this is an intervention.

I think Nico will go nuclear on my ass as soon as the other five step through the door.

"Nah, I'm good," I lie through my teeth, itching to throw him out of here and let Cassidy out of the garage.

Again, if I had taken a second to think, I would've sent her upstairs, but my mind was thrown into overdrive when I saw Nico standing outside the front door on the security system app.

"Work as always," I add. "Care to tell me why everyone is coming over here tonight?"

"We would've met at my place if you answered your phone." There's no amusement in his eyes. It's not like he ever smiles, but given the circumstances, I tense even more. "Patience, bro. I'll tell you when everyone gets here."

The doorbell rings five minutes later, and the triplets pour inside, not waiting for an invitation. To be honest, I'm surprised that Nico hadn't just barged in. I don't insist on them knocking the way Theo does. He's very particular about privacy. Even more so since he met Thalia, which is understandable, I guess.

I wouldn't risk walking into their house without knocking in case I'd walk in on my younger brother getting his dick wet.

Colt and Conor banter down the hallway before entering the living room. Cody hugs a case of beer to his chest, his hair long enough to be tied into a ponytail at the back of his neck, but it's not Cody's hairstyle that has Nico and me frowning.

"What happened to your face?" I ask, glaring at Colt's black eye and split lip. "You let some asshole hit you?"

"Quite a few times before I arrived at the scene to help," Conor says, blowing the curly mane out of his eyes. He looks like Harry Styles back in 2013. One of these days, I'll get him drunk beyond comprehension and cut his hair myself. "I got punched in the ribs." He inflates his chest proudly and lifts his t-shirt to reveal a purple, dusky bruise the size of my hand. "We won, though."

"Why were you fighting?" Nico forces the words past his clenched teeth.

"How did you not know? They *live* at your house!"

"I've not seen them in three days, Logan." He turns back to Colt. "Why did you get hit? Have I taught you nothing?"

Cody opens the case of beer, handing out bottles to the other two. "Give him a break. The guy was your size and raging."

"And where were you when they were getting their asses handed to them?"

"Making sure the girl that fucker drugged to rape at the back of *Q* was okay," Cody seethes, murder on his mind as he dares to *glare* at Nico. Bold move. "Any more fucking questions?!"

I've never heard him snap. His chest heaves, and his hands ball into tight fists like he's getting ready to knock Nico out if he says one more word. Good luck. He'd end up in the ICU if he'd dare to throw one punch. Nico would knock him out before Cody's fist would come near his face.

The door to the house opens again, saving us from an awkward situation.

"Anybody home?!" Shawn laughs, walking into the living room with a bottle of vodka in hand. "How's your friend?" he asks the triplets. "Is she going to testify?"

"We're working on it," Cody admits, his tone back to normal. "She's shaken up, but she's a tough one. She'll be okay."

"Tough one?" Shawn scoffs. "She puked all over Colt's shoes, bro. She's not tough."

"She was almost *raped*!" Cody booms again, scrambling to his feet. "Did you expect her to laugh it off? Give her a break! We'll have her at the station on Monday. You make sure Asher doesn't walk away with a warning, alright?"

"Asher Woodward?" I ask, recalling the guy who got his nuts kicked by Thalia two years ago. She saw him spike someone's drink and got in his face.

"Yeah, same one. I should have enough now to send him down for a couple of years."

"A couple of years?" Conor scoffs, raking his hand through the mess he calls hair. "I should've knocked out a few more of his teeth."

The last of the seven arrives with more beer. This is turning into a typical Hayes rager. They won't leave for hours. I want to send Cass a text, but if the volume on her phone is on the highest setting, the guys might hear it ping.

My leg bounces on the floor. "Right, what's this gathering all about?" I ask Nico once everyone has a beer or drink in hand. "Are we celebrating something?"

The room falls silent. My heart beats like a conga drum while he takes his sweet time, building on the anticipation and tension. He takes a wad of papers from his jacket pocket and hands them to me with a stoic face. I feel sick when I unroll the papers, expecting pictures of Cass and me making out in the doorway to her apartment.

There are no pictures, though.

My brows knot in the middle. *Purchase Agreement* is written at the top in bold ink, and *Country Club* catches my eye among the mass of text. "Is that," I start, staring at Nico. "You *bought* the Country Club?!"

He bobs his head, his face no longer impassive. In fact,

he's sporting a real fucking smile. "I made the jackass an offer he couldn't refuse."

"You spoke to Jared?!" Theo booms.

"Through my lawyer. Anyway, this," he takes the paperwork from me and slaps it on the coffee table, "isn't why I wanted you all here. "This is." He fishes another wad of papers out and hands out six copies.

I briefly read through mine, my eyes bulging out of their sockets. Nico split the Country Club seven ways, giving us fourteen percent of shares each.

"Why?" Shawn gets out of the initial shock first.

Nico shrugs, but I know there's a solid reason. He never makes any moves without planning and thinking it through. "You're married with a kid. You don't have much time for us anymore. Theo's married, too, and soon we'll all have families. You think we'll ever get together, just the seven of us, to sit and drink like we are now?"

"Hell yes!" Colt booms. "Bros before hos!"

The line earns him a whack across the back of his head from Theo. "Call my wife a *ho* again, and you'll be picking your teeth off the carpet, *bro*."

"We'll see each other, sure," Nico continues. "But it'll be birthdays and Christmas and Mom's get-togethers. Running a business will keep us close. Mandatory management review meetings are factored into the agreements. Two weekends a year in an undisclosed location."

Theo smirks, patting Nico on the back. "So, you basically drew up a legal document to let us get away from our wives and kids for the weekend."

"*Sweetie, it's work. I swear. Yes, we're going to Vegas, but... shit, just look at the contract. I have to go!*" Cody dramatizes.

I can't believe my brother spent a few million dollars to make sure we'd have a reason to get away from our lives and spend time together, just the seven of us.

"Shit," Shawn says, wiping his eyes with the back of his hand. "You're making me tear up, asshole."

We laugh it off, but the truth is, there's a clog in my throat, too. I can't imagine my life without the six of them, and it makes me painfully aware that the time has come to end the dalliance with Cassidy. At first, I was fine with casual, but for the past week, I struggled to focus, willing the hours away so I could drive over to her flat and spread her on the kitchen counter.

I'm balancing on the edge of the knife. One false move and I'll come tumbling down. The question is, will I hit the sharp or the blunt edge?

I thought I'd have my fill of her by now, but the longer we continue the arrangement, the more I crave her body. And lately, the erotic thoughts aren't limited to my dick sliding in and out of her. I imagine kissing her. I imagine locking her in my arms and stroking her back as we lay breathless on the small, uncomfortable bed in her bedroom.

She's a parasite I can't get rid of, and I have to. The longer we continue, the bigger the risk that my brothers will catch onto the secret.

We celebrate for a few hours, talking, catching up, and laughing at Shawn's stories about Josh causing undeniable mayhem. They leave around one in the morning, and as soon as the last car disappears at the end of the street, I cross the hallway and yank the garage door open, flipping the light on.

"Shit, I'm so—" I pause, glancing around the empty room. Where the hell did she go?

A small, silver gift bag lies on the floor. I pick it up, my eyebrows knotted together when I pull out a card.

Thank you for helping with the floor. And thank you for listening. The seats aren't as good as you'd pick, but I hope you'll enjoy the day.

Two tickets to a Los Angeles Dodgers game a few weeks from now are in the bag. My heart wrings itself out again. Here I am, ready to cut her loose, and she chooses that moment to buy me tickets to see my favorite team play.

I take my phone out of my pocket and check the security app to see how she managed to get out of here unnoticed. I'm relieved to see she emerged from the side of the building at the front of the house, which means...

I glance from the screen to the personnel door on the opposite wall. I've used that door twice since I moved in. Maybe it'd be wise to lock it. There's nothing in the garage to steal, but I don't lock the door that leads inside the house, and there's plenty to steal in there.

She's probably asleep by now, but I send her a text anyway.

Me: I'm sorry. That was a dick move even for me. Thank you for the tickets.

Delivered changes to *read* under the message almost instantly, but three dots are nowhere to be seen. A minute goes by, two, five. No reply.

Me: Don't ghost me. I should've told you to go upstairs, but I wasn't thinking.

Again, *read* but no reply. She's mad as hell. To be honest, I deserve the silent treatment. Locking her in the dark, cold garage, wet and still scared after she went under, was fucking low.

Me: Come on, don't be like that. I'm sorry.

The three dots start dancing. I leave the garage and head upstairs, my eyes on the screen while she types. And it seems she's typing a whole dissertation on the topic. I strip off my clothes, brush my teeth and get in bed, all the while waiting for her to finish scolding me and hit *send*.

The dots stop, then start again, and it takes at least ten minutes before my phone pings.

Princess: I'm fine. Goodnight.

A kind of slow, stubborn, unquenchable guilt sweeps through me. Fuck. That hurts.
She's not fine. Not by a long shot.
She's upset again.
Because of *me*. *Again*.
The image of her tear-stained face flashes before my eyes. I try to swallow the shame burning the back of my throat, but it's lodged there like a chunky piece of an apple.
I need to let that girl go. I don't want to be another person in her life that's there to take and give little in return.

EIGHTEEN

Cassidy

Mary-Jane, Kaya, and I enter Rave at ten in the evening. The latter called to invite me out at the last minute, but with no other plans, I took her up on the offer.

I can't remember the last time I went out with the girls. Most of my time recently was spent with Logan, and while I wouldn't change that, my anxiety grows tenfold with every day of silence on his part. It's been three days since he locked me in the garage, and other than the half-assed apology in the middle of the night, I've not heard from him.

He didn't come over to fuck.

I shouldn't have made him feel bad about locking me up. He wasn't thinking... he panicked.

I hate that I'm making excuses for the jerk, but more than that, I hate that he's not been around. I miss him. I don't want us to end... but deep down, I know he's done with me.

Still, I cling to the excuses. Maybe he's busy? Or not in the mood for sex? Maybe he had a family emergency?

No, you idiot. You're over.

God, why does it hurt so much?

Kaya elbows my side, strolling past me, dressed to impress in a tempting number covered in silver sequins that reflect the strobe lights, changing colors like a kaleidoscope and catching the attention of most men within eyesight.

It's not sequins that grab their eyes. It's the narrow, low-cut cleavage that reaches her belly button and no bra on her impressive implants.

"Drinks first!" she yells, aiming for the bar. "What are we drinking tonight?"

I lean over the counter so the bartender will hear me over the roaring music blasting from the speakers around the club. "Kiwi daiquiri, please."

Kaya scrunches her nose before placing her usual order—a bottle of bubbly. I used to do the same, but now that I own a business and watched my best friend spiral into alcohol addiction, I cut back my intake.

I check my phone while we wait, hoping to see a text from Logan, but no notifications are waiting.

"I'll wait upstairs," I tell Kaya when she eyes a guy standing beside her. She'll end up making out with him in less than a minute, and I don't want to watch her cheating on her husband.

With a drink in hand, I head to the staircase on the other side of the room but don't make it halfway there before I freeze mid-step, my pulse roaring in my ears.

Logan stands no more than ten feet away, dressed as usual in a jersey and jeans, a baseball cap hiding his dark hair. My stomach drops, and bile climbs to my throat.

He's kissing some girl.

Their lips work in breathless sync, his hands groping her ass, barely covered by the tight bodycon dress she wears. She sways to the music, weaving her fingers through his hair and pressing herself closer to the man I love.

I don't know what kills me more, that he's touching her or that he's doing it in public. A high-pitched ringing starts in my ears. The world slowly splinters apart around me as I watch, unable to tear my gaze from them. He's kissing her in the middle of the club for anyone to see.

She's not a secret.

He's not ashamed of her...

Tears prickle my eyes when the brunette smiles against his lips, her cheeks pink, a drunken, blissful look on her pretty face. She winks and spins around, pressing her ass to his crotch, grinding as if Logan's her pole.

He holds her in the straitjacket of his arms, supporting her bouncing boobs as he dips his head, biting her ear.

Kaya stops beside me, following my line of sight. A hot glow of anger works its way up to her face before she rolls her eyes at me. "Jeez, still not over the idiot? Give up already, Cass. It's been three years."

It's been three days, but Kaya doesn't know that. She only knows about the one night we spent together. Back then, she was a different person. Caring, loving. When I called her, bawling my eyes out, she burned through the city and knocked on my door twenty minutes later, armed with ice cream and wine.

She glances around, scanning the dancefloor to check how many more Hayes lurk in the darkness. Nico is undoubtedly here somewhere. He and Logan grew closer since Theo got married, and they rarely go out separately.

It's pathetic that I know this. He never told me. I simply

pay attention to his life, scavenging for scraps of information.

The brunette in Logan's arms spins around again, her small hand sliding down his chest to cup the inseam of his jeans. A hot ball of jealousy, hurt, and disappointment burns behind my ribs. The way his eyes hood over rips me wide open.

More tears well in my eyes, but I swallow hard, snapping a mask of indifference in place just as Logan turns our way as if he can feel my eyes burning holes in his head. We lock eyes across the dancefloor and the utter lack of emotion on his face freezes the blood in my veins.

He steps away from the girl, but he's not fazed by my presence, not ashamed of his actions, not mortified by being caught.

I grit my teeth, fighting not to let Kaya or Mary-Jane see how distraught I am inside and not to give Logan the satisfaction of crying right in the middle of the dancefloor.

I knew it was just sex, even if I let myself hope for more, time and time again, but I thought we were exclusive. He was in my bed every other day, but apparently, that's not enough, and he needs another girl to fill in the gaps. How many more has he slept with since we started hooking up?

Oh, God... I fucking trusted him not to use a condom!

"Come on," Kaya yells over the blazing music, her tone annoyed as she hooks her elbow with mine. "We have a booth reserved upstairs."

"You want to stay?" That's the last thing on my to-do list right now. "I'm sure Nico is upstairs." *Please, let's leave.*

She drapes her long hair over one shoulder, pushing her chin higher. "So what? He can leave if he doesn't want to see me, but I'm not moving. I like it here."

I'm not falling for that. Kaya's been seeking Nico out since a week after her wedding. She's honestly delusional, but she's hoping he'll give her another chance.

Why marry Jared if he's not the guy she wants? Why sleep around with half of Newport instead of earning Nico's trust back and begging for forgiveness? Maybe I'm dumb, but I can't wrap my head around her choices.

I want to turn around and run with my tail between my legs, but before I can come up with a believable excuse to feed Kaya, I think better of it.

I'm *not* giving Logan the satisfaction.

Kaya and I ascend the staircase leading to the upstairs bar and get into the booth that happens to be directly opposite where Nico sits with Toby. Neither spares us a glance, but the way Nico's jaw works in tight, furious circles, I know he noticed Kaya sauntering over here as if she owns the place.

"What the hell is that?" she snaps, scrunching her cute-as-a-button nose at the kiwi daiquiri in my hand. "You're supposed to get drunk, not fit, bitch. I'm getting us shots."

She heard me order the drink at the bar and saw the bartender hand it over. The only reason she's making a problem now is to have an excuse to get up and walk past Nico's booth again, swaying her hips left and right.

Not that he cares. His eyes don't move from the screen of his phone. Kaya won't admit it aloud, but she'd turn back time if she could and never cheat on him.

I'm pretty sure she'd get sober for him, too, but it's too late, so she continues to party like she's sixteen.

"Jared would lose his fucking mind if he knew Nico's here," Mary-Jane says, plopping down beside me. "Should we tell him? He's an ass, but—"

He *is* an ass, and there is no *but* to follow. "Do what you want, MJ. I really don't care."

She pulls a face, crossing her arms. "Alright, spill it. I'm sick and tired of your attitude. You've been happy and sad, and everything in between on repeat for weeks. What's going on?"

"I'm fine. Just tired of Kaya's bullshit." That's not a lie, but not the truth Mary-Jane wants. I can't tell a living soul about Logan and me, regardless of how hurt and pissed off I am.

"Yeah, right. You've been putting up with her bullshit for years, babe, don't tell me you only now realized she's a piece of work. I know something's wrong. Who will you tell if not me? Is it a guy?"

I down half of the daiquiri and sit straight even though I want to crawl under a bed and hide like I used to when I was younger. It didn't keep Zack away then, so it sure won't help my bleeding heart now.

"An asshole, not a guy. It doesn't matter. It's over. It never really began, so... yeah." I glance around to check Kaya's location. She is my friend for all intents and purposes, but she's the last person I want to know about my mystery non-man. "Don't mention it to Kaya. I don't want to spend the rest of the night dodging her nosy questions."

MJ pulls her lips in a thin line. I think she's hurt that I didn't confide in her, but she must sense my foul mood and decides not to push for answers.

Thank God. Just thinking about Logan rips me to shreds and boils my blood at the same time.

"You know what you need?" She playfully pushes me away. "Rebound guy. A hot *mudstuffin* to help you forget about..." she pauses, leaning closer, eyes big and round, then sighs when I don't fall for the trap. "Trust me. A good orgasm is what you need."

That's *not* what I need. It's not like there's another man in

Newport as skilled as Logan. Not possible. Men like him come once in a lifetime and ruin you for whoever takes their place until the end of time.

Cuddling is what I need.

Netflix, a bottle of wine, a fluffy blanket, and a warm chest to press my cheek against. Someone to play with my hair while we watch a movie. Someone to stay the night, kiss my head, and whisper the three words I'm yet to hear anyone say to me.

Twenty-five years old, and I've never heard *I love you*. Not once. Not from my parents, foster families, not from my friends. What a sad, *sad* life.

I don't tell Mary-Jane any of that because, in my peripheral vision, I catch a glimpse of Logan sliding into the booth occupied by his younger brother.

He's not alone.

The brunette sits beside him, sipping from a tall glass, long fingers scraping the nape of his neck.

"I think you're right," I tell MJ, forcing a smile onto my lips. "I need a guy."

If Logan can parade his newest hookup in front of me, I'll give him a taste of his own medicine.

As if on cue, Kaya arrives, armed with four men. One carries a tray with at least twenty shots, and the other three place bottles of prosecco and six glasses on the table. She's married but has no problem fucking a stranger in the men's room.

If Jared doesn't know about his wife's antics, then he must be the most gullible person to walk this Earth.

"This is Mary-Jane and Cassidy," Kaya introduces us when the four of them force me and MJ to scoot over.

I end up facing the booth occupied by Logan and his new toy. He's not touching her but does nothing to stop her from touching *him*. I make a mental note not to glance in their direction. Instead, I focus on the guy on my right. He's got a piercing in his lower lip and a set of deep, stormy-blue eyes.

"Cheers," Kaya beams, grabbing a shot and urging us to follow. "Here's to those who wish us well…"

"All the rest can go to hell!" Mary-Jane and I finish in sync.

I'm not a fan of vodka, especially when paired with other alcohol, but tonight I'm throwing inhibitions and reason out the window, ready to face the consequences in the morning.

And those will be severe if the last time I drank vodka is any indication of what I can expect.

"Come on, you need something less alcoholic to wash the vodka down," Rush, the guy beside me, says in my ear, pointing toward the bar.

Normally, I'd say *no*, but A: I want to kick Logan where it hurts, and B: I spotted a familiar face at the bar and want to say *hi*. I nudge Mary-Jane so she and her friend for the night move to let us out of the booth. She texted me the day after she ditched me for Adrian outside *Q* that he's an asshole and not worth her time. *Love* didn't last long.

My eyes are on Rush's lips to ensure I don't look past him at Logan. We rest against the bar to the left of the balcony, and Rush calls the bartender over while I scan the crowd, looking for a head of dark blonde hair.

She was *just* here. Where did she go?

"What are you having?" Rush asks.

"According to you, something non-alcoholic. Coke."

He bobs his head, leaning over the counter to place the order. I can't unglue my eyes from his piercing moving as he speaks. There's a kind of odd sensuality about his lip with the silver ring in it. I wonder what it would feel like pressed against my lips... or my clit.

"You're staring, Cass," he says in my ear, then moves his hands to grip the counter on both sides of my body, leaning over my back. "At my lips."

"You play with the piercing. It draws attention."

He smiles against my neck, the metal ring grazing a sensitive spot below my ear. I really want to feel it dig into my lips.

No. You want to get back at Logan.

True. And it's not fair to Rush. Or Logan, for that matter. He's not mine. Never was and never will be. He didn't promise me a relationship or a set time frame for our sexcapades. Besides, if I'm being honest, I know Logan doesn't care that Rush is invading my space.

I shouldn't feel bad about flirting. I should cut the misery short and use the handsome stranger as an ad-hoc anesthetic. I spin on my heel, and words catch in my throat when he scrapes the lip ring with his white teeth.

"Stop staring," he rasps. "You make it damn near impossible not to kiss you when you look at me like that."

My sadistic mind pushes the image of Logan kissing the brunette to the front as if to fuel my anger and force my hand.

Kiss Rush to get back at Logan.

The problem remains—Logan won't care. I'm not important enough. I'm a warm, wet hole he can stick his dick in whenever he feels like it. A living, breathing blow-up doll.

"Are you afraid I'll bite?" I tease.

It doesn't come out flirty. No wonder. I don't feel like flirting with the guy. I'd much rather be at home, crying into my pillow until I cry Logan out of my system.

Rush smirks. "I hope you'll bite, babe, but I'll torture myself a little while longer."

Babe. One word with a hidden meaning when coming from a guy you meet at the club. Loosely translates to: *I just want to fuck you real quick, so don't get your hopes up.*

The bartender sets a glass of coke and two shots on the counter. We down them in sync, and I grab Rush's hand. "Come on. Dance with me. I'll stare at your lips for a very inappropriate amount of time." My head is spinning just a little, and it looks like three shots in twenty minutes make me courageous.

Rush places his hand on the small of my back as we forge a path through the crowd. "We'll see how long it takes before I snap."

Strobe lights jump across the room, and I let my eyes follow them for a moment, the everchanging colors captivating as we take the staircase to the dancefloor.

"Safari" by J. Blavin booms around us, the place packed beyond capacity. Rush doesn't need space. He pulls me into his arms until I press my back flat to his chest.

I don't feel the music tonight, but it's hardly the DJ's fault. It's mine. I can't get into the groove, and not even three songs later, we're back upstairs.

This time, I fail to keep my eyes from wandering to Logan. The brunette is no longer there, replaced by two others, one of which I know. She looks at me, a big smile stretching her lips.

"Cass! Hey, girl!" Aisha jumps out of the booth, wrapping her arms around me. "How are you?"

"I'm good. How are you?"

She shoots me a knowing look, grips my hand, and drags me away, back toward the bar. "Please tell me Nico's not taken," she squeals in my ear, then backs away, stealing glances at their table. "He's so fucking hot!"

"Nico?" My eyebrows pull together. I mean, he's good-looking, but he's not a guy most women willingly approach. On the other hand, Aisha's as spirited as they come, so I doubt she's afraid of him. "Um, no, he's not taken, but—"

"Good. He's mine tonight." She casts another look his way, seductively biting her lower lip. "He'll be my new muse."

"He's not into blondes, Aisha, and besides, he's very..." I trail off, unsure how to put Nico into words.

"Broody?" she supplies with an ever-growing smile. "Sexy? Arrogant? I know! That's why I like him. And believe me, tonight, he'll be all about blondes. One in particular." She winks, leaning in to peck my cheek. "Me."

Who am I to say *no*? Maybe Aisha has a way of making men fall at her feet. "Have fun. Oh, and do me a favor, don't mention to Nico that Logan was posing for your cover, okay?"

She props her elbows on the bar, signaling the bartender. "Why? Is he shy?" She chuckles, but then her eyes grow wider. "Shit, are you two a thing or something? Secret love affair?"

Damn, she's good. I meant well trying to cover for Logan, but I didn't take a second to think what kind of questions my statement would prompt. "No," I laugh it off. "He just wanted to surprise them but didn't have time yet."

"Ah, gotcha. Sure, no worries. It's not like I can seduce the guy by showing him pictures of Logan's bare chest."

"What the hell is taking you so long?" Kaya snaps, stopping beside us. "We're all waiting for you. I want to play a game, and Rush might start oozing sperm from his ears if you don't get your ass back in there right now."

Aisha narrows her eyes at Kaya, and Kaya shoots back with the same glare. God, *please* don't let Aisha mention Nico.

"We'll catch up soon, okay?" I tell Aisha before any damage is done. "Call me when you've got time for coffee."

TOO WRONG

"I will, babe." She's talking to me, but she's looking Kaya over, one eyebrow raised, the gesture laced with mockery. And then, recognition flashes across her face as if she realizes who this beautiful woman beside me is. "Have fun tonight, Cassidy." Her eyes cut back to Nico for a second. "I sure will." She turns to place an order with the bartender, but before I take Kaya back to our booth, Aisha grabs my hand. "Nico drinks Corona, right?"

I groan internally. No way Kaya didn't hear that. And considering how territorial she gets about Nico, especially when she's had a few drinks, *this* will not end well.

A few months ago, she slapped a girl about at *Tortugo* when she saw Nico buy her a drink. The second he left the bar with his friends; she ambushed the girl in the bathroom and tore a handful of her hair out. I wasn't there that night, but I got a detailed retelling of the events from Amy.

I don't understand what Kaya's trying to achieve, acting bat-shit crazy. I also don't know what that power play on Aisha's part is about, but I do know I'm the one who has to calm Kaya down before all hell breaks loose.

I don't get a chance, though.

Kaya's bright red, nostrils flared. "Nico?" she asks, getting in Aisha's face. "Sorry to clip your wings, *Barbie*, but Nico doesn't fuck blondes."

"Time to show him what he's been missing," Aisha bites back with a sweet smile. "I hear brunettes aren't doing him any good."

"What's that supposed to mean?!"

"Come on," I clutch Kaya's arm, holding her back like a dog on a leash. "Nico's not yours, remember?" I lean closer to speak in her ear. "And if you want him back, you're not doing yourself any favors right now."

She clenches her jaw, murderous gaze fixed on Aisha for a few more seconds before my words sink in, and she steps away, ironing her dress with both hands, her chin raised like she's trying to show off she's the bigger person.

Hardly.

Without another word, she turns on her heel and marches away. Aisha offers me a small smile before turning to the bar, and I'm left standing there, too tired to ask what she's playing at.

NINETEEN

Cassidy

Logan's eyes lock with mine when I return to our booth. He briefly glances between me and his phone on the table, tapping the screen three times before moving his attention to Nico.

Not one word.

Not even a proper look my way, just a cryptic nonverbal order to check my phone. The Hayes brothers are arrogant, spoilt, and players, but there are good qualities among the flaws.

Loyalty to their family sits at the very top. By sleeping with me, Logan's abusing their trust. My connection with Kaya is enough reason to hate me, even without adding Theo to the mix.

I take a seat, accepting a shot from Rush, itching to check my phone, but after pondering the idea for a minute, I leave my bag where it is on the table, in plain view, so Logan knows I disobeyed his indirect order.

If he thinks he can *booty-text* me after I caught him making out with a random girl, he's got another thing coming.

"We need more shots," Kaya yells, her hand draped over Rush's friend, Jason, who nods and gets up, heading for the bar. "Alright! Let's play that game." She grabs the bottle of prosecco, downs the remaining three fingers of bubbly, and lays it flat on the table. "Spin the bottle!" She grins, watching the neck land on Aaron, the guy next to MJ.

No one protests. No one bats an eyelash when Kaya leans across the table. Aaron doesn't hesitate, closing the distance to press his lips to hers for a hot and very inappropriate kiss. She's a married woman, for crying out loud.

A married woman who's hell-bent on making her ex jealous. She's eyeing Nico every few seconds, checking if he's watching, but he doesn't pay her any heed, engrossed in a chat with Aisha.

I need another shot if I'm to survive this evening.

MJ grabs the bottle, which lands on Kaya, and again, neither hesitates before they engage in a make-out session. God, we'll end up in a seven-way orgy at this rate.

Jason comes back with another tray of shots and, thankfully, a few glasses of lemonade. I grab one, clutching it close to my chest, feeling sick from the vodka and kiwi daiquiri.

Not the best combination.

It's Aaron's turn to spin, my palms clammy when the neck of the bottle misses me by one person, landing on Rush.

"No way," he yells over the thunder of bass. "I'll drink a penalty shot."

"Penalty shot?" I ask, clinging to the idea.

"Yeah, if you don't want to kiss someone, have a shot."

There are five people at the table, and only one I'd consider kissing. Although with Logan twenty feet away, even that's unbearable. Either I walk out of here drunk off my ass or subject myself to kissing strangers and my friends.

The table vibrates under my hand. I cast a casual glance to the bar, my eyes skimming over Logan, whose phone faces up, the screen lit. Toby's busy making out with one of the girls while Nico's grinding his teeth and glaring at Aisha.

I guess he doesn't want to check what he's been missing.

A heartbeat later, I cave, curious about what Logan has to say. If he wants to come over tonight, I think I'm drunk and brave enough to fight him. I pull my phone out to check the messages and lean back, making sure no one can see the screen.

Logan: Very mature. Lose the asshole.

Logan: Don't fucking test me. Get up and go home.

Logan: You think he'll walk out of here unscathed now that you let him touch you?

An unhealthy thrill washes over me, and my heart picks up pace. He's annoyed. I bite my cheek to stop the smile that wants to rip my mouth wide open. He cares. Only for my body, but he cares enough that he doesn't want to share me with anyone else.

He should've thought about that before he kissed the brunette in the middle of the dancefloor.

A few ideas for a reply spring to my head, but each sounds pathetic, jealous, or challenging. Each can be used against me, and all I want is to sever our minuscule connection with a scalpel: nice, clean cut, not a botched cheese knife job. No arguing, begging, or crying.

Nothing to hurt me anymore.

Too Wrong

A small cheer erupts, rolling around the table like a wave. I lift my head, checking what got everyone so excited.

Rush watches me, toying with his lip piercing, and motions to the bottle, its neck pointing at me. Adrenaline ignites my nerve endings when he smirks, eyeing my lips.

He leans closer, close enough that I feel the warmth of his breath fanning my cheek. "What will it be, babe? You want a shot or a kiss?"

I look away, straight ahead, my eyes locked on Logan. He's gauging his fingers into the glass bottle as if he wants it to explode in his palm. He holds himself wound so tight; I can tell his muscles have no give in them. His shoulders are rolled back, eyes narrowed, jaw squared.

I'm captive to his gaze. Butterflies take flight in my tummy, and a wave of blazing heat slides down my spine and travels lower to caress the backs of my thighs.

How long can I keep this up? How long before I can't get back up after people knock me down? When will I stop settling for being expendable? All my life, I've been just a means to an end. Never anyone's priority. Never cared for or loved.

Used.

Neglected.

Abused.

Discarded.

Forgotten.

A never-ending cycle of hurt spinning round and round like the Merry-go-round. First, my parents. The money they got from the government for having a child was more important than me. Then, the foster families who took me in to cash the cheques. Next, too many friends who only remember about me when they need help.

Hundreds of small, invisible cuts and bruises on my heart and my mind. Endless nights spent crying. Endless days spent living in fear.

But I rise every time and face another day with a smile because I have hope. I believe that one day, the Merry-go-round will stop and spin in the other direction; that happiness will fine me if I wait long enough.

Until then, I have no choice but to fight for myself. Protect my heart and mind from more hurt because I'm not sure where my limit is. I might be dangerously close to the point of no return.

I swallow hard, mustering the remnants of strength to turn away from Logan.

We were never meant to be. It's time to let him go, cry, and stop living a fairytale fantasy. Happily ever after only happens once upon a time.

"I need both," I tell Rush.

He reaches for a shot and watches me drink while sipping his lemonade. As soon as I place the glass back on the table, he grips my jaw, closing my lips with his, the kiss hard, hot, and sweet thanks to the lemonade I taste on his tongue. His piercing digs into my lower lip as I kiss him back as best I can.

I feel nothing, though. No butterflies, heat, or tingling in my chest. Nothing, but vile shame sinking deep into my bones.

He stamps a cute peck to my nose, releasing his firm grip on my jaw. His lips part, but no words come out when my phone vibrates in my hand, forcing Rush to move away.

I unlock the screen, doing my utmost to uphold an impassive expression while I read the text.

Logan: Two words, one finger. We're done.

TOO WRONG

The words hit me like an iron fist. Logan knows exactly what to say to inflict the most damage, to twist the knife and draw as much blood as possible. One sentence and all that's left of me is a shell missing its pearl.

My instincts take over, and I fight to ease the pain resonating through me like the lowest A note on the piano.

A sob threatens to tear out of my chest while my heart is on its way down to my knees, but I move the phone lower, under the table. I pump my fists and inhale a deep breath through my nose, faking the most genuine smile I can muster.

Me: Thank you. I hope one day you'll find someone who'll be your priority, not just your option.

TWENTY

Logan

Everything about tonight is wrong.
Me and the brunette?
Wrong.
Cass seeing me kiss her?
Wrong'*er*.
Thinking I can just flush Cass out of my system with the first easy girl I lay my eyes on?
Wrong'*est*.
As soon as I saw her, a sense of calmness seeped through the cracks of my edgy mind, setting me back on track for the shortest second.
My thoughts turned into a Mario Kart race when I realized she saw my hands groping the brunette's ass.
She saw me *kiss* her.
Should I care? Nope. We're not together. I did nothing wrong. I'd never top her stunt with Theo. I'm a fucking saint

in this situation, but... a dense stillness fell over me when our eyes locked. Her smile dimmed, slipped, and even from a distance, I saw her face twist with hurt.

Only for a moment, but it was there: disappointment.

Then, she marshaled her expression into that spoiled look she wears so often—a mask designed to hide her insecurities.

I wanted to chase after her, but how was I supposed to explain myself? *Shit, I didn't expect you to be here* is no fucking excuse. It's not like I should explain, anyway. Cassidy knew the rules. She knew we were a sex-only deal. No emotions, no attachment. It's not like I cheated on her... so why does it feel like I did? Why does my stomach feel so tight, twisting and rolling? Why do my lungs struggle to take in air?

I press my fingers to my temple, massaging in small circles for a moment before I drop my hand back down, squeezing my beer. Ten feet to my right, Cruella DeMon spins a bottle on the table in their booth, her dark eyes glancing over here, zeroing in on my brother every few seconds.

My hands grow cold and numb the slower the bottle spins. Anger riots through my system, heading straight for my chest where it'll set camp in my heart, and the liquid wrath will blast through my fucking bloodstream.

I can feel it gaining momentum, growing at an alarming rate like a snowball rolling down a steep hill. Nothing will save the asshole who dared to touch Cassidy on the dancefloor if he decides to lay one fucking finger on her again.

She's mine.

No one touches her but me.

The problem with that train of thought? It's a lie. Cassidy isn't and will never be mine.

I grind my teeth, fighting to keep my shit intact as frustration tugs at my mind. The ball of nerves lodged in my throat makes it hard to swallow.

How did I get here? Sex was what I wanted from the get-go. Just her body. The smoking hot, lean, toned, and skillful body, but suddenly, I crave more.

I'm jealous.

I worry.

I constantly want to see her, be around her, touch her, kiss her, and fucking protect her from the entire goddamn world.

It can't be happening. Not now. Not with *her*.

Cass and I can't happen. Ever. That's why kissing the brunette seemed like a great plan. One night to re-wire my brain, forget the beautiful blonde I can't get enough of, and channel my obsessive thoughts toward some nameless bimbo. One night to screw my head back in place.

Too bad it didn't work and opened a can of worms named *Rush*. I know him. His older brother is a friend of mine, and Rush isn't the kind of guy Cassidy needs around her. He's a player—a *collector*, as he calls himself.

Collector of pussies.

I stood on the balcony when they danced downstairs and fought my instincts to keep my ass in place whenever his hands touched her stomach or waist. I imagined breaking those hands ten different ways, and I'm *this* close to lashing out. It's a miracle I've managed to control my temper as long as I have. Deep down, I know I have no right to mess Cass about.

Our purely sexual relationship isn't working for her.

I *shouldn't* mess her about, but here I am, my phone in hand, already three texts sent. My leg bounces impatiently when it's Rush's turn to spin the bottle. He looks at her as often as Kaya looks at Nico, and he's pissing me off to my back fucking teeth.

The only consolation is that Cass focuses her attention on her phone, reading my texts.

Nico's too busy, glowering, snapping, and losing his patience with Aisha. She straddled him a moment ago, whispering sweet nothings in his ear and rolling her hips in his lap. He's not paying attention to the booth directly opposite ours. And he's too riled up to notice I've been stewing since I sat down.

The bottle spins slower and slower, finally coming to a halt and pointing at Cassidy. Of course, it does. It's Karma at play, I'm sure—*Ha! Take that, you prick.*

A thumping pressure starts at my temples, my body wound up so tight I can't move a muscle, but I damn near double over and throw up when Rush leans closer to Cass. His lips move, so I know he's speaking, a gentleman of the highest order checking if he can put his mouth on hers.

No, he can't. Not if he still wants to have teeth by the end of the night.

She says something back. And that anger, that thumping pressure in my head... *fuck*!

I can't pull down a single breath when he grabs her jaw, and their lips connect. I'm *this* close to smashing a bottle on his head, then carrying Cassidy out of the club fireman style. I'd take her home to remind her who she fucking belongs to.

The problem with that train of thought? Yeah... it's a lie too. She doesn't belong to me.

I wince as the pressure inside my head ups the stakes.

Game over.

The end.

With my eyes cast downward, I take a few very deep and very calming breaths. It does fuck all to cool the lava burning through my veins, but I put on a mask of indifference, rein in the violence coiled around me, and send her another message.

Me: Two words, one finger. We're done.

I glance over there again, checking her reaction, expecting her lips pulled into a line, eyes watering, but no. She *smiles* at her phone, riling me up beyond comprehension.

Have I misread her intentions? Until now, I was certain she wanted more than sex, but the smile lighting up her gorgeous face tells a different story, and so does the text she shoots back.

Princess: Thank you. I hope one day you'll find someone who'll be your priority, not just your option.

Thank you? What is she thanking me for? And way to twist the knife a little bit harder.

Cassidy: 1. Logan: 0.

She's right. She's not my priority, and she deserves to be someone's. Despite the shitty labels people stick to her behind her back, she's amazing. Passionate, smart, caring. Naïve and too trusting, which comes back to bite her time and time again. People use her good heart and take advantage of how much she craves human interaction after years of neglect and being treated with cold, harsh reserve.

My head is spinning when I dim the screen and shove the phone back in my pocket.

Hell just froze the fuck over.

***

She's tipsy. She's downing shots like nobody's business, refusing to kiss anyone else at the table. While I'm glad about that, I'm reeling every time she smiles at Rush.

Around midnight, I watch as she marches toward the corridor leading to the bathrooms, her steps awkward, the alcohol impairing her motor functions.

I glance at Nico, checking if he's paying attention to the booth opposite, but he's squabbling with Aisha. I heard him point-blank tell her he won't fuck her, but she brushed him off and keeps getting on his nerves as if seeing steam come out his nostrils is the best form of entertainment.

With the two of them occupied and Toby on the dancefloor, I bite the bullet, following Cass. She needs to get the fuck out of here, go home and sleep. She's had enough for one night.

The air is stuffy, the stench of piss, booze, and sweat assaulting my nostrils as I prop myself against the wall opposite the girls' toilet, waiting, chewing my own fucking teeth.

As soon as Cass is out, I grip her wrist and drag her into another corridor to my right. It's empty, dark, and out of the way. Perfect for a chat.

"What the fuck are you doing?" I clip, manhandling her until we're by the *personnel-only* door at the far end. My chest is heaving. The touch of her skin, the smell of her perfume, and that curve-hugging dress she wears stir a brand-new riot inside my head. "And what the hell is *this*?" I push her against the wall, tracing my finger along the edge of the fabric on her cleavage.

I can barely see her in the dark. Nothing but faint light from a LED strip above the door illuminates her face and her tits that almost leap out of the flimsy dress she wears.

"This," she says, touching the fabric I just touched. "This is called a dress."

"This is called *inappropriate*. You got any idea how many assholes have been eyeing you up? You look like every pervert's wet dream!"

She looks down, deep grooves marking her forehead. "I'm not showing off anything, asshole. Your *friend* wore less, but I didn't see you busting her ass—"

"She's not my responsibility!" I snap before I mull the words and take a second to realize how messed up that sounds. "Neither are you," I quickly add, backing myself into a corner. There's no rational way of explaining why her dress bothers me so much. "You can't be here," I continue, navigating back to the main issue, my ears ringing. My hands shake, and the riot of my pulse drives me nuts as I tower above her. "You're drunk, Cass. You need to go home." But instead of pushing her away, my grip on her wrist tightens. "You think I don't know what you're doing with Rush? You're trying to make me jealous, aren't you? You gonna fuck him to prove a point? Drop it. We're done. Over."

She twists her arm, struggling against my hold. *Good luck, princess.* I'm not letting go until I know she'll head straight for the exit.

"You think so highly of yourself, don't you?" she clips, shoving me a step back. "What if I like him? You're not the only guy in Newport, you know? I don't need *you* to get laid."

"Yeah, you'll just fuck one of my brothers instead, right? Triplets are legal now, so—"

She retaliates.

She hurts me the only way she knows how.

She slaps me so fucking hard my head swings to the side. The sound of her palm connecting with my cheek echoes throughout the empty space.

What the actual...

I press my fingertips against the burning flesh, speechless for the first time in a long time, as the words I spoke bounce around my head.

Fuck.

That was uncalled for.

"Cass, I'm—"

"*Don't*," she clips, yanking her hand out of my grasp.

Fresh tears pool in her blue eyes when she pushes me away with both hands, and seeing her like this—close to tears—guts me like a fucking fish. I watch, glued to the floor, frozen, motionless. What the hell just happened?

Why did I say that? I don't... shit. I don't *think* that. I got over her and Theo. She didn't know me when they landed in bed. I know she wouldn't have looked at him if we had met first. Cassidy's attention was on me since we first looked at each other three years ago, but... but I'm a fucking asshole.

My blood's been boiling for two hours, jealousy kicking up a hissy fit in my head as I watched her in that tight, beautiful dress, smiling at that sorry-excuse-for-a-man.

I snapped.

She takes a step away, but I grip her hand again, my heart rate skyrocketing. "I'm sorry."

She's not looking at me, eyes cast down. "Let me go," she whispers.

I read her lips more than hear the words. Shame curls around my stomach, and it feels like someone just throttled me. The music still pumps around us, the bass shaking the floor, but the sound seems distant, as if coming through a sheet of thick glass.

I take her face in my hands, wiping the tears I feel under

my thumbs. Her chin quivers. A small, pained whimper slips past her lips, and my stomach drops to my knees. "I didn't mean it."

"You did." She slaps my hands away, stepping back again. "I thought I reached the limit of how small and unwanted a person can feel when I was tossed back and forth between foster families, but you showed me I was wrong when you texted me three years ago." Her voice breaks—another kick right in my balls. She swats her tears away, pushing a steady breath past her lips. "I thought I found the bottom back then. But you proved me wrong again when you threw me out of your house. And then again, when you locked me in the garage… three nights ago, and tonight… I'm not worthless, Logan. I don't deserve to feel like this. I've never intentionally hurt you."

"Cass—"

"What?" she grinds out, standing a little taller. "You're sorry?" she jokes through tears, but there's no humor in her voice, just an ocean of pain. "You're not sorry. At least have the decency not to lie to my face."

With that, she spins on her heel and marches away.

I don't put up a fight.

I don't chase after her.

We're done. Over. We've been at it for too long as it is, but the weakness in my limbs can't be shaken.

Is the goddamn world imploding?

TWENTY-ONE

Logan

Cassidy's booth empties around one in the morning, but she's been gone for an hour now. She was no longer there when I finally forced my feet to move and came back to sit with Nico.

It's just Rush and one of his buddies left there, and just me and my brother left here.

Toby took a cute girl home ten minutes ago, squeezing her ass on the way out. I expected the same game plan from my brother. Once he got rid of Aisha, a nimble brunette took her place and spent an hour dry humping his zipper. She looked like his type, but he sent her away, forfeiting perfectly acceptable pussy for no reason whatsoever.

At least, I hope there's no reason. I hope Cruella's presence and the blatantly obvious, seductive glances she was casting at Nico any chance she had didn't spark a fire in his head, or so help me God, I'll break his fucking jaw if he even thinks about chasing after that bitch again.

"What's the deal?" I ask him, moving closer, not to shout over Ava Max and "The Motto" pumping through the speakers. "Why did you send that chick away?"

He finishes his beer in one tug, angling his head to me. "She let it slip that she's in college."

"College chicks are wild, bro. You should've gone for it."

He shakes his head once, slamming the empty bottle on the table. "Too young, too clingy, and too annoying. And don't get me started on Aisha. What a piece of fucking work."

I smirk, peeling the label off my beer. "Don't say you didn't enjoy her. I know you too well."

"I wasn't far off ringing her neck, Logan. She's annoying, to put it mildly." He snaps, but a very rare, minuscule smile curls the corner of his lips. "Why aren't you hunting tonight?"

I shrug, drying my eighth Bud Light. "I'm too busy up here..." I tap my temple, "...with the shit grandad wants me to go through before he retires."

I wish I could tell him about Cassidy. Him, or any one of my brothers. I'm way out of my element, and they always know what to do. I could use their advice, but I can't talk to them. I'm alone in this, navigating a dark, creepy labyrinth with no way out.

I should've never touched the brunette. The kiss was sloppy and off-putting, thanks to the botched lip-filler job. My dick didn't stir when she curved into me, rolling her hips and rubbing her ass against me.

I felt nothing, even though she was perfectly fuckable.

Jesus. It's not even been two hours since I told Cassidy we're done, but I'm gloomy like a graveyard on a wet, misty morning... but luck might be smiling down on me as I spot something that might lift my mood.

Rush heads for the bar, giving me a great opportunity to let some steam off. I couldn't just get up and nail him while he sat in the booth without making my brother suspicious, but I know how to get my revenge now that he's at the bar.

All I have to do is provoke the asshole to throw the first punch, and I'll be golden. I'll even let him land it.

"You want another beer?" I ask Nico and get a sharp nod in return. "I'll be right back."

He pulls his phone out as I get up, cracking my neck and knuckles. The thought of making the fucker bleed eases the chain wrapped tightly around my ribcage.

I stop at the bar, a strategy already in place, as I rest my elbow between Rush and some other guy, shoving them aside and fetching Mick, the bartender. I'm petty as hell, but I don't give a flying fuck right now.

"Same again, man," I say, perfectly aware it's not my turn.

"There's a line," Rush snaps.

We never got along, which proves an advantage tonight. I can't just connect my fist with his jaw without prompting Nico to ask questions or jump to his own conclusions. He's smart and observant. He'll figure this out, and then I'll be the one bleeding.

"You know the rules don't apply to me," I shoot back, eyes straight ahead as I watch Mick grab my beers.

"You mean Nico. It's *his* club, not yours."

Technically, Adam Banes is the owner. Nico's just a silent partner. Or he likes to think so. In reality, everyone in Newport knows he bought Adam out at the start of this year and appointed him the general manager.

Casting a sideways glance at Rush, I shrug. "Tomayto, tomahto. The point is, I get served; you wait. It's called a hierarchy, and you're sitting quite low on the ladder."

Mick slides two bottles toward me. "I'll pop it on your tab."

"Thanks, man, and," I grip Rush's shoulder, gouging my fingers into the bone, hard enough to bruise as I point my chin at him. "He can wait until you're done serving everyone else."

Rush yanks himself out of my grasp and—*thank fuck*—gets in my face. "What the hell is your problem, Logan?" He grabs a fistful of my jersey.

It's not a punch, but I'll take it. I mean, you saw him. He started it, right?

Nico will think so too.

I hope.

Either way, I don't have an ounce of self-restraint left inside me. I grip his wrist and twist back until his hold on me loosens, and a pained scowl taints his features. "Careful who you put your hands on," I growl, meaning both Cassidy and me. "Touch the wrong person, and you'll bleed. Tonight, you bleed twice."

I move my hand to his neck, sink my fingers into his skin and smash his face against the countertop. He stumbles back, bouncing off a few bystanders, but raises his clenched fists, ready for more. And more he'll get.

I've punched many people in my life, but *this* punch is *the* fucking punch. I'll forever remember how my elbow falls back, then shoots through the air, landing on target.

Not his jaw. Not his nose. Not even his cheekbone. His *lips*. Lower splits, oozing blood, and both swell immediately.

That's for kissing her.

I strike again, dodging a half-assed punch he's trying to land, and my fist connects with the side of his face this time.

That's for touching her.

"You done?" Nico asks, stopping beside us, ever so casual,

the beers I ordered now in his hand. "What's this about?"

"He cut the line!" Rush snaps, angling his body away from me, fearful, pleading eyes trained on my brother as if he'll help him. "Just get the fuck off me, Logan," he adds, gripping my hand that holds him by his shirt.

I shove him back, letting him go, and he hurries away, his order long forgotten. I want to follow. I'm nowhere near done. I didn't even break a sweat, but Nico clasps his hand over my shoulder, steering me back to the table, so I have no choice.

"You lose your cool way too fast," he muses, sitting back down in the booth.

I cock an eyebrow, gulping two hefty sips. "Look who's talking," I motion to his knuckles, not yet healed after he nailed a random asshole last week at *Tortugo*.

I still don't know what that was about.

"Case in point," he admits, looking over his shoulder to the crowd of bodies moving on the dancefloor.

I nailed Rush, but the facts don't change.

Cass and I are over.

TWENTY-TWO

Cassidy

TLC all weekend long.

    As expected, I woke up with a headache on top of a headache and a migraine, too. The headaches were from the alcohol, but the migraine was from crying. I fell asleep dehydrated, hurt, and exhausted. If I could show Logan how awful he makes me feel, how worthless and expendable, he'd never be able to look me in the eyes again.

    My bedroom was spinning until late afternoon on Saturday when I risked getting out of bed to swallow a handful of painkillers and wash them down with a glass of tap water. Neither stuck with me for long. Less than three minutes later, I threw up the tablets, water, shots, and the kiwi daiquiri.

    Too weak to move, I nodded off, resting against the wall in the bathroom. And what a good choice that was... I puked on and off until late into the night. By Sunday afternoon, I started holding down tiny sips of water, my body limp as I lay on the sofa with a wet towel on my head. I hadn't had food since Friday, but my stomach wasn't asking for it, and I was too scared to eat in case I'd throw up again.

The good thing about feeling like I spent an hour in the washing machine on spin cycle and swallowed a bucketful of bleach is that I had no strength to think about Logan. If I'd let him in my thoughts, I'd cry and scream to let it all out.

Two words, one finger. We're done.

Done. Funny... I remember him saying we never began.

I nodded off most of the day, the TV on as background noise, but at some point, I fell asleep for good and didn't wake up until six on Monday morning.

The headache is gone, but I don't feel good enough to eat and settle for a cup of black, bitter coffee, stomping around the flat, looking for my phone. I find the pesky thing under the pillow and plug it to charge while I grab a shower to wash off the stench of alcohol, puke, and sweat.

The last time I got so drunk was at college. I have a newfound respect for Kaya today. She's always so fresh and rested the morning after a wild rager, and she functions like a normal person regardless of how wasted she is the night before.

It must be a skill. Either that or she developed an ultra-high tolerance, and hangovers don't bother her. Or maybe she downs a glass of bubbly instead of coffee every morning.

I hear it helps.

I considered the *stay-drunk* route on Saturday, but one glance at a bottle of Corona in the fridge was enough to turn my stomach.

Showered, dressed, and smelling nice and clean, I sit cross-legged in front of the mirror in my bedroom, attempting to hide the dark circles under my eyes with concealer and foundation. It works to an extent. Enough that I'm not ashamed to leave the house or schedule an OBGYN appointment for nine in the morning.

Logan failed my trust, and while I don't believe he'd knowingly risk my health, I'm not stupid enough not to get tested for STDs. He better hope he didn't give me chlamydia.

Although... I guess out of all the sexually transmitted diseases, chlamydia wouldn't be so bad.

I text Luke to let him know I'll be late for work and hop in my car, heading to the clinic on the other side of town. The receptionist greets me with a smile, and the nurse ushers me into a private room within minutes.

"Here's your gown. Get changed and hop on the bed. The doctor will be with you in a few minutes."

I fold my jeans and t-shirt, hide my pink panties in between and sit on the bed, holding the back of the blue gown in a tight grip. I'll show my lady parts to the doctor in a minute, but I'll hang onto my modesty for now.

Graphic posters of woman's reproductive system and tell-tale signs of breast cancer dot the walls among an array of reassuring lines. They're supposed to make you feel at ease and comfortable about discussing sex and STDs with a stranger while he shoves a plastic tube in your vagina.

The door opens a moment later, and I'm relieved to see a familiar face. Dr. Jones, an older man in his sixties, has been my doctor since I moved to Newport. I'm glad he's not retired yet, but he can't be far off now.

"Good morning, Cassidy," he chirps, pushing his rectangle glasses up his long, crooked nose. "What brings you over? Just a check-up?"

"I wish. I need to get tested for STDs."

"Okay, we can do that." He pulls a stool closer, not a hint of condemnation visible on his face. I'm sure he's seen it all during however many years of practice, and nothing can surprise him anymore. "How long has it been since you had unprotected sex? Some infections take time to show up on the tests. It might be better to wait a couple weeks before we draw blood."

"If I caught something, it'll show," I assure, ashamed that I allowed Logan between my legs for three months despite all the hurt he purposely inflicted. "I doubt there's anything to worry about, but better safe than sorry."

I don't think Logan gave me an STD, but I don't trust him anymore, and I'm not stupid enough not to get tested.

Stupid enough to let him ditch the condom, though.

My life has been on a downward spiral since I was born, but *this* is a brand-new level of low. How did I end up here?

I blame it on Thalia and her stupid, considerate, caring husband who threw her a party. If not for that party...

I shake my head, dismissing the thoughts. What's done is done. I can't turn back time, so there's no point in dwelling on what's out of my control.

"I was also thinking of getting an implant."

Dr. Jones flicks through my medical history and scribbles in the notepad, nodding along. "Any reason why? Are you not feeling well on the pill?"

"No, but implants are less hassle."

"We can talk about this once we've got the results back. You've not had a check-up for a while, so I'll do a quick exam while you're here, get a swab, and then you'll pee in the cup, and we'll draw blood." He gestures to the bed, inviting me to get comfortable or as comfortable as one can be at a gynecologist's office. "Are your periods regular? No issues?"

"Yes, no changes there. I hardly bleed on the pill. Will I have normal periods again when I'm on the implant?"

He reaches for a speculum and covers it with lubricant, spreading me open with his fingers dressed in latex gloves. I hate this part; the gel is cold and the speculum stretching me so Dr. Jones can take a good look gives me the visual of a can-opener for some reason.

"It's hard to predict," he mutters, lifting his head from between my legs. "You might have normal periods or not have them at all. It varies." He dives back down, his gray hair all I can see. "How's work?"

Yeah, why not have a casual chat while he's looking deep inside me? That'll surely take my mind off what he's doing and why I'm here.

As promised, the exam takes all but five minutes. With the swabs taken, my insides checked, and my boobs felt for tumors, I lock myself in the bathroom to pee in the cup and change back into my clothes.

Isn't this every girl's dream come true?

A real-life fairy tale: fall for the perfect man, make love to him all night, and then check if he gave you gonorrhea because he's an asshole who can't keep it in his pants.

"We should have the results by Wednesday," Dr. Jones says, meeting me in the foyer once a nurse draws my blood. "We'll call you once they're here to book you in for another appointment. Do you want to book in to have the implant, too?"

"Maybe when I come back," I say, nervous for the first time since I walked through the door, as if my brain is only now catching up to the horror. "I'll wait for the call."

He pulls a strip of colorful condoms out of a big fishbowl on the reception desks and hands them over with a cheeky grin. "Rip it, grip it, and roll it."

I force a chuckle, hiding the condoms in my bag. "Thank you. Too bad it's a little too late for that."

***

I'm jolted out of sleep by a loud bang. My heart kicks into the highest gear even before my eyes fully open.

Bang, bang, bang!

I frown, glancing at the phone on my coffee table, a little confused that I dozed off on the couch. It's not even nine in the evening yet. A few unread messages wait on the screen, but one thing at a time.

The banging continues, shaking the windows in my tiny apartment. It's Tuesday evening. My neighbors won't appreciate the disturbance, while most need to be up for work at five or six in the morning.

"I'm coming," I mutter, kicking the blanket aside.

I should've checked the messages before I flung the door open because they're probably from the same person, and had I known, I would've pretended not to be home.

"Leave, Logan," I say, holding onto the door, unsure whether to slam it in his face or open it further. The mere sight of him floods my system with endorphins. "Leave," I say again.

It's my only line of defense, but my tone lacks resolve. Even I don't believe I want him to go. He's vile. He hurts me and makes me feel worse than anyone else in my life, but I miss him. His scent, dark eyes, the firm touch of his hands worshipping my skin...

"Please, just leave me alone, okay? You said we're done."

"Yeah, I remember." He lets himself in, bursting past me

into the kitchen. "I also said we'll only fuck once, and look what happened. Why haven't you replied to my texts?"

"I was sleeping, and I have nothing to say to you," I clip, feeding off his anger that rekindles mine. "Leave, Logan."

He rests against the kitchen counter, jaw squared, eyes narrowed. "Not until you explain why you kissed Rush."

I fold my hands across my chest, mimicking his stance. "You had no trouble sticking your tongue in the brunette's mouth, and I don't hear you explaining." I step closer, my chest heaving. The anxiety associated with the test results I'll get tomorrow blends with hurt and anger, creating an explosive mixture. "I guess we weren't exclusive. You could've told me that before you fucked me without protection!" I shove him toward the door. "Leave. Right now."

He grips my forearm, yanking me closer. "We were exclusive. We *are* exclusive. I kissed the brunette, but you kissed Rush, so call it even."

I try to shrug him off, but his hold on me tightens. "The only thing we are is *done*, Logan. You think you can come here like nothing happened? Like you didn't say all that shit you did on Friday?!" I stab his chest with my finger. "Get out of my house! And better pray you didn't give me an STD, or I swear I'll kill you as soon as I get the results!"

He lets go of me at that; his eyebrow raised, utter disbelief painted across his stupid, handsome face. "You got tested? Why? I'd never touch you if I wasn't sure I was clean. You know that, Cassidy. You trust me!"

"*Trust?*" He has to be kidding. "I *don't* trust you, and I don't want you coming over here. Leave and don't come back!" I shove him again. "Two words, one finger. Get out!"

Silence sprinkles the room, and Logan's animosity washes

away like chalk drawings in the spring rain. "I'm sorry about what I said on Friday. I really am, Cass. I don't want us to part ways like this," he says, heaving a heavy sigh. "I kissed that girl because—"

"I don't care! Even if you didn't, we—" I cut myself off, biting my lip. There is no *we*. "*This*," I gesture between us, "would end soon anyway." I inhale a deep breath because the anger subsides, and hurt takes its place, threatening to bring me to my knees. "You got what you wanted, Logan, and you tossed me aside like a broken toy. We're done. You said it. Now get out."

"I'm not tossing you aside." He yanks the baseball cap off, griping a fistful of his hair. "You know the drill. You agreed to sex only, and now, what? You want more? You're besties with *Kaya*, for God's sake!"

"Don't forget I fucked Theo."

He grits his teeth, pinning me down with a pained stare, his face a picture of devastation. And then, his attitude changes before my eyes. His features soften, and he glances at my lips, a look of unwavering determination in his brown eyes a second before he cuffs my wrist and yanks me to him.

I react the way I always do to his touch, with a fit of shivers and heat pooling in my stomach. As if he can sense my resolve wearing thin, his lips capture mine. The softness and familiarity of his mouth tear apart the tall wall I've been building around me for days. The first thought to push him away vanishes faster than it appeared, leaving no trace.

When he holds me, when his lips battle with mine, his kisses greedy, downright ruthless, I don't know why I was mad at him in the first place. It's a blur. An unfocused, faded memory. A thing of the past that's less than one minute old.

A needy whimper escapes me, and Logan drinks that sound straight from my lips, his tongue teasing mine in a more sensual, calm way. "I know I'm an asshole. I know I keep hurting you, but... I don't want us to end this while we're mad, okay?" he whispers, moving his lips to my neck, grazing the flesh with his teeth. "We'll make up in bed, and then we're done, I promise." He grips my wrists in one hand, tracing the other down my side until he finds my waist. "You're amazing, baby, you know that? I'll make you feel good. I always do."

There.

That sound...

The cracking in the background.

That's my resolve; my determination not to let him close, not to let him touch and brainwash me, shattering.

I can't fight him.

I love him, and I want him, and I need him.

He hauls me onto the countertop, lips on mine, hands climbing my thighs until his fingers disappear under the hem of my nightdress and his breathing hitches.

"So soft," he murmurs, nipping my lower lip. "So warm. Open, baby," he coaxes. "Nice and wide."

I spread my legs, my mind devoid of rational thoughts. It's just me and him.

Him.

Nothing else matters.

He moves my panties aside and slides two fingers in slowly as if he's afraid I'll lash out if he's not careful. "I'm going to fuck that anger out of you right here, but first..." he curls his fingers, stroking my G spot. "...you'll come for me. I want to feel you dripping on my fingers."

I part my lips, resting my forehead on his shoulder, eyes

closed, boobs flush against his chest. I can't stop this. There's no strength left in my body to push him away, to protect my mind that's almost gone now.

I'm not in control when he's close. I only attempt to control the situation when there's distance between us, so I shouldn't have let him in tonight. I shouldn't have opened the door. I can scream and fight when he's a foot away, but I can't defend myself when he's touching me.

And I don't want to.

I'm lost in this man. In his tenderness and his fierceness. In the affection reserved for the short moments when we're alone, dead to the world.

"I missed you," he whispers, pressing his lips to my temple while his fingers bring me higher. "I missed you like crazy."

My heart swells, surrounded by a pleasant warmness. I'm not naïve enough to think this is significant. That maybe he wants more than sex, but his words act like a soothing balm over hundreds of cuts and bruises on my neglected mind.

He won't ever see me as more than a hookup, but when he holds me close to his chest, one hand draped over my shoulder blades as if to cuddle me into him; as if to protect me and take care of me, I can't bring myself to fight him.

I'll cry another river tomorrow, but for now, I savor his closeness, the peace he brings, and the happiness he evokes.

No other man could get me to the brink of an orgasm as fast as Logan. He's attuned to my body. He knows what to do, where to press, and where to push to get me to the highest high. To make me moan and cling to him.

My gasps fill the air, growing more audible. The cramps in my abdomen intensify, and I buckle against him with each precise, targeted stroke of his fingers.

"It's okay, baby. It's okay," he coos in a soft voice. "Let me have it." He holds me closer, tighter, his lips firmly on my temple when I come on his fingers, still and silent before I bite his shoulder. "There you go. Don't fight it. Don't fight *me*." He inches away, retreating his fingers, caressing my thigh before he cups my face, his eyes boring into mine. "Better?"

I nod, too afraid to speak in case I'll burst into tears. He doesn't expect me to speak, though. His lips catch mine again, the kiss slow, deep, almost affectionate. As if he wants to soothe me. As if he's trying to apologize with gestures because he knows I don't believe his words.

"*I* make you feel good. No one else. Only me, princess." He stamps a kiss on my head and drops his hands to my thighs. "I changed my mind. I want you in bed."

My legs have nowhere to go other than around his waist when he slides me off the counter and into his arms. Worked up to the limit, almost blinded by lust, I try to take off his jersey, but my moves are too uncoordinated. Logan's not helping me focus, kissing my neck and biting my ear. I yank the fabric up, pushing my hands underneath, touching his immaculate abs.

"So impatient," he murmurs, throwing me on the bed. He tears his jersey off in one move before his body covers mine.

I devote myself to the moment, driven by passion and longing. I fight for his touch as our clothes fly across the room until we're both naked, and I cling to his hot skin. As soon as I meet his gaze, Logan pushes his hips forward without warning, filling me with every stiff inch. A piercing shudder shakes my body, the sensation almost unbearable in all its perfection.

"Hold me," I utter, clawing at his back. "Please just—"

He shushes me with a kiss, his arms boxing me in, skin on skin, chest to chest, as he slowly retreats and thrusts back in.

"One more," he says in my ear, making my heart skip a beat and a wave of heat flood my thighs. "I want to hear you, baby."

I graze my teeth on his shoulder, planting open-mouthed kisses in the crook of his neck, but every desperate, hard thrust that scoots me up the bed brings me closer to another orgasm. I can't keep the soft, almost inaudible moans quiet any longer.

Logan watches me between kissing every inch of my skin within his reach. The low grunts and shallow breaths force a fit of shivers down my spine.

God, I never want to see him in a different state than the one he's in now, watching me with dark, lustful eyes as if I'm the only person in the world he needs.

"There it is," he rasps when the orgasm hits me, painting the backs of my eyelids with a stark whiteness. "Good, that's it... I love seeing you like this."

I pull him as close as I can while my body's in his possession and falling apart in the sweetest way. A satisfied, peaceful smile curls his lips before he reassumes the excruciating tempo for a few more thrusts until he stills, coming in *my* arms just as hard as I did in his.

His lips find mine again as if he missed me despite having me right here all this time. He pulls out slowly, holding onto my hip, and the most unexpected thing happens... he collapses beside me, wraps me in his arms, and takes a deep, calming breath.

***

The bed creaks under Logan's weight when he sits, flinging his legs over the edge. He cuddled me into his chest after wild sex, and I must've dozed off, too comfortable with his warm body beside me.

I didn't expect him to stay, but here he is, rubbing sleep away from his eyes. My insides swell, and hope reappears. Is this the first step to more?

I turn onto my side, prop my head on my elbow, and ghost my fingers down the line of his spine, feeling his muscles bunch under my touch. It's dark outside, the clock on the bedside table showing just past four a.m.

"I didn't mean to wake you," he says, arching away from my touch before he stands, grabbing his jersey off the floor.

I'm still half-asleep, and it takes me a moment to realize why he's up in the middle of the night. He's sneaking out before my neighbors wake up, so no one will see him leave in the morning.

A gross feeling that I'm filthy coils itself around my neck.

I curl into a ball, digging my nails into my hands to stop the oncoming tears. How many more ways will Logan find to break me? To give me hope and snatch it away with one small gesture?

I watch through tears as he slips into his jeans, buckles the belt, and shrugs on his jacket. Then, he leans over me to press a tight-lipped kiss to the crown of my head.

I want to move away.

I want to jump out of bed, toss everything within reach at his face, and kick him out of here, screaming at the top of my lungs, but I'm frozen in place, afraid to move a muscle.

I'll lose my composure, and instead of fighting, I'll beg.

"I'll see you around," he whispers into the darkness before he walks away.

No one will ever stick around.

No one will ever love me.

No one will ever care.

TWENTY-THREE

Cassidy

I check my phone every ten minutes from the moment I wake up on Wednesday until Dr. Jones calls at half-eleven. A sense of dread blooms in my stomach when I hide in the kitchenette while Luke snaps pictures of a new collection of shoes from a local designer.

I take a deep breath before sliding my thumb across the screen. *It's fine. You're fine. Relax.* "Hello?"

"Good morning, Cassidy," Dr. Jones says, the usual lightness gone from his voice, replaced by a formal tone with a sharp edge.

A tumult of anger dances up my spine, and my heart kicks into the cardiac arrest range. Something *is* wrong.

Fucking bastard!

I'm going to castrate him; I swear to God. He won't get a chance to stick his beautiful, long cock inside any woman ever again.

"Good morning," I say, a body-wide shudder running over me. "By the sound of it, you don't have good news."

The flash clicking on Luke's Nikon is the only sound breaking the heavy silence.

"Cassidy, can you come by the office today?"

Another riot of nerves wrings my stomach, and I picture how I'll torture Logan for this mess. "Should I be worried? What do I have?"

"I'd rather it if we could talk face to face. What time can you be here?"

I glance at the calendar on the wall, checking my appointments for the day. Pulse throbs in my ears, muting the sound of Luke's camera and the traffic outside the window.

I've got a family photoshoot booked in half an hour and a toddler session at four in the afternoon, but I won't be able to take one decent picture today with the unspoken STD diagnosis hanging over my head like a brewing tornado.

"If I can reschedule my clients, I'll be there in half an hour."

"Okay, that's fine. I'm dealing with paperwork today, so any time is good. I'll see you soon." He cuts the call before I can pester him for more information.

An oppressive silence rings in my ears. God, please don't let it be HIV. *Please.* I'll *never* look at Logan again, I swear. Just *don't* let it be HIV.

I squeeze the phone with all my might, taking deep breaths and doing my best to keep calm, but the unshed tears are once again threatening to spill.

How much can one person cry before the tears dry out? Since Friday, I've cried two rivers, but the waterworks still work just fine. I wish the plumbing in my flat was as reliable as my tear ducts.

I call my client to reschedule the morning appointment to next week, and once that's taken care of, I swing my bag over my shoulder. "I'm off," I tell Luke, my legs feeling a little spongy. "I'll be back later. I've got a toddler photoshoot at four."

He's in the zone, glaring between the camera and a pair of cute, pink, strappy heels with little bows at the back as if he's willing the shoes to pose better. I'm not sure if he heard me, but the answer is silence.

With every step closer to my car, I'm shaking more until the anger rising in my chest is like a cornered, scared animal trying to claw its way out. And a way out I show it when I sit at the wheel and send Logan a text.

Me: Thanks a lot, asshole! Don't come near me again, or I'll cut your dick off. Better let your girls know to get tested.

I toss the phone on the passenger seat and start the engine, pulling out onto the main road. The hands-free system activates, filling the car with the ringtone I assigned to Logan after the evening we spent in his pool—"Swim" by Chase Atlantic. I send him to voice mail seven times, but he's not getting the hint.

"What?!" I snap, answering on his eighth try. "I've got nothing to tell you!"

"Whatever you have, you didn't get it from me, so *you* call *your* guys to let them know."

I scoff, pressing my foot harder to the floor. "I've not been with anyone in over a year, Logan. You gave me this shit! Don't you dare show your face around me again. We're done. Over! You got that?! OVER!"

A loud bang sounds on his side of the line. "I got tested before we happened, Cass. I was good, so you gave..." He trails off, his voice changing from anger to controlled annoyance. "What did you test positive for?"

"None of your business!"

Even if I knew which STD he oh so graciously shared with me, I wouldn't tell him. He deserves to experience the humiliation of walking into a clinic, peeing in the cup, and getting swabbed. The mortification of receiving the results.

I'd pay good money to see the almighty Logan Hayes hanging his head low in shame.

"I never had unprotected sex until you, so don't blame this mess on me. You think I'll make this easy for you? Ha!" I shift the gear, pressing my foot back down. "Forget it! If you want to know what treatment you need, you'll have to go through the whole fucked-up process just like I did! Call your doctor!"

The light on the junction ahead changes to red. I've riled myself up so bad I've not noticed the climbing speed or how hard I've been pressing on the gas.

I'm doing over sixty miles an hour in the heart of Newport, and I have no chance to stop in time. There's no room to veer right or left and avoid the standstill Mustang no more than twenty yards away.

"Shit!" I cry out, slamming the brakes.

The sound of tires skidding on the road pierces my ears. I lose control of the car a second before a huge blow jolts my little Fiat. Time slows down. The force of impact throws me forward, my arms in the air as if gravity ceased to exist.

A deafening, crushing sound of metal bending and glass braking fills the air.

The airbag explodes in my face.

The seatbelt blocks, shoving me back against the seat.

A waterfall of glass cascades down on me before the world

fades to black.

And then... *pain*.

So much pain.

It's the first thing I register before prying my eyes open. My vision is blurred as if I'm looking through a pair of four-diopter corrective glasses with a twenty-twenty vision.

I blink, trying to adjust, to *see* my hands which I'm holding out in front of my face. A high-pitched ringing in my ears drowns out other sounds, and warm and wet blood trickles down my face. I lift my hand to touch it, pulling in a breath that'd have me doubling over if there was enough room. A sharp, stabbing pain rips through my ribcage.

A cold shiver slides down my spine, and pulse triphammers in my neck when my vision starts clearing by the second.

I'm covered in blood.

My hands, blouse, legs... covered in crimson blood and tiny shards of broken glass. I swallow hard, inhaling quick, shallow breaths that don't hurt as much.

"Cassidy?! Are you okay?" Someone bends down by the car, peering inside through the window—or what used to be a window. There's no glass there now. "Fuck!" He clips, turning around. "Conor! Call an ambulance!"

Staring straight ahead, my mind is in a hazy daze of confusion. The back of a Mustang I remember smashing into isn't there anymore. Instead, I'm mindlessly gawping at a shopfront of a hardware store. The front of my car folded at the impact like an accordion.

I blink, replaying the crash. There definitely was a Mustang. Where the hell did it go?

I glance to the side again at the young boy beside my car. He looks familiar. Dark eyes, dark hair, sharp features.

Logan.

No, too young.

His brother.

"I know you," I say, the words like razor blades on my tongue. "Cody, is... is anyone hurt?"

"You banged your head pretty hard, so I'll let that slide," he smirks, the corner of his mouth lifting slightly.

Logan...

No, too young, but they look so much alike.

"It's Colt, Cassidy, and you're the only one hurt. What were you thinking going all Schumacher on my ass?"

"Colt," I echo, wincing as pain strobes behind my temples. My mind is still half-stuck in slow motion. It takes three times the usual time to process and understand his words. "What is Schumacher?"

He smirks again, and I want to cry.

Logan.

I'd give my arm to have him here. I'm so confused.

"He used to be a Formula 1 driver. Back in 1998, he crashed into the back of another F1 car—" He pauses and waves me off, noticing my baffled expression. "Never mind. What's the rush?" He shoves his head further inside, glancing at the dashboard. "Wow. Forty at impact. I heard the tires screeching when you hit the brakes, and I looked in the mirror, but it was too late to move out of your way. How fast were you going?"

"Um..." I press my fingers to my temple, pain lancing through my head. It feels like a bomb had gone off in there. "I don't know. Sixty, I think." I glance around again. Where is Colt's car? My neck is too stiff to tilt my head and look through the back window. "I crashed."

"Yeah, no shit. How you're still alive is beyond me, girl.

You smashed into the back of my car, and this..." he wrinkles his nose, angling himself back to eye my Fiat, "...*toy* was thrown out and spun twice before it stopped here."

"The ambulance is on its way." Another boy stops beside the car. Conor, I think. Or maybe it's Cody. I can't tell them apart right now, but he looks like Colt, so he must be one of the triplets. "Hey there, Schumacher. You good? You need to stay where you are until the ambulance gets here."

"Don't bother, Conor. She doesn't get the reference," Colt says, unhappy with my lack of F1 knowledge. "Don't move. Fuck knows how badly you're hurt."

I tremble. Cold shivers run up and down my entire body as if I were dipped in an ice hole on a frozen lake. Why is it so cold? The sun is shining, and it was eighty-five degrees when I left the studio.

"What is that?" Colt asks, pushing his head inside again. "Is that... radio? No way that's still working."

I focus on the quiet melody—"Swim" by Chase Atlantic. "It's my phone."

Logan.

The deafening blare of police sirens swallows the melody seeping from my phone. Colt and Conor step away, revealing a crowd of onlookers standing nearby on the sidewalk, snapping pictures and gawking at the scene.

No one's trying to help. They stand there, appalled and curious, as if this isn't a real-life accident but a stunt performed by a movie crew.

I assess my position and the damage to my body, glad to see that there aren't any metal parts sticking out of me. That's reassuring. My hands and arms are covered in cuts where the glass broke my skin, but nothing major. Nothing that requires stitches. I touch my face, tracing the trickle of blood up from my chin until my fingers find a gaping wound over my left eye.

That might need stitches.

My legs are trapped under the steering column that's digging into my thighs. Shit, what if I don't have legs? What if I'm in shock and can't feel the pain?!

The theory is overthrown when I start to panic and inhale another deep, sharp breath. The agony ripping my ribcage wide open proves I can, in fact, feel pain. Excruciating pain.

I wriggle my toes, checking if they're there, and breathe a sigh of relief, feeling them move in my sneakers.

I'm okay.

I've got legs.

I'm alive.

Colt is right. It's baffling that I'm not severed in half. I want to kiss the *toy* with a decent crash zone for saving my life, but before I try to hug the wheel and thank the piece of metal, Shawn bends down, sticking his head inside the car.

"Hey there, Cass," he says, his voice gentle, calm, and soft as if he's talking to a frightened child. "How are you feeling? Can you move your hands and legs?"

"Yes. I'm okay. God, I'm so sorry, I wasn't paying attention to my speed or the road and—"

"Hey, calm down. Shit happens. My brothers are fine, so let's focus on you now, alright?" He assesses the car and tries to pry the door open, but it's stuck. "We might have to cut you out of here."

"No, no, no. If you open the door and slide the seat back, I'll get out on my own. I'm not that hurt." I lift my hands, twirling my wrists and bending my elbows. "See?"

He smiles, shaking his head, then straightens up, shouting

someone over. Three firemen approach the car, playing tug-of-war with the door. All the while, "Swim" by Chase Atlantic plays in the background on repeat, not stopping for longer than three seconds at a time. The melody fills the cracks in my composure like warm honey, helping me stay calm.

The paramedics clasp a neck brace around my neck as soon as the door is cut open, and the seat is pushed back to free my legs. A young man dressed in an EMT uniform shines a light in my eyes and asks dozens of questions before hauling me onto a stretcher despite my protests.

I can walk.

I'm not that hurt.

My ribs are killing me, and my head feels as if it's split wide open at the back, but my legs and my spine are fine.

"Colt!" I yell, seeing him stand to the side with one of the firemen. Conor's there, too, snapping pictures of my car. Colt jogs over, forcing the paramedics to make a short stop. "My phone," I pant. "Can you please get my phone? It's somewhere on the passenger side."

"If I can find it," he mutters, looking me up and down with genuine concern in his eyes. "You'll be alright, Cass."

I'm not sure which one of us he's trying to reassure. The triplets are identical save for their hairstyles, but somehow, each resembles one of his older brothers more than the other.

Colt has the same eyes as Logan. Deep, rich brown with a single speck of gold in his left iris. A skitter of dread prickles my skin like a rash, and the thin outer layer of my composed, forced calmness begins to shiver and crack. I wish Logan was with me right now.

I wish he'd hold my hand and just be here.

I'm scared. I won't admit it out loud, but I'm terrified of

what will happen at the hospital. One of the paramedics wore a disturbing look on his face when I described the pain in my ribs and how every breath feels as if my lungs are pierced with a blade. That can't be good.

Colt jogs over to the Fiat, and I'm hauled into the back of the ambulance. The smell of antiseptic irritates my nose while I stare at the roof, refusing to check what the EMTs are doing around me.

"There, I got your bag, too," Colt jumps in, placing the bag beside me, and pushes the phone into my hand. "Take care, alright?" He squeezes my fingers, a small smile curving his lips. "And slow down, Schumacher."

I chuckle, nodding as much as the cervical collar allows, and close my fingers on the phone that's no longer ringing. I want to call Logan and beg him to come to the hospital, but the memory of him sneaking out of my apartment in the middle of the night flashes before my eyes, and I don't dial.

That's not how our relationship works.

That's not how my relationship with anyone works.

I'm alone in this. No one but myself to count on.

Colt gets out of the ambulance, and a second later, the paramedics shut the door, the siren blaring overhead.

"You can call your family if you want," one of the crew, a woman in her late thirties, says, buckling up in her seat.

"No family," I mutter but hold the phone up to see the screen and dial a number.

"Good afternoon, Newport Beach OBGYN. How can I help?" The receptionist's melodic voice sounds in my ear, the line well practiced.

"Hey, Darcie, it's Cassidy Roberts. Could you put me through to Dr. Jones?"

"Yeah, sure. Hold on a second." The on-hold music starts, but thankfully, it's not as annoying as other places, and ends after a few seconds when Darcie's voice fills my ear again. "Sorry, he nipped out to grab a bite to eat. Do you want me to give him a message?"

"Yes, tell him I won't be able to make the appointment today. I'll call him tomorrow to reschedule."

"Sure thing. I'll let him know. Take care!"

A little too late for that piece of advice...

TWENTY-FOUR

Logan

"Pick up!" I snap, not for the first time, dialing Cass's number on repeat for twenty minutes. "Fuck! Pick *up!*"

I pace the office, dry wood termites gnawing at the paper-mill of my mind. The way she cried out *shit* right before the call dropped has me worried to my back fucking teeth.

She was driving when we talked, but I refuse to let the dark scenarios infest my mind.

She's okay.

She's just pissed off and doesn't want to talk to me.

Not that she should be. I sure didn't give her an STD. No way it was me. I was clean. I get routinely tested every year, and it just so happened that my appointment was the day before Thalia's birthday.

I was clean before I touched Cassidy.

Now, I'm not. All thanks to her and whatever dirty asshole she fucked while sleeping with me.

TOO WRONG

The anger is pushed to the background for now. My stomach churns with dread as I dial and redial her number. Five more tries before the cell pings in my hand—a message in the Hayes group chat. Before I even open the app, three more messages arrive.

Conor: Colt's not having a great day. Just his fucking luck.

I study the picture he sent of Colt's Mustang, the rear bumper and the left light smashed.

Nico: You good?

Theo: Shit, how did he do that?

Conor: Yeah, we're good. You should see the other car. Cody's is unscathed in comparison.

He sends another picture. A yellow Fiat is scrunched up as if it collided with a truck, not Colt's Mustang. The front is almost unrecognizable, the hood folded like a pancake, the windscreen and left wheel missing.

Bile comes up to my throat. My hands shake so hard I can't read the messages that keep coming. I know that car.

Cassidy.

Instead of her, I call Conor, ignoring the incessant pinging.

"You're such a sweetheart," he laughs in my ear. "We're alright, Logan. Chill. Not a scratch on Colt or me. Cody's not here. We nipped out for coffee and *bam*! You should've seen Colt's face, bro!" He laughs again. "We're cool, Shawn's here, and I know a guy who'll—"

"Conor!" I snap to stop his rambling. "I'm glad you're fine. What about Cassidy? Is *she* okay?"

There's a short pause on his side. Long enough to fucking choke me. I close my eyes, blocking another wave of dark scenarios, but they flicker on the backs of my eyelids, and my eyes pop back open.

She's okay. She's okay. Don't freak out.

"How do you know it's her?" he asks, weighing every word.

"I know her car. How. Is. She?"

"She's alive... somehow. The clock on that toy she drives stopped at forty miles an hour on impact. I've no idea how the hell that tiny car took the blast the way it did. It got thrown onto the fucking sidewalk!"

"For fuck's sake!" I boom, my teeth grinding with every next word coming out of his mouth. "Focus, Conor! *Cassidy*. Is she okay? Is she hurt?"

"Jeez, who pissed in your cereal?" he mumbles, royally annoyed with me now. "I said she's alive. Battered and bruised. I think she broke a few ribs, and she's got a nasty cut on her face, but she's better than I'd expect after such a blast. The fire crew got her out of the car, and—" The ambulance siren goes off in the background stopping Conor mid-sentence. "Yeah, they're taking her to the hospital."

"Thanks. I'll call you later." I snatch the keys from the desk, storming out of the office without a *bye* in the receptionist's direction when I pass her desk.

***

"What do you mean *no visitors*?" I growl at the nurse, who refuses to let me see Cass. "Visiting hours don't end until half five!"

TOO WRONG

She shifts her weight from one foot to another. "I'm sorry, but the patient asked not to let anyone in. She does have her phone, so maybe try calling. I know she's in her room now, but she's due a few more tests soon. If she tells me you can come in, I'll take you up there, but—"

"Fine," I huff, taking out my phone.

It's not like I've not tried calling or texting a dozen times already. She's not answering.

I stroll to the cafeteria, ready to wait until Cass lets me visit. The assaulting smell of antiseptic, citrus floor wash, and latex fails to mask the odor of sickness and death lurking in every corner of this place.

"A black coffee," I tell the cashier and grab a sandwich while I'm at it. I have a feeling I'll be here for a while.

As he moves away to fetch my coffee, I send Cass a text.

Me: Why don't you want to see anyone? I'm not leaving until I see you, princess.

My phone keeps pinging, the chat about Colt's crash still ongoing. I've glanced at the messages a few times since I got here to make sure Conor hadn't made my concern for Cassidy the number one topic, but thankfully, he hasn't mentioned it yet.

I hope he won't. I don't have the time or the energy to come up with an excuse for my sudden interest in her well-being.

Me: Your Guardian Angel needs sacking. He's disgraceful.

An hour goes by while I eat and drink coffee, staring at the screen and willing Cassidy to read the messages. At least the engaging subject of Colt's smashed Mustang runs its course, and the pings aren't eating away my battery which sits at twenty percent. I might need to visit the gift shop to buy a charger.

Me: Still here. Just tell me you're okay.

Time drags.

Everyone around me is going through a tough time. Whether it's a disease or watching a loved one die slowly, people chatting quietly over the tables put my problems in perspective. A young girl sits nearby, her head shaved but a brave smile on her tired, pale face. She smiles at her mother, who keeps kissing her head and squeezing her arm.

Life is so short, yet people don't realize it until it's too late. We're blind to the obvious. Too blind to see that life is about moments. Too scared to step out of the line and say *fuck it, this is my life and my choices.*

Instead, we chase the unattainable. We want more: money, recognition, respect. But the truth is that in the end, no one will remember the cool car you drove or the brand-new sofa you spent five grand on.

You won't see expensive gadgets or a five-bedroom house when you're gasping for your last breath and life flashes before your eyes. You won't see material things.

You'll see *people*.

Moments.

Memories.

The smile of someone you love. Their laughter. You'll remember what it felt like to be happy.

People don't need much to be happy, but we complicate our lives on purpose. We're raised in a society that cares about appearances more than human interactions.

TOO WRONG

Two more hours pass and three empty cups sit on the table. I bought a charger, too. And one more sandwich. And a slice of pie. It's close to half past five before *Delivered* changes to *Read* under the last message I sent. I grip the phone, waiting for three dots to start dancing.

A minute goes by.

Five.

Ten.

And finally, she starts typing.

Princess: Two fractured ribs, three stitches, and a mild contusion. I'll live. My angel quit the day I let you back into my life. He knew I'll end up crying and signed off ahead of time. Go home. I don't want to see you.

I stare at the text message for the longest time as if it's written in Greek. *I don't want to see you* jumps out from the screen, cutting me in ways I've never been cut.

Stitches. Fractured ribs. Contusion.

That hurts, too. Picturing Cassidy in bed, in pain, alone and scared drives the knife that much deeper, but that one line hurts more than I'd ever expect words to hurt: *He knew I'll end up crying and signed off ahead of time.*

Fuck.

I never wanted to hurt her. We were supposed to have fun. We were supposed to fuck, because we do it so well but add feelings into the mix, and that's the kind of mess neither of us needs on our hands.

I should go. I should move on, but I can't until I see her.

Me: Say it to my face, and I might believe you.

The three dots flash, then stop on repeat for a whole minute, but no messages come through. I have the sudden urge to toss the cell across the cafeteria.

It'd bounce off one of the patients' heads, though.

"Excuse me." The same nurse who didn't let me in to see Cass before stops by my table. "Cassidy said you can visit now if you—"

I'm on my feet before she finishes. "Lead the way."

A fond smile curves her lips, emphasizing the wrinkles around her eyes. "Normally, we don't allow people in after five thirty, but you've been here all day, so I'll make an exception."

My mouth is too dry to grace her with pleasantries. I'm grateful she's letting me in, but at the same time, I'm jittery inside, unsure what to expect.

The nurse leads me out of the cafeteria, and we take the elevator to the fifth floor. I keep pumping my fists to rid the irrational tension, anxious to see the state of Cassidy. The few pictures of her smashed-up Fiat that Colt sent to the group chat confirm it's a miracle she's alive. Two broken ribs are merely a surface scratch after a crash like that.

"You only have ten minutes," the nurse says, opening the door to Cassidy's room. "Make it count." She winks, gesturing for me to enter.

I stop two steps inside the room, my eyes on the girl half-sitting, half-lying in bed, propped up by a few white pillows.

I suck in a ragged breath, taking in the stitches under her eyebrow. Half an inch lower, and she would've lost her eye. Hairs on the back of my neck rise, and I feel sick, scrutinizing her olive skin covered in cuts and bruises.

"Don't look at me like that," she says, her voice calm but weak as if she's exhausted. "You asked to come up here. Did you expect to find me in full makeup, pretty as always?"

"You're just as pretty without makeup as you are with red lips and a smoky eye." I walk further in, my legs a little spongy as I take a seat in the uncomfortable chair beside her bed. "How are you feeling?"

She's ghastly pale, her lips a faint milky pink, and shadows under her blue eyes. A heavy chain girds itself around my chest. She looks so fucking fragile.

"I'm fine. The painkillers are working, so I can hardly feel my ribs now." She brushes her blonde hair back with her fingers, meeting my gaze. "Why are you here, Logan? Why can't you just let me be?"

Because I worry. I'm confused and can't figure out how to tackle what I feel. I don't *understand* what I feel, but I know those feelings aren't welcome. They push me another step closer to losing my family.

"Did you mean what you said in the text?"

"I want to mean it," she admits on a sigh, toying with the corner of the comforter covering her frail body. "We knew this... *us* had an expiration date. We're past that now."

Us. It's been a long time since I was a part of *us*. Ten years to be precise, but the college flings weren't meaningful. Not that Cass and I were supposed to be meaningful, but here we are. Three months of sex, and I'm way out of my depth.

"Plans change, Cassidy. It's not like either of us has anyone to come home to." *Don't end this. Not yet. I'm not fucking done with you.* "What's wrong with what we have?"

"There's nothing wrong. Nothing *right,* either." She steadies her breathing and wipes her eyes, getting ahead of tears, and I want to crawl out of my skin. "The longer we keep this up, the more I get hurt. There's only so long I can pretend."

"Pretend?"

"That sex is enough. It isn't."

I grit my teeth, pushing away the contradicting emotions. She's slipping between my fingers, and I can't decide whether to spread them wider or close my fist.

"Why did you agree if casual isn't what you want?" I ask, letting annoyance shine through. It's my safest bet right now. Anger is familiar. Disappointment isn't. I don't know how to deal with that glum mist of dysphoria blanketing my thoughts. "Why did you come to me when I said it'll only be this once?"

A small smile tugs her lips, but there's nothing joyful about it. She looks like she gave up, stopped fighting for herself, and accepted what life has in store, regardless of how much it hurts.

"For such a clever guy, you're awfully oblivious. I'll *always* come to you if you let me, and I'll always take you back no matter how much it hurts to watch you sneak out at night." She looks me dead in the eye, her voice soft. "I'll cry, and promise myself that I won't let you near, but I can't push you away when you show up." She bites her cheek, first silent tears sliding down her cheeks. "It's sad," she whispers, her eyes holding me hostage. "But no matter how often you leave, I want you to come back, Logan, because I love you. I've loved you for *years*."

I... I... God, I can't fucking breathe.

I've heard those words before. So many times from my parents, grandparents, and even my brothers. I've heard them from a few drunk chicks back at school too, but it never hit me the way it does now.

Those three small words act like a bullet. They penetrate my armor, pierce my chest, and stop in my heart, breaking it clean in two.

TOO WRONG

A cacophony of contradicting emotions burn beneath my skin as if someone set a slow and steady match deep in the pit of my stomach. Words stick to my throat. I'm afraid I might spontaneously combust at any moment. A primal flight reaction, or something like it, kicks in: a giant flood of adrenaline fills my veins like a drug.

I've never felt more alive and more defeated.

Cassidy watches me with big eyes. She's silently coming apart, tugging on the comforter, and sinking her teeth into her lower lip to keep on top of her emotions. Confessing her feelings to me, the cold, arrogant fucker who brings more pain than good, sometimes without knowing, couldn't have been easy.

"The cards are in your hands," she continues quietly. "You decide whether I'll cry once and by some miracle move on or whether I'll cry time and time again."

I don't want the cards.

I don't want to exploit her feelings and vulnerability, but I don't know if I have the strength to let her go...

Maybe if we spend one more night together, I'll get my fill. Maybe that'll be enough. *Fuck.* She shouldn't have told me she'll give in to me every time.

How am I supposed to step aside?

A soft tapping on the door jolts me from the weird trance I've slipped into. The door swings open, and the same nurse who let me in here stands in the doorway with the same fond smile twisting her mouth.

"I'm sorry, but it's time to go. You can come back tomorrow at eight-thirty."

My legs feel as if I ran a marathon when I haul myself up to my feet, eyes back on Cassidy. I feel so fucking raw under her gaze, like there's no skin left on my bones, and every movement of air is pure agony.

I take one step, lean over the bed and press my lips to her forehead. It takes all I have, every ounce of determination, will, and courage to walk out of the room without one word.

Without acknowledging or dismissing her confession.

But I do it.

One leg after the other, I leave Cassidy to lick her wounds in peace.

TWENTY-FIVE

Cassidy

For the first time in a week, I don't cry when Logan leaves.

He sat there so, *so* still. Silent. Eyes on mine, but face not hinting what was going through his head.

I expected words. Any words would've sufficed. Any reaction at all, but he gave me *nothing*. No indication whether we're done or if I should expect him to show up at my apartment in a few days. *Nothing*, until he kissed my head.

No words were needed after that. The gesture spoke volumes. It screamed at the top of its lungs.

It was his way of saying *goodbye*.

Maybe telling him that I love him was the wrong choice. I could've fed him a generic answer that neither of us would believe, but why bother? What has keeping my feelings unspoken achieved so far?

At least by telling him, I was taking a step. God knows in what direction, but a step, nonetheless.

I didn't shed a single tear all night. I didn't sleep, either.

My body and mind feel numb, partly thanks to the painkillers coursing through my bloodstream and partly because I accepted that Logan is gone for good this time. Instead of the expected relief, I want to curl in a ball and mourn.

Luke is the first to come by early in the morning with an unexpected but much-welcome visit. It doesn't do me any good to be alone with my thoughts.

"Holy mother of baby Jesus," he huffs before he properly closes the door. "You look like hell, babe. Now I know why you didn't want me to come over yesterday. I wouldn't want people to see me like this." He gestures to me, pulling a face. "Damn, you look like you lost a fight with a bus. How are you feeling?"

"Better than expected," I admit, sitting up when he hands me a take-out cup of coffee from the café near our studio. I smile, popping the lid and inhaling the heavenly, bitter-sweet aroma. The coffee they serve at the hospital tastes like feet, so *this* is a godsend. "You're a lifesaver. Thank you. I'm drugged up, so I feel okay. No pain for now."

He takes a seat in the chair Logan occupied a little over twelve hours earlier. "I moved most of your appointments to next week, and I'll cover the two couples who don't care you almost died and refused to be postponed."

"I'm not sure if I'll be able to work next week. Once they let me out of here, the nice drugs stop, and you have no idea how much broken ribs hurt." I consider getting out of bed to kiss his cheek but send him an air kiss instead. "Thank you for covering for me yesterday. I'm sure you had so much fun with the toddler."

He scowls, but amusement shines in his eyes as he playfully pokes my shoulder. "Actually, he wasn't half bad, you know?

He tore that stuffed, gray bunny's eye out, though. I've ordered a new one."

I get a minute-by-minute rendition of the photo shoot, then spend ten minutes explaining how I crashed the car before Luke leaves to start his day, leaving me alone again, texting back and forth with Kaya.

She's *oh so very sorry*, but she's snowed under with work and won't be able to come over. She also hopes I'll get better soon and promises to visit *when work is more manageable*. Read: once my ribs heal and I won't ask her for help.

Not that I would. Life taught me to be self-sufficient.

"You've got another visitor." The nurse peeks into the room close to two in the afternoon. "Not the cute guy," she adds in a sweet voice before my heart starts racing, and hope dares to fill the cracks in my heart like medical glue. "Thalia Hayes. Can she come in?"

"Yes, but before you go, do you know when I'm getting released?" I've been waiting for the doctor to sign the release paperwork since this morning, but so far, no show.

"It won't be long now. The doctor is out of the theater and will be doing rounds shortly."

I've heard that three times already, but I smile instead of calling her out on something she has little control over. I don't feel like smiling, but I realized it gets me things. An extra pudding at lunchtime and coffee from the nurse's lounge instead of the awful, lukewarm, brown water I had with breakfast.

"I'll send your friend in."

Thalia enters the room, her curly mane bouncing as she strolls across to my bed with a big bag flung over one shoulder and a smaller one in her hand. "We've got to stop meeting like this," she huffs, dropping the bags on my legs. "What the hell were you thinking? Theo said your car is totaled. Why were you speeding?!"

"Hello to you, too."

She leans over to peck my cheek, brown eyes roaming over my face, her anger fading as she ghosts her thumb along the stitches under my eyebrow and sighs. "How are you feeling?"

"About just as good as I look," I mouth because the concern written on her face hits me all wrong, and I'm struggling to keep my smile genuine.

She cares. Like, *really* cares about me. My stomach ties in knots, tears welling in my eyes again.

"Thank you," I mumble.

Thalia pulls her eyebrows together. "What the hell are you thanking me for? I haven't given you anything yet, but—" She holds her finger up, looks through her bag, and pulls out Milk Duds. "There, I wanted to bring wine, but," she gestures around us, "can't have you drunk *and* drugged."

I chuckle, wiping my eyes. "I love you; you know that?"

"Why, I'm very lovable." She winks, plopping down in the chair beside the bed. "Okay, I'm all ears. Talk, Cass. Get it out of your system. I know you're hiding something. You've been a trainwreck for weeks! Is it still about that mystery guy?"

It's not the first time she's ordered me to talk, but it was easier to brush her off over the phone when she called for chit-chat than face-to-face. I'm too tired and too hurt to fight her.

She cares about me, and if there's anyone I trust enough to share secrets with, Thalia's it.

"If I tell you something..." I look up, meeting her eyes. "Will you swear not to tell anyone? And I mean anyone, Thalia. Not even Theo."

Especially not Theo.

She holds three fingers up. "Scout's honor. Come on, you know you can trust me. Talk."

I bite my lip, inhaling a shaky breath. "That guy I've been hooking up with for three months now..."

She rolls her eyes, tilting her head expectantly. "Yeah?"

"It's Logan."

"Logan," she echoes, drawing her thick eyebrows together. "As in... my brother-in-law? *That* Logan?"

"*That* Logan." My head hits the pillows, and I gun the ceiling with a pointed stare. "I thought I could do it." I grit my teeth, throwing my arm over my face. That's a lie, and I'm not lying to her. "I hoped if we kept it going long enough, he'd want more, but he only wanted sex. The longer we hooked up, the harder it got to watch him sneak out after dark."

She grips my hand, grazing her thumb over my knuckles. "That's the last thing I expected. Why did you keep it a secret so freaking long?!"

"Part of the deal. I was just his dirty secret. No one knows, and no one can know, okay? Please, don't tell Theo."

"I promised," she clips. "You've been sneaking around for *three* months, Cass. That's not just sex."

Oh, but it was.

"I told him I love him," I whisper, close to tears. God damn my waterworks. I'm so fucking tired of crying. "And now he doesn't even want sex."

"What an ass," she huffs, squeezing my hand too tight.

The dam bursts and I spend an hour filling her in on the rollercoaster that the last three months were. She listens mostly in silence, muttering profanities when I tell her Logan threw me out of his house the first time I was there and locked me in the garage the second time.

TOO WRONG

I'm lighter when I finish. Purified, somehow. I needed to let it out. Not necessarily to hear an opinion, just to talk and be heard. The harsh reality is that Logan is gone, and he won't be back this time. I stepped over the line confessing my feelings.

"What did he say when you told him you love him?"

"Nothing," I say on a sigh, recalling the pure mortification on his face at the sound of the three words. "Absolutely nothing. He got up and left. I've not heard from him since, and I'm sure I won't."

"I don't know what to say," she admits.

"There's not much left to say. We're done. I need to pick myself up again and keep going."

TWENTY-SIX

Cassidy

My bed isn't the most comfortable, but ten times better than the hospital one. Now, safe in my own flat, I lay awake since five in the morning, staring at the ceiling and trying to figure out how to move on. How to proceed with my life and erase Logan.

I miss him so much I feel like my sanity is splintering. It's unhealthy, to say the least, but at the same time, a tiny, lackluster part of me reveals that he won't be showing up again. That I won't watch him leave in the middle of the night.

We can go back to being civil, to acknowledging our existence with a polite nod whenever we bump into each other in town. It'll be fine.

It sure won't feel like my heart is being torn right out of my chest because I've had him, even if briefly, and now we'll be perfect strangers.

At eight, I drag myself out of bed, rolling and squatting to protect the ribs, and by nine—after a painful shower and even worse attempt at getting dressed—I arrive at the clinic in a summery, button-down dress. No amount of makeup would cover the stitches under my eyebrow, so I didn't bother covering the bruised cheekbone.

"Dear God!" Darcie shouts, rushing from behind her desk. "What happened to you, sweetheart?"

Her sudden outburst summons Dr. Jones, who emerges from his office, eyes narrowed and two deep wrinkles marking his forehead as he looks me over.

"I'm okay. I had a car accident, but thankfully I only fractured two ribs. I've been at the hospital since Wednesday, which is why I didn't come over sooner."

"Oh, you poor thing!" Darcie squeezes my shoulder. "That must've been awful!"

Dr. Jones rolls his eyes behind her back. "Come on, Cassidy. We'll talk in my office."

My heart picks up a higher rhythm. He doesn't sound casual and cheerful as always. The mild unease rolling around me until now quadruples in seconds. What if this isn't about the STD tests but the Pap smear? I inhale as deeply as possible without bursting into tears from the pain knifing my ribs.

I push a slow breath out, calming myself down. I try not to let my mind wander to the six-letter word no one wants to hear, but it's impossible.

Cancer.

"Take a seat," he says, pointing at the chair in front of a narrow, white desk. "How are you feeling?"

I've heard this question too many times over the past two days. "Honestly, I'm okay. The ribs hurt, but painkillers take the edge off, and," I gesture to the stitches under my eyebrow, "this will heal in no time."

He bobs his head, lost in thought. "What tests have you had done at the hospital?" His tone is soothing as if he's trying to ease me into a false sense of security before he drops a bomb. "Did they draw blood? X-rays?"

"Both. Why?"

"What medication are you on now?"

"Just painkillers. Why?" I ask again, squirming in my seat. "Is this about the results? What's wrong with me? God, please don't tell me I have HIV and infected half of the hospi—"

"Cassidy," he says in a strained huff, his voice back to the formal doctor-patient tone he rarely uses. He peers up from the notepad on his desk and rips the ground from beneath my feet with one sentence. "You're pregnant."

My thoughts come to a sudden halt the same way my Fiat stopped when I crashed. The words echo in my ears like a looped voice clip.

Cassidy, you're pregnant.
You're pregnant.
Pregnant...

"No, that's not right," I whisper, gathering my thoughts and clinging to the idea. "It's a mistake. You know I'm on the pill. It's not possible."

"Everything is possible." He ties his fingers together, resting his hands on the desk. "Pills fail from time to time. Maybe you didn't take them regularly or took medication that weakened their effectiveness. I don't know, but I ran the labs twice myself. You're definitely pregnant."

This is a dream. A bad, *bad* dream.

I find my thigh and pinch hard enough to break the first layer of skin with my nails. It's *not* a dream. My chest tightens, my lungs compress, and I can't pull down a breath. The sharp stabbing in my ribcage mixes with fear, the weight of the news crushing me inside out.

"It's okay," Dr. Jones says, getting up to fetch me a cup of water. "All other tests came back negative, so you don't need to worry about STDs. We'll do an ultrasound to see how far along you are and get you started on prenatal vitamins..."

He's talking.

Saying I need to stop taking painkillers and that he'll write me a prescription for pregnancy-friendly medication and that I need to rest and...

I'm not sure what else. I'm only half listening. I can't focus. On the outside, I'm well put together, eyes on his, head nodding whenever I think it's the right thing to do, but on the inside, I'm screaming.

I'm pregnant with the man I love more than life.

Can I keep the baby? Raise it by myself? Does Logan have the right to know?

Maybe.

Will I tell him?

I don't know.

I'm scared of his reaction. Not one scenario will work in my favor. Either he'll stay with me because he'll want to do right by his child, but he'll hate me when his brothers stop talking to him, or he'll tell me to book an appointment at the abortion clinic, and then he'll cut me out of his life.

I wish there was a third option. One where he'd smile down at me, excited, *happy*, and in love. One where he'd kiss me and then drop to his knees to kiss my tummy.

I move my hand to my abdomen for a moment, then yank it away. This isn't the time to get attached to someone I might never meet.

Maybe I shouldn't tell Logan. He'll hate me, and while I can handle indifference, I don't think I can handle hate from the one person I love.

"Cassidy," Dr. Jones's voice breaks through the turmoil of my disarrayed thoughts. "I didn't think to ask the question when you came here on Monday, but... when you asked me to test you for STDs, was the sex consensual?"

"Oh God, *yes!*" I yelp, digging my nails into the backs of my hands. "Yes, it was, but I can't understand how this is possible. I never missed a pill, and they're supposed to work!"

"I don't know what to tell you." He pushes the paperwork on his desk aside, leaning closer to me. "It happens. Not often, but it does. Let me do the ultrasound, and you can go home and think about your next step, okay?"

"Okay," I whisper, nodding like a bobblehead dog on the dashboard before my eyes widen. "What about the car crash? What if—"

"Don't think ahead," he warns. "You're not showing, so you can't be too far along, and with no internal damage other than the broken ribs..." he trails off. "Any bleeding or pains?"

I shake my head *no*.

"That's good. Can you remember when you had your last period?"

I shake my head again but open my mouth, too. "No, they're not regular on the pill. Sometimes I don't have one for months, so I don't pay attention."

"Okay, what about unprotected sex? When was that?"

My cheeks heat in an instant.

I'm counting, trying to come up with a number. How long ago did Logan and I have sex for the first time? Thalia's birthday was in March. Express dates, the first week of April. It's

TOO WRONG

the first week of July now."

"Um, first time about three months ago."

Thirteen weeks. I'd be showing at thirteen weeks, wouldn't I? No way I'm that far along. I've not been sick or tired or had any cravings. I feel *normal*.

I wish I knew when my last period was and how to count when I'm ovulating. Maybe if I were nauseous, I would've realized sooner. Maybe if my periods were more regular or if I craved weird food, but I'm pregnancy-symptom-free so far.

He's not fazed by the answer, and I'm grateful for his impeccable professionalism. "Okay, you can't be further along than the first trimester. We can do a normal ultrasound first, but I'd recommend a transvaginal. It'll show us the pregnancy, even if it's only a few weeks old. Do you want me to get a nurse to help you get changed?"

"No, I'll manage."

It takes longer than usual to shimmy out of my dress and into a gown, but the moment of solitude gives me a chance to breathe and think. I gawk at my reflection in the mirror, eyes fixed on my tummy. I turn left and right, checking for any roundness, then press my fingers there, frowning. Was my abdomen always so firm? Was this slight curve here before?

"Are you okay there, Cass?" Dr. Jones taps on the door.

"Yes, sorry." I shove my hands into the sleeves of the gown and try to hold the back closed because there's no way I'll reach behind to tie it up. "I'm much slower now that I need to watch how I move."

"I broke a few ribs when I was younger, so I know how it hurts. You're handling it like a champ, believe me. I was more theatrical."

I lay down on the bed with a bit of help, and Dr. Jones

repositions my legs: ankles together, knees apart.

"Okay, try to relax. It'll feel cold."

As always. He rolls a condom on the wand, covers it in clear gel, and then hauls a monitor closer before slowly sticking the wand inside me.

It's a surreal experience.

I've not had time to come to terms with the news yet, to stop and understand that a tiny person is growing inside me. A tiny person with Logan's eyes and dark hair, my nose, and lips. His cleverness, my passion, and...

The warmness spreading around my bruised heart is close to what I feel when I'm with Logan... *happy*. I've learned not to hang onto that feeling.

It never lasts.

I shut my eyes, blocking the enticing images of a baby lying in a crib beside the large bed in Logan's bedroom.

Dr. Jones wiggles the wand around for a while before it stills, and he smiles wide enough to highlight the wrinkles in the corners of his eyes. "Okay, I found the little one. Don't move. I'll do the measurements. Do you want me to put the sound on? You can hear the heartbeat."

My eyes prickle with tears when I shake my head. I want to hear it, but if I decide not to keep the baby, the sound will haunt me forever. I bite my lip, glaring at the ceiling.

"I know it's a surprise pregnancy, Cassidy, but give yourself time, okay? Don't go making rash decisions. Think, and think again, and when you're certain you know what you want to do, I'm here to help any way you decide."

Words don't get past my lips. They're stuck in my throat, behind a big lump that makes swallowing painful. I'm fighting not to burst into tears for the duration of the ultrasound that takes all but five minutes.

"From the measurements, you're nine weeks and three days. The baby looks healthy and is developing as it should at this stage. I see no cause for concern."

Nine weeks. I've been pregnant for two months, and I haven't noticed. I bite the inside of my cheek, tasting copper pennies on my tongue.

How could I not have noticed?! What kind of a potential mother does that make me if I didn't even realize I'm pregnant?

"I've been drinking," I say, my voice breaking. "I didn't know, and I've been drinking and partying and stressing and lifting and—"

Dr. Jones squeezes my hand reassuringly. "The baby is fine, Cassidy. Do you think you're the only woman who didn't know she was pregnant? I've had women not realize until halfway through the second trimester. You can't go back and change things now, so don't beat yourself up. Make sure you take care of yourself going forward. No drinking, no lifting, no stressing, and lots of rest." He squeezes my hand again when I wipe my face. "Get dressed. I'll print the pictures and write a prescription for folic acid and vitamins."

He helps me to a sitting position, a fond look across his face that does little to help me cope. I lock myself back in the bathroom, shedding the gown with trembling hands.

"I don't have any symptoms," I say loud enough for him to hear me. "I've not been sick or had cravings. Is that normal?"

He chuckles softly, the sound barely reaching me through the closed door. "Every pregnancy is different. Some women puke and some don't. You should be glad you've had no morning sickness. Many women would give up their arm and leg not to throw up every day. That's not to say it won't come.

There's still plenty of time."

Maybe my symptoms are mild? Or easily mistaken. I've been tired and low on energy lately, which resulted in more hours spent in bed, but I associated that with long days at work and late nights with Logan.

"Darcie will book you in for another visit in four weeks, and she'll give you a pregnancy pack at the desk," he tells me when I'm back in his office. "Get over to the pharmacy today and start taking the folic acid and the vitamins right away. I've printed a few pictures." He hands me a prescription slip and a sealed A4 envelope. "Just in case you want to have a look. Call me if you have any questions."

I have one hundred questions, but Dr. Jones doesn't have the answers.

Only I do.

TWENTY-SEVEN

Logan

A day goes by.

Two.

Three.

I'm losing my sanity.

Each day is a struggle. I mentally spar with myself every goddamn hour not to text Cass, not to call, not to get in my car and drive over to her flat.

My head is full of her. My thoughts circle around the beautiful blonde non-stop. I've hardly had any food since I left the hospital on Wednesday evening. I'm surviving on coffee, apples, and beer. I don't know *why* apples, so don't fucking ask.

It's Saturday now, and I'm not sure how much longer I can cope with the incessant back and forth my head is playing.

Go and see her.

Don't go.

Admit that you care.

TOO WRONG

It's just a crush.

I want to see her and make sure she's okay. I want to check if she needs help with anything. Shopping, maybe. Or getting her car fixed. Although I doubt it can be fixed. She needs a new one. I could help with that.

I'm drinking alone for the first time in a very long time. It's not like I can call one of my brothers to keep me company in my misery, so a case of Corona and Ghost it is.

He doesn't give two shits about me, curling himself around the armchair.

I spill my beer, jolting out of my seat when my phone pings on the coffee table, thinking—fucking *hoping*—it's Cassidy, but no. It's just the Hayes group chat.

Nico: Logan, meet me at Rave *in an hour.*

Colt: What about me? I want to go, too.

Cody: Yeah, and me.

Nico: Let the record show I voted against adding 3Cs to the chat before they turn twenty-one.

Me: Thanks, bro, but I need to pass tonight.

*Shawn: *Dun dun dunnn* The plot thickens...*

Theo: Record shall so reflect. Not that anyone cares. You were outvoted, Nico. And why am I not invited?

Nico: Because I pay attention. It's the first weekend of the month, and that means wifey time. Date night, isn't it? You're grounded, bro. And Logan? You can pass if you're fucking or dying. Which one is it?*

Fucking dying.

I'm dramatic as shit, but a part of me feels like it's fucking dying right now. I dim the screen and throw the phone on the seat beside me. The incessant pinging doesn't stop, and I know the six of them will show up here if I stop replying. I grab the phone again to tell them I'm busy with some chick, so they leave me the fuck alone, but I almost choke on the sip of Corona instead. Among a gazillion notifications from the chat, there's a message from Cassidy.

My Princess: Turns out I don't have an STD. Unless you lied when you said we were exclusive, I guess you're fine. I'm sorry I screamed at you.

I tap out a reply, my heart beating out of my chest with a hammer, and my soul sitting on my shoulder, watching the unfolding scene with arms crossed and a dubious look.

Me: I didn't lie. How are you feeling? Do you need anything?

My eyes are glued to the screen the whole time the three dots dance. It takes half a minute before a reply comes.

Three words.

Three fucking words that kill me dead.

My Princess: A time machine.

My Princess: I'm fine. I'll see you around.

Fuck, that hurts. She throws the line I whispered in the darkness of her bedroom time and time again right back at me, and it pierces through my composure with a sniper's precision.

My head hits the back of the couch while the phone keeps pinging. It's not Cass, though. It's my brothers blowing up the group chat.

I try to imagine cutting her out of my life, going back to the way we were before Thalia's birthday party, but I can't.

There's no going back.

I don't want to go *back*. I don't want to pretend she hadn't told me she loves me. I want to move forward; check what we can make of this. *Us*. I want to man up and stop fighting the overpowering feelings; stop pretending we're just physical.

That ship has sailed.

No, it sunk to the bottom of the ocean.

The last three days were pure torture. I powered through, working and keeping myself distracted during the day, but there were no distractions to stop my mind from wandering while I sat in my silent house, alone.

I miss her.

Not sex.

I miss *her*.

The smell of her hair, her sweet smiles, her voice, her lips, and the way she tastes. I miss seeing her, being around her, watching her tuck the blonde strands of silky hair behind her ears and chew on her bottom lip when she's uncertain.

I miss hearing her voice and seeing her smile or scrunch her little nose. I miss the warmth of her body, hooded eyes, and my name on her lips sounding like a prayer. I miss how she plays with my hair when I lay with my face buried in her boobs right after I come and I'm catching my breath.

There's so much I miss. So much I love about that girl.

I sit up, my eyes wide open.

Love?

My heart beats faster, trying to match the pace of my thoughts, and my chest constricts like it's cramping.

Am I...?

Is this what it feels like?

The constant worrying, my thoughts spinning around her like a vulture that spotted a wounded animal, the need to be with her all the fucking time... is that *it?*

My heart swells, fluttering like a caged bird.

Holy shit.

And as if at a touch of a magic wand, my mind empties the static and clutter. I discard the thoughts of my brothers hating my guts for pursuing Cassidy.

Love me or fucking hate me.

There's not a single thing I wouldn't forgive them.

Not a single thing would make me turn my back on either one of my brothers, and I hope it works both ways.

Even if it doesn't, I shouldn't have to choose between them and *her*. They should be there for me no matter what. My happiness can't be conditional on their approval.

I grip the phone to shoot Cass a text and let her know I'm coming, but sixty-nine notifications on the screen steal my attention. "Shit," I hiss under my breath, seeing that five minutes of no replies on my part was enough for the Hayes to assemble like fucking Avengers.

They're on their way to my house, but I don't have time for this right now. They can wait. I need to talk to Cassidy first. I snatch the keys, lock the house and reverse out of the driveway, tires squealing when my foot drops the pedal to the floor.

TWENTY-EIGHT

Cassidy

Several parenting pamphlets lay spread out on the coffee table. The vitamins and folic acid are by the kettle, ready for me to take every morning. I took the first dose last night and another one today.

I've not decided what the hell I'm going to do, but for now, while I come to terms with the clusterfuck, I take the vitamins, drink decaf that tastes like cardboard and try not to stress. Easier said than done.

It's been twenty-four hours since Dr. Jones threw me off the cliff with the news. It's still so new. So *odd* to think a person is growing inside me.

A boy, I hope.

A little carbon copy of his daddy with dark eyes, high cheekbones, and a strong jaw. My nose, though. And my face shape.

Will he have dark hair or light like mine?

Dark. Definitely dark. The Hayes genes are too strong for

my measly blonde to win the fight.

Among the happy, heartwarming pamphlets filled with pregnancy milestones, dos and don'ts, and drawings of the baby at different stages until birth, there are two other pamphlets. The not-so-happy ones. White covers with no pictures, drawings, or text. Just a plain sheet of paper to disguise what's written on the pages hiding underneath.

I've flipped one open but didn't stomach more than the two questions written in bold ink at the top of the first page.

Are you pregnant but not sure if you want to have the baby? Do you need more information about abortion?

The thought of terminating the pregnancy turns my blood cold, but the choice is as valid as going through with it and having the baby. There are pros and cons to both options. The choice itself is a blessing most women in America no longer have. Here, in California, we're still allowed to make conscious decisions about our bodies. We're allowed to *not* become mothers just because we got drunk and forgot a condom.

Shit happens, and the fact we're not forced to raise babies we don't want makes for a healthier society.

I want to read through the leaflet and know my options. How long before I need to decide? How long before it's too late? Will it hurt? What is the process like?

I know the other side of the coin—the pregnancy leaflets were a breeze to read through. I soaked up the information, making mental notes, forgetting for a while that this baby is not a planned miracle. It's a surprise. An accident.

A cup of green tea in hand, I sit on the sofa, glaring at the still-sealed envelope among the pamphlets. A part of me wants to rip it wide open and stare at the pictures inside: the first pictures of my baby. A different part of me knows I shouldn't touch that until my mind is made.

A knock on the door has my head snapping in that direction. Without taking a second to think, I cross the room and yank the door open. And just as I do, I realize the pamphlets are still on the coffee table in plain sight.

Blood drains from my face when I see Thalia. Her smile morphs into a scowl a second before I shut the door in her face.

"Give me a sec!" I yell, hurrying to hide the leaflets. She can't find out. Not until I decide whether to tell Logan. "Come in!" I yell again, stuffing the evidence of my new, blessed state into the drawer in my bedroom.

"What's going on?" She asks from the kitchen, her tone clipped. "Why did you almost break my nose?"

"Sorry, I had to put something away." I come out of the bedroom and stop-mid step.

Thalia stands by the kitchen cupboards, a bottle of wine beside her, two glasses in one hand...

My prenatal vitamins in the other.

Why didn't I think of that?!

"I-I... those aren't—"

"Not yours?!" she snaps, eyes wide and horizontal creases lining her forehead. "Don't you dare lie in my face!" She gawks at the bottle and glances briefly at the one filled with folic acid. "You're pregnant."

This isn't how anyone was supposed to find out. *No one was supposed to know!* I'm furious at myself for not thinking to hide the vitamins and furious at Thalia for showing up here unannounced. If she had given me ten minutes' notice, I would've remembered to hide the pills.

The anger isn't as intense as relief, though. I want to talk, to hear an unbiased opinion, and just *tell* someone because my mind is all over the place, changing ten times a minute.

"I only found out yesterday," I admit quietly.

She closes the distance between us and flings her arms over my shoulders, pulling me in for a hug. "I'm so shocked I don't know what to say. I want to say *congratulations*, but I have a feeling you're not far off crying, so I'm guessing you're not in the right frame of mind for that yet."

"Not yet," I say in her hair, that tickles my face. "I don't know what to do… I'm so confused." I step away to pour her a glass of wine and hide the vitamins and folic acid in the cupboard in case anyone else decides to pay me a visit.

"How far along are you?" she asks when we sit on opposite ends of the couch. "Does Logan know?"

"No. I've been trying to decide whether to tell him or whether to… you know. *Not* have the baby."

Her eyebrows meet her hairline, and her mouth falls open as if she wants to talk but decides to take a large gulp of wine instead. I'm sure she wants to scream at me, grab the phone and tell Logan to haul ass here right now, but that's just it—Thalia *is* my best friend. Instead of acting on her beliefs and ensuring her family is protected, she takes a second to think about *me*.

"Okay." She shakes off whatever stiffness her muscles held. "Have you made your mind up? Talk to me, babe. I can't help you if I don't know where your head is right now. I know Logan, so I might be able to put your doubts to rest."

I curl my feet under my bum, fighting the maternal instinct of placing my hand on my tummy. I've not done it once yet, but it's hard. Especially that when I scrutinized my belly this morning, I grew more confident that the faint rise on my lower tummy *is* a bump.

It's tiny, and probably no one would consider it a baby bump, but I know my body, and that rise is new.

The pamphlets say that some women start showing as early as eight weeks, depending on their physique. I'm skin-on-bones skinny, which means I'll probably be showing sooner than, say, Thalia, when she decides to get pregnant.

I press the rim of the cup to my lower lip, holding it with both hands to keep them occupied. "I'm scared."

"That he'll tell you to get rid of the baby?" she demands, finishing the rest of the wine. "Looks like I'm getting drunk for the both of us tonight."

"I'm scared he'll step up and hate me for ruining his relationship with Nico, Theo, and the others. I've always been disposable. Always a nuisance to people around me. My parents, the foster families, even most of my friends."

Thalia's all ears while I talk, telling her things about my past no one but Logan knows. I paint a vivid picture of the neglect and abuse and how powerless it made me feel for years. How hard it was to get back up time after time and face the world with a brave face.

"I don't want to feel unwanted forever," I admit quietly, and I'm hit with the thought that the baby inside me would *want* and *need* me forever. I'd be important to someone. Irreplaceable. "I love Logan, Thalia. With everything I have, but he's loyal to his brothers, and I'm foul air to them. If Logan steps up, which I'm pretty sure he will, they won't stand by him, and at some point, he'll blame me for losing them."

"What makes you—" she stops, shaking her head. "Let's rewind. What makes *Logan* think his brothers won't have his back?"

TOO WRONG

My cheeks heat. Thalia knows I slept with Theo long before she moved to America, but we never divulged the subject. "Theo, for one," I say as vaguely as possible, but the way she presses her lips together tells me she got the hint. "And Nico, obviously. I'm friends with Kaya."

"So what? It's not like *you* cheated on Nico."

"I know, but he's pretty much ready to murder me with whatever he has in hand whenever he sees me, and—"

"He always looks like he wants to kill someone, Cassidy. He's not your fan, sure, but not because he holds a grudge against *you* personally. He's just trying to steer clear of anyone who reminds him of Kaya and Jared, but he'll get over himself. He's got a short fuse, but once you break through that tough exterior, he's a good guy."

Nico Hayes a good guy?

Nope. She's only saying that because he is a Hayes and family is the most important thing to her.

She sits back down in the wingchair, turning my Ficus the other way around, so it's not in her face. "I think Theo's so stiff because he's scared I'll be jealous if he talks to you." She takes another sip of wine. "I told him I'm not, by the way. We all have a past."

"Maybe you're right, or maybe you're a helpless optimist... I'm back and forth about telling Logan."

Thalia toys with her glass, deep in thought for a moment as if trying to put her thoughts to words and not sound bad. "I won't tell you what to do, babe. This is your life, and you need to make this decision alone, but if you care about my opinion, I think Logan deserves to know. It's not just your baby."

Every time she says *baby,* my heart flutters. Hearing the word makes it real. Not that it's not real, but... I don't know, it just solidifies the fact.

***

A loud bang sounds on the door close to nine in the evening, not long after Thalia left. This time, I know exactly who stands outside. There's no mistaking the urgent knock, but this is the worst time for him to show up because my cheeks are stained with tears.

I plucked the courage to read through the abortion pamphlet, and my imagination works overtime, envisioning the process, the pain, and the blood. The feeling of loss crept in on me, and I hold my hand protectively cupped around my tiny bump.

My resolve not to tell Logan wore thin while I read. He needs to know. He has the right to know and help me make a conscious decision. We're both adults for crying out loud. We can work this out.

Just not tonight. I'm too distraught. Too vulnerable to fight.

I stand by the door, wiping my face. Until the lock is turned, until there's distance between us, I have the strength to stand up to him. "Not tonight, Logan," I say, resting my head on the door, tears resuming their journey down my face like little rivers. My voice breaks, coming out strained, but I can't stop the sobs burning my throat. "Please. Not tonight, okay? Go away."

"Are you crying?" he asks, tension vibrating in his voice. "What's going on? Are you not well? Let me in."

"Go away."

"Open the door, Cassidy. Let me in. We need to talk."

Yes, but not tonight. "Go away," I choke, whimpering and

shuddering all over.

"Fuck that. No way I'm leaving. Move away from the door. I'm coming in."

"Go away."

A soft thud shakes the frame. It's not powerful enough for Logan's tall, toned body, so I assume he banged his forehead against it. "Let me in, baby. You're upset. Talk to me. Tell me what's wrong."

"Go away."

It's all I can say, silently choking on tears. He doesn't reply for the longest time, but I know he's still there. I can feel him. My body tingles whenever he's close, but those tingles aren't pleasant tonight.

Tonight, small insects crawl under my skin, the unease like a living, breathing organism taking up residence in my heart and mind. I slide to the floor, clutching my knees. At some point, he'll give up and leave. He won't spend the night out in the hall.

I sit there, doing my best to get a hold of myself for what feels like a long time. There's no movement outside the door, but I can still feel his presence.

The screeching of the balcony door sliding open has my head snapping in that direction, my heart in my throat for two long seconds before Logan enters the flat in the darkness of the night like a common burglar.

My pulse accelerates, resonating in my head and the tips of my fingers as he slides the door shut, eyes on me, a frown carving a deep eleven between his eyebrows. I scramble to my feet, wiping my face with the back of my hand.

"What's going on?" he asks, concern tainting his features as he comes closer. "Why are you crying? What happened?"

I shove him back with both hands, biting my lip hard enough to bruise and hard enough to stop crying. "Go away."

The sheer panic in my voice rings loud and clear.

It's pathetic. I'm so tired of the emotional turmoil and tears that won't dry out.

My eyes widen, and a small, disturbing chuckle rips out of my mouth when I realize why I've been acting so out of character, bawling my eyes out like a scared little girl.

I've always held my own. I lived through enough pain and neglect not to let myself get hung up on the hurt thrown my way, but for a while, I've been an emotional trainwreck.

Stupid hormones.

"Please, Logan. Leave, I can't do this today," I utter, planting my feet on the floor while trying to push him toward the door. Toward the *exit*.

I'd have more luck moving a brick wall.

He cuffs my wrists, pulling me to him, and locks me in his arms, one hand cradling my head, pressing my cheek to his chest, the other around my lower back. "Shh, baby. Calm down."

I'm shaking. My body's so detached from my mind it feels as if I'm standing in the middle of the Arctic Pole while my brain's in the Amazon, overheating. Bile comes up my throat, the vile, acidic taste burning like battery acid. I try to jerk myself away from Logan, but he only pulls me closer to him.

"I'm not letting you go. Not until you calm down and tell me what the hell happened to get you so upset."

The tears come on stronger, dripping down my nose and chin even though my eyes are shut to stop them from escaping. I shove at Logan again, driving my fists into his sides, trashing like a crazy person.

Not the best move considering my broken ribs scream in

agony, rendering me motionless and speechless three punches later. I bite down on Logan's arm in an involuntary reflex as I grip the back of his t-shirt and squeeze as hard as possible to transfer the pain.

"Shit." He moves his hands to my hips and lifts me into his arms. "Breathe, baby. Just breathe through it for me." He sits on the loveseat, curving me into his chest. "Is that okay?"

I readjust my position ever so slightly, melting against his chest, the blinding pain acting like a sedative to my crazed mind, shushing the screams and halting the tears.

"We need to talk," I say, sucking in a slow, careful breath. "I don't want to do this today, but you're here now, and I'm losing my mind."

"We sure do need to talk, but," he pushes me away and curls his fingers under my chin, forcing me to meet his eyes. "You'll have to *look* at me while I talk."

"Me first," I plead, sliding off his lap to take a seat on the other end of the loveseat like a schoolgirl in front of the principal's office. I dig my nails into my knees. This shouldn't be so hard. Not at all how any woman imagines breaking the news to the father of her baby, but here I am, so nervous my stomach whips. "We're nothing more than casual fuck-buddies and—"

Logan leans forward, his jaw set tight. "It'll be better if I talk first."

I shake my head, biting my lip to stop a new wave of tears. God, how long does this teary, emotional side effect of pregnancy last?

"You need to shut up and listen because this is as hard as it gets, and if you keep interrupting me, I'll keep crying, and this will be a mess."

He narrows his eyes, but shuts up, readjusting himself in his seat, his attention focused, the room so still and silent you'd hear a pin drop. "Okay, but don't call me your fuck-buddy, Cass."

"I don't want to be the reason you stop talking to your family," I start, weighing every word. "I don't want to destroy your life and I don't want you to hate me." I'm not making sense yet, but soon, he'll understand. "I love you, Logan, and I only want the best for you, but I've been through enough hurt. I need you to consider my feelings, at least on some level, okay?"

"Cass, I—"

"Not done yet," I say, rising to my feet, too jittery to sit still. "Just know I didn't do this on purpose. I *never* lied to you. And don't act all noble for the sake of it. No one has to know."

I leave the room to fetch the ultrasound pictures. I don't want to see them, but if he questions my words, I'll have proof to hand him. I drop the envelope on the coffee table in front of him, and he moves to grab it.

"Logan," I urge, standing there like an orphan.

His eyes snap to me, and the change of my tone from a teary mess to a resigned whisper stops him from closing his fingers around the envelope. "Just say it. Are those the test results? What the hell do you have?"

A single tear rolls down my cheek as I brace for the unknown. "I'm pregnant."

TWENTY-NINE

Logan

There's an earthquake.

In my head.

I'm pregnant reverberates through the deepest recesses of my mind, heart, and soul if that even exists.

She's pregnant.

My eyes drop to her abdomen, but there's no roundness. No visual representation of her words. It's an out-of-body experience as I sit here in a state of deep fucking shock.

My vocal cords are tied, and I can't unglue my eyes from her tummy as if staring long enough will let me see inside.

"Say something," Cass urges, taking a seat beside me on the edge of the loveseat. I think she's afraid to startle me if she comes closer. "I know this is unexpected. If you need time to think, that's okay, just—"

"You were on birth control," I cut in, remembering that fact. "How can you be pregnant?"

TOO WRONG

She sucks her bottom lip between her teeth but holds my gaze. "I swear I didn't do this on purpose. I took the pills every day like I was supposed to. You can check the calendar, I mark it every day, and I can show you the tablets I have left, and you can count them to see I haven't missed a single one," she rambles, eyes wide, hands knitting an invisible sweater. She's so scared of my reaction that she trembles like a cornered animal, her eyes pooling with tears. "Dr. Jones said it happens. Rarely, but it does."

I take a deep breath, doing my best to calmly assess the situation and think through what comes out of my mouth and *how* it comes out. "And you're sure it's mine."

It's not a question.

There's not an ounce of accusation in my voice. I know the baby is mine. She wouldn't be sitting here, shuddering, gawking at me with big eyes if the baby were someone else's.

"I've not been with anyone else in over a year," she says quietly. "I wish I could tell you we have more time to make a decision, but we don't. A week is all I can give you."

My brows knit together. "What decision? There's no decision to be made here. You're pregnant. It's done."

She tucks her hair away, struggling to look me in the eye. I can't stand seeing her so vulnerable. It's a side of her I've seen before, and one I can't comprehend exists underneath the confidence and smiles she wears daily.

She's normally so positive and amazing, but the weight of the world sits on her shoulders right now. The mental scars she usually hides are on display, showcasing that beneath her will to put the past behind and not let it affect her present, there's still a girl who feels unwanted.

"I'm pregnant *now*. Your family hates me, Logan. And I

know how important they are to you. Please don't step up just because you think it's the right thing to do. We're not in the eighties. Try to think about me, too, okay?"

I tear myself out of the seat, my blood boiling, bubbling, fucking *overflowing*. "What are you talking about?! Of course, I'm going to step up!" I yank the baseball cap off and rake my fingers through my hair back and forth. "You think I'll let you raise my baby alone?"

"I've been through enough," she whispers and chews on her lip, glaring at her fingers. "I don't want to be another bad decision. If we keep the baby—"

"If?" I mouth only now understanding where she's coming from. "*If*?!" I boom again, pacing the room. "There's no *if*! How can you consider *not* having it? You said you love me!"

More tears spill from her eyes, mouth opening and closing a few times before she swallows hard and wipes her face for the umpteenth time, attempting to stop the tears that trickle down her pale cheeks on their own accord.

"I do, and if you're sure you can handle whatever your brothers will do when they find out, then I'll have the baby. You'll see it whenever you want. I won't make it hard for you, but I don't want you to start hating me down the line. If we end this now, no one has to know."

Her words ring in my head like a church bell.

Her train of thought unfolds and makes more sense by the minute. She thinks she'll be a single mom. That we'll draw up a schedule of who'll take care of the baby and when.

I can see why she thinks that. I've done nothing but hurt her, intentionally or not, since the start. Even when I tried to help her overcome the fear of water, I locked her in the garage straight after like she was a fucking mistake.

Tonight, I came here with one goal in mind. It hasn't changed with the news. If anything, my determination to show her that I care about her more than I've ever cared about any woman grew tenfold.

She's pregnant with *my* baby.

Everything I ever wanted sits on the loveseat... crying.

"If my brothers can't accept my choices, then to hell with them." I crouch beside her, taking her hands in mine. "I came here to tell you I don't want us to be sex buddies. God, baby... you're all I think about. You're all I want, and I'm falling in love with you so fucking fast I can't keep up."

She stills.

Stops breathing.

A long, silent moment passes with her staring at me blankly before a small, pitiful whimper slips past her lips, and her whole body shudders. "You want me?" she utters, her face a picture of disbelief. She looks from my eyes to my lips, cheeks, nose, and back to my eyes. "Are you sure?"

Her choice of words is another low blow to my stomach.

Are you sure?

She looks and sounds like she can't fathom that anyone could want her. Like she's been living under the assumption that everyone is out to take but never give anything back.

I wish I had noticed sooner that all Cassidy wants is for someone to give a damn. She wants to be important to at least one person in her life. Beneath the tough exterior hides an anxious, neglected woman who was never put first.

"I'm sorry." I wipe the tears from her face with my thumbs, cupping her cheeks. "I know I've hurt you, but I'll do better. You just have to give me a chance to prove myself."

She leans out, hope glistening in her teary eyes when she

presses her lips to mine. "I love you so much," she whispers, weaving her fingers through my hair and deepening the kiss. "I'll make you happy, Logan. I promise you won't regret this."

I'm fucking reeling.

Hating myself more with every word she speaks.

She's afraid. I feel how fast her heart is going, and my chest tightens painfully. *I should be the one making promises, not her.* I'm the one who took her for granted.

"You already make me the happiest man alive," I move my hands to cup her thighs and lift her into my arms, holding onto her for dear life. "I swear I'll do better. I'll do my best, princess."

Nothing else ever mattered as much as the blonde in my arms. The first time I looked at her, I knew I was as good as gone. I've wasted three years holding a grudge over something out of our control.

She could've been mine for *three* years.

She should've been mine.

She *was* mine…

I just didn't know it.

I take her to bed, resting my back on the masses of decorative cushions, and pull her close, careful not to hurt her ribs. She curves into me, her back to my chest, and I wrap one hand across her collarbones, my lips on her temple.

"I'm sorry. I'm so fucking sorry I put my brothers first when it should've been you all along."

She covers my hand with hers, the rhythm of her heart slowing down the longer she's with me. "They're your family," she says, toying with my fingers. "A casual fling isn't worth risking your relationship with them." She angles her head, kissing the underside of my chin. "It's not too late, you know? You can still leave."

Instinctively, I hold her a little tighter. She fits in my arms like she's been made for me. How have I not noticed sooner? "We're not casual. I don't think we were for long. And this isn't a fling. You're mine, Cassidy. You're pregnant with my baby."

I lower my free hand and push it under her t-shirt, spreading my fingers over her abdomen. There's a slight bump there already. Not big, barely a suggestion of what's to come. It's firm to the touch, the curve ever so slight, but it's there.

Hands down, this is the most surreal and amazing moment of my life. I've been nagging Theo to start a family since he married Thalia because my paternal instinct has been in the highest gear for a while, and now... I'm going to be a Dad.

"How far along are you?"

"Nine and a half weeks. I only found out yesterday." She wriggles in my arms enough to turn her body and look me in the eye. "I didn't know when I went out last weekend. I wouldn't have had a drink if I knew, but I—"

"Is the baby okay?" I cut in, brushing my fingertips up and down her arm. "What did the doctor say?"

"He said it looks healthy and the right size, and the heartbeat is nice and strong."

"Then that's all that matters." I press a kiss to the side of her head. "God, Cass... you're *pregnant,* princess." I kiss her again. "You're pregnant with *my* baby. I'll take care of you. Both of you. I'll make this as easy as breathing. I'll get up in the middle of the night to buy pickles and hold your hair when you puke." I hold her closer, kissing her head over and over again, my chest inflating like a balloon. "We'll move your things over to my house tomorrow."

She jerks away too abruptly and grabs her side, hissing under her breath. "We're not moving anything," she pants through gritted teeth, her eyes shut tight. "Don't rush. We've got time. The baby won't be here until February."

I pull her back to me, cradling her until the pain subsides. "What do you want to wait for? I've wasted three years already. You're mine now. I want you close. We'll live together sooner or later, so why not sooner?"

"Because... because you need to be sure you want this."

She doesn't say it out loud, but I can tell by the grimace tainting her pretty face and how she nervously pinches the comforter that she's scared I'll change my mind and put her out the door a few days from now.

Not a chance. I might've been an idiot all this time, but when I realized I'm falling in love with her, a fundamental change happened in the blink of an eye. She's *mine*.

Mine to care for. Mine to keep *safe*.

After all that I've put her through, I don't blame her for not believing my words. Instead of telling, I need to start showing her I mean what I say.

***

Cassidy is asleep when I wake up, entangled in the sheets and her arms and legs. She clings to my side, one hand across my chest, one leg bent at the knee and draped over my thighs. She nuzzles her face in the crook of my neck, a veil of messy, blonde hair scattered around her peaceful face.

I've not seen her like this before, and I take a few minutes to openly stare and commit to memory everything about her. The slight pout of her lips, light eyelashes, every beauty mark. She's so fucking beautiful curling into me.

I slide my hand under the duvet and push it between us,

caressing the tiny bump with my thumb. That's all I've done all evening, and for at least an hour after Cassidy fell asleep.

My heart swells three sizes when the thought hits me once again: I'm going to be a Dad.

It feels like I've been waiting for this moment for years, and now that it's finally happening, I can't contain the overwhelming joy. I pull my hand out, sliding out from under the duvet, and cover Cassidy back up.

The curve of her hip and waist melts my brain and the morning wood I'm sporting becomes painfully hard. My chances at sex are extremely low, considering she's got two broken ribs, so instead of making the cock situation worse, I kiss her forehead and tug the same t-shirt I wore last night over my head.

A sense of dread hits me as soon as I spot my phone on the coffee table. I switched it off last night at some point because my brothers were blowing up the group chat, but I can't keep hiding here forever.

I grab the phone and switch it on. Dozens of notifications pop up immediately, and I find out why they were so fucking relentless in trying to reach me last night. They spent a few hours at my house, waiting for me to show up.

A spare key is in a safe box by the main door, and every one of them knows the combination, but...

Me: The key is for emergencies.

Ping, ping, ping.
Ping.
Ping, ping.
They swear at me for not replying to their messages last

night and swear at me for making them worry, and swear at me for not having enough beer in the fridge to accommodate six uninvited guests who'd dry a well.

I wait until the *fucks, shits,* and *assholes* are out of their system, and the first decent question arrives.

Shawn: Are you alright? Where were you last night?

Me: I'm good. I was busy. We need to talk, but this isn't a chat we can have over texts. Can you all come over around noon?

Shawn: Wink if you need an alibi.

Nico: Are you home now?

Me: Not yet. I should be back in an hour.

A feeling of impending doom settles over me when they reply that they'll be there at ten o'clock sharp.

A part of me is terrified of losing them. I can't imagine what my life will look like without them. I've never been alone. They were always there by my side, always available when I needed help or advice and the grim possibility of losing their trust and acceptance fills me with mild panic.

But, at the same time, a different part of me that sprouted overnight won't put their approval before my baby or Cass.

It's still surreal to think I'm going to be a Dad. Surreal, scary, and exhilarating. My protectiveness toward the life sprouting inside Cassidy is already overpowering. The same words replay in my head like a broken record.

My baby.

TOO WRONG

Mine.

My *family*.

God, I can't believe my own fucking idiocy. I could've had this, the most incredible feeling in the world, for three years now. I could've loved and cared for her all this time.

What a fucking waste of life that's already so short.

The sound of the coffee maker pulls Cassidy out of bed. She enters the kitchen, tightening the straps of her gray robe around her waist.

"You're still here." She nuzzles into my chest, peppering my chin with soft kisses. "Good morning."

"Morning, baby. The door was closed, so I couldn't sneak out." I smirk, kissing her head. "Of course, I'm here. You're stuck with me now. I do need to go out for a bit, but I won't be long, and when I'm back, I expect to find you packing your bags." I hand her a cup of coffee and fetch another pod. "No lifting, though, okay?"

It took two hours, but I convinced her last night that she should move in with me. We looked through the ultrasound pictures, too. I expected something different than a bean-shaped blob among white noise, but I stared awestruck at the tiny arms and legs for the longest time.

"How about I pack a bag or two with essentials for now? I need to give my landlord a month's notice, so we don't have to move all my stuff right away."

I wrap her tighter in my arms, ready to argue, but a lone thought pierces my mind before I say one word. I want her to feel safe with me; that won't happen until she sees I won't give up on her, so I need to make adjustments.

"Will you feel better if we do this in stages?"

She nods, eyeing the coffee in her hand. "Which pod did

you use? The blue one?"

"I don't know. Why?"

"I can't have normal coffee for now." She opens the bin, takes out the pod I threw away, hands me her cup, and grabs a fresh, blue pod. "It's decaf."

"Decaf, got it."

I make a mental note to send my cleaning lady shopping tomorrow. She's versatile like that: she does more than cleaning. I bet there are more things Cass needs now apart from decaf, and Mira will probably know all the pregnancy must-haves, having raised four kids herself.

Ten minutes later, I kiss Cass and promise to pick her up in a couple of hours. I don't want to leave even for a few minutes, but it's time to face the fucking music.

I hop in my car and head home to grab a shower and a change of clothes before my brothers raid the house. I know they won't be late today, and I almost break a leg trying to get ready before they arrive.

The doorbell rings just as I descend the stairs pulling a fresh jersey over my head, my hair still damp. And as if a switch has been flipped, my stomach twists with nerves.

One deep breath is all I need to get a hold of myself before I let Nico and the triplets inside.

"What's going on? Why the rush?" Colt sheds his denim jacket in the hallway and tosses it over a narrow side table, readjusting his silver watch. "You don't look so good, bro."

"Don't ask questions. I won't repeat myself, so we'll have to wait for the other two to get here, alright?" I lead them into the kitchen, my palms sweating already. "You want coffee?"

Nico's eyes follow my every move as if he can guess the problem by reading into my gestures and expressions. Usually, he can riddle out what's going on, he has this sixth sense about him, but it'll fail him today. No way he can deduce what brand of fresh hell I'm about to unleash.

The triplets bicker between themselves, sitting by the island while I get the coffee maker started, my mind skipping ahead to visualize my brothers' possible reactions to the news.

All I hope at this point is that the conversation won't drag.

I want to be with Cass. I want to hold my hand across her tummy, kiss her head, and show her that I meant every word I said last night.

I told her I'm falling in love with her, but the truth is I'm already in love. How did I miss when it happened? How have I not known until the realization hit me square in the jaw last night?

I squeeze the bridge of my nose, pushing the annoyance aside. No point in fixating on what I can't change.

Theo and Shawn arrive ten minutes later. The atmosphere immediately shifts to heavy, but my mind is made and calm. Cass is what I want. She's what I need. My brothers will either accept that or they won't. Simple as that.

I rest my back against the countertop, watching six of them scattered around the kitchen, all equally tense, suspicious, and silent.

"Go on, bro," Cody urges, holding his cup with both hands and blowing the steam away. "What's this gathering all about? And why so fucking early?" He chuckles, trying to lighten the mood. He's the resident tension-breaker, but he fails miserably this morning. No one is in the mood to laugh. "I crawled into my bed four hours ago. Spill your guts. What's going on?"

The Holy Trinity is least involved in the matter, but whatever the older three decide, the younger three will mimic. It's just how it works among us.

We're usually a united front in the face of problems, but whenever we argue about how to proceed, the triplets stay to the side, waiting until we agree on a course of action.

They're still finding themselves, learning how to navigate the world and when big-boy pants are required, they trust us more than they trust themselves.

I've rehearsed the start of this conversation a hundred times before I fell asleep last night, long after Cass nodded off, and I've not stopped rehearsing it since I left her flat.

"I love you all," I say, holding my cup in both hands like Cody, to stop myself from squirming.

"Well, shit. You're gay, too?" Conor huffs, one eyebrow raised. "Jesus, why so grim? It's cool, Logan. We love you. Chill the fuck out, bro. You're paler than pale."

"Shush," Shawn clips, whacking Conor across the back of his head, then gestures for me to keep going.

"You're my family," I recite the rehearsed statement, "and regardless of how this ends, even if you won't talk to me again, just know that if either one of you ever needs me, be it five, ten, or thirty years down the line, I'll always be here for you."

Shawn shifts from one foot to another. His focused look slowly morphs into two vertical creases lining his forehead. It's the same look on all their faces.

"You're starting to freak me out," Colt says, crossing his arms and straightening his back. "Just get it out in the open. What's going on?"

"Did you kill someone?" Conor chips in. "Are you going to jail or something?"

"Zip it," Nico clips, the authoritative note in his tone ringing loud and clear. He leans against the doorframe closest to the exit as if he senses that what will come out of my mouth affects him most. "Drop the bullshit. Cards on the table, Logan."

He's not the oldest. He's actually the middle child, but he always commands the room, and we all respect his word most, which is why I'm at a huge disadvantage here.

I reach into the back pocket of my jeans and do put something on the table. Not cards, though. I pull out one of the ultrasound pictures and toss it across the island toward Theo, who sits opposite where I stand.

He grabs it, gawking at the white noise, a blizzard of confusion flashing across his face. "Is that—" his eyes snap to me, growing wider just as Colt snatches the picture out of his hand. "You got some chick pregnant?"

I nod, biting my teeth. "She's due in February."

"Fuck me sideways!" Conor exclaims. "Are you serious right now? Bro, that's *good* news! Why do you act like someone died? Who's the—" He halts, sucking in a harsh breath when he adds two and two together. "No way..."

"Who's the Mommy?" Shawn finishes for him. "You never told us you're seeing anyone. What's that about?"

I glance between Theo and Nico, ejecting all air from my lungs. "I wasn't exactly seeing her per se. We were casual for three months, but it grew out of control. I'm in love with her."

"That's still *good* news, Logan. You're making no sense." Cody says, the picture in his hands now. He turns it upside down and tilts his head as if it's an optical illusion only visible at a certain angle. "What's the bad news?"

"There is no bad news." I shift from one foot to another. "Just news you won't like."

"Fuck," Nico seethes, nostrils flared, black eyes shooting daggers my way. "Tell me it's not who I fucking think it is."

There. The reaction I expected all along. The reason why I didn't want to let myself *feel* for Cassidy sooner.

As disappointed as I am to know I was right, I'm also not fazed by his curt tone.

"I'm sorry," I say on autopilot. "It just happened, Nico. I don't even know when. I thought I could stop seeing her at any mome—" The words pile up on the tip of my tongue when he charges at me, fists clenched.

Theo jumps out of his seat at the last second, acting like a barricade and stops Nico from knocking out my front teeth.

"You better let me go, or you'll get one in your jaw, too," he snaps, trying to shove Theo away, but he's not about to knock him out for no good reason, so he glares at me over his shoulder instead. "How many times have you called her a psycho bitch? Fucking unstable. Manipulative. Sorry excuse for a woman! And now you got her *pregnant?!*"

His outburst doesn't surprise me. In all fairness, I expected him to get to me faster; before Theo had a chance to get in the way. And him jumping to my aid *is* a surprise. Short-lived, though, because once Nico's words sink, I know this isn't close to being over.

He's got it all wrong.

"I'm not talking about Kaya," I say. "I wouldn't touch her even if you fucking paid me."

The anger drains from Nico's face in a flash, confusion taking the stage. He folds his arms over his chest, stepping back from Theo. "Then who are you talking about?"

"Cassidy," Conor supplies, sporting a self-assured smirk. "Right? That's why you were so bent out of shape when she crashed into Colt's car."

"Yeah," I admit. The weight of the confession falls to the

ground with a thud, but instead of feeling lighter, I feel heavier. Defeated. I'm facing a life without their support, and I'm fucking sick to my stomach at the thought. "We've been a no-strings-attached kind of deal since Express Dates. I thought I could stop seeing her anytime, but I can't, and I don't fucking want to. I'm in love with her... and she's pregnant. I'm gonna be a Dad. I love you all, but my priorities have shifted overnight."

They're silent for a minute, either waiting for me to speak again or processing the news. I have nothing more to add.

The ball is in their court.

Time slows. Seconds stretch until they feel like minutes, and *no one* is reacting.

Not one punch from Nico.

Not one frown from Theo.

It's like waiting for the guillotine to drop.

"You're making no sense, Logan, and you're giving me a migraine," Shawn huffs, squeezing the bridge of his nose. "Explain that opener. Why would we never talk to you again?"

I set my cup aside, no longer needing a distraction. "Her history with Theo, for one, and—"

"That was three years ago!" Theo snaps, slamming his fist on the marble countertop. "Get over yourself. I've apologized like a hundred times already. You didn't know her when we hooked up. What else do you want me to do? It's not like I can turn back time, bro!"

My eyebrows knot in the middle. "You... *what?* I've been over it for a long time, Theo. It's all of you who despise her for it. When has either one of you said one word to her? Huh? And you?" I glare at Nico. "You couldn't even sit at her table for five minutes! So yeah, I know this is a problem, but guess what? Love me or hate me. She's mine, and I'm not letting her go."

Nico's jaw works furiously, nothing but murder on his mind as he balls his hands into tight fists. I'm waiting for another outburst, another lunge forward to land a precise punch on my face that'll leave me with a dislocated jaw at best, but instead, Nico dents my fridge with his fist.

"You're a fucking idiot," he seethes, pointing his finger at me. "There's a reason why I wanted *you* to take over my time with Cass at the Express Dates." He's no longer stewing.

Well, he is, but it's the good kind of energy bubbling inside him. I can tell because he's almost *smiling*. Almost. It's not a full-blown smile, but the slight curve of his mouth is more than I've seen on him in a long time.

Ever since the Kaya and Jared fiasco, Nico's emotions range from annoyance to fury ninety-nine percent of the time, but here he is, almost smiling.

"I saw how you watched her at Thalia's party and how panicked you were when she wasn't breathing," he continues. "I've seen you with many women, Logan, but Cassidy is the only one that makes you tick. You were miserable for weeks when you found out she hooked up with Theo first."

"Because I liked her!" My heart starts beating a touch faster as Nico's words bounce in my head.

He wanted me to go after Cassidy? He tried to help?

Have I fallen into the rabbit hole and emerged in an alternate reality? It sure feels like it. I've imagined fifty different scenarios of this conversation, but not one looked like what's happening right now.

They're not fuming.

They're not swearing.

They're pissed off, alright, but for an entirely different reason than I expected.

"No shit!" Theo chuckles, shaking his head. "I can't believe you thought we'd stop talking to you if you end up with Cassidy. Come on, bro. We've been through so much shit together! How stupid are you?"

"We don't despise her," Cody adds, leaning back on the bar stool. "I don't even know her all that much."

"I steer clear of her because of Kaya and Jared," Nico says, sounding apologetic. "Not because I hold a grudge. Shit, does she think we all hate her?"

Everyone in her past did...

I bob my head, my jaw set tight. It strips me of my sanity to know just how vulnerable Cassidy is and how I exploited her weaknesses without realizing. "Why wouldn't she? Did any one of you say one word to her at Thalia's party? You treat her like thin air. She's *afraid* of you two." I point at Nico and Theo.

"Great," Theo mumbles, fiddling with his thumbs. "Thalia's going to kill me. Listen, I don't talk to Cass because Thalia knows we hooked up that time, and I thought it'll be safer for my marriage if I didn't entertain her with a chat." He rakes his hand through his hair. "I honestly have nothing against Cass, Logan. Thalia loves her to bits, and if that's not a statement in Cassidy's favor, I don't know what is."

"It's not easy to impress your wife," Colt agrees.

"Well, you're all assholes, but don't put me in the same bag as them because *I* did talk to Cass at the party, and she sure isn't afraid of me," Shawn says, pleased with himself.

His smile slips fast when Cody bursts out laughing.

"No one's afraid of you. Not even your son."

The atmosphere starts to relax, and my muscles along with it. I didn't know just how scared I was of losing them until now when I know I won't. It'd be a challenge trying to navigate life without their support.

"Let the record show," Nico says, glancing at the triplets. "In case either one of you has similar dumb ideas in the future as this genius," he points at me. "There isn't a single thing you could do to make us turn on you." He looks at me again. "Even if you'd have that baby with Kaya, I'd still be here for you. I'd break your jaw first, sure, but I'd be the favorite uncle regardless." Tension leaves my shoulders and neck, and my heart almost bursts out of my chest when he pulls me into a hug. "Congratulations, bro. Let's hope your kid is smarter than you."

They take turns playfully punching my shoulder, pulling me into tight hugs, patting my back, and calling me an idiot. They're right. I am an idiot for doubting them.

We're a *family*.

We're Hayes, and we're fucking indestructible.

THIRTY

Cassidy

Newport Beach has been my home for three years, but I've never had as many people knock on my door during one twenty-four-hour period as I do now.

I fling the door open, blood draining from my face instantly. I expected a Hayes, and a Hayes is here, but it's not Logan. It's Nico.

He was always the one to make my bones shiver, but ever since Kaya, he downright scares me. The way he moves as if he's a lion on the hunt; the way he glares at everyone and weighs every word has me bracing for an attack.

And he's *here*, standing in the doorway to my flat, the sleeves of his black t-shirt stretching beyond the capacity of the cotton strands, his jaw squared, eyes narrowed, a vein throbbing down the column of his tattooed neck.

A part of me wants to slam the door in his face and push the loveseat against it to stop him from getting inside. It borders on insanity, just like my weak knees, but I can't fool my brain and the dismay filling my veins with ice-cold liquid.

"Will you let me in or...?" he asks, standing there and taking almost the whole width and height of the doorframe.

My skin's crawling, my mind like a beehive. "Is something wrong?" I manage, muscles in my neck and shoulders harder than stone. "Why are you here?"

"To talk," he denotes, his voice like a growl of a vicious dog ready to rip out your windpipe. "Stop acting like you want to have a baseball bat in your hand right about now."

As if a baseball bat could freaking stop him. Every muscle in his body is toned to perfection, his chest broad, shoulders square. I'm half his size at best.

The pregnancy symptom that eluded me since the start, now arrives in full force: nausea. Possible reasons behind Nico's unannounced visit flood my mind. He's probably here to tell me that either I move out of the way or Logan will lose his family, and it'll be my fault.

Forcing my legs to work, I open the door further, moving out of the way to let the wolf in the hen house. He enters, the smell of his cologne soaking the air and intensifying the unease whooshing in my head.

Logan hadn't called or texted since he left and Nico's presence in my flat means he knows about us.

"Why are you afraid of me?" he asks, casually leaning his back against the fridge, his tattooed arms folded across his chest. "Have I ever given you a reason?"

"You're very..." I pick a piece of lint from the sleeve of my sweater, mouth dry. "...intimidating."

He cocks an eyebrow. "Intimidating... alright, I get that a lot, but that's no reason to act so skittish. I've never hurt you,

Cassidy. I never said one foul word your way. I've never raised my voice, either, so help me out here because I sure as fuck don't understand why you look ready to burst out crying."

"I... I don't feel so good." I clasp my hand over my mouth and bolt into the bathroom.

My knees hit the tiled floor just in time. A coffee and a bagel I had this morning, and the toast from last night pour out of my mouth. Cold sweat breaks out at the back of my neck, the acidic bile setting my throat ablaze with every wave of puke landing in the toilet. Shuddering, I press the flush button on the wall and fall back on my ass, tucking my hair behind my ears.

I'm so glad I skipped morning sickness thus far.

"Here," Nico crouches beside me, pressing a wet towel to my forehead. "Are you done, or is there more to come?"

"I'm done." I brace one hand against the tiles to haul myself up, but Nico grips my forearm, his touch bordering on painful as he helps me up. By the look of him, I don't think he knows he's squeezing too hard. "Thank you," I mutter, my eyebrows drawn together when he dabs a bit of toothpaste on my toothbrush and hands it over.

"Don't act so surprised, Cass. You know nothing about me."

I brush my teeth and wash my face before we move back to the kitchen, my body weak and feeble. "Why are you here, Nico? What do you want to talk about?"

He grabs a bottle of water from the fridge and passes it to me, apparently feeling at home. "I want you to understand that me avoiding you has nothing to do with *you*. I don't hate you, Cass. And neither do the other five."

"Logan told you about us," I mumble more to myself than him. A rush of inordinate relief hits me right in the gut.

They won't turn their backs on him. He'll still have his brothers despite choosing me.

"Yeah, he did. Just like you, I don't know you enough to trust you, which is why I steered clear. That's no longer a possibility, so you'll have to learn not to be afraid of me so I can get to know you."

My eyes pool with tears when the corners of his lips curl into a ghost of a smile. "You chose the wrong day to pay me a visit," I whisper, wiping my eyes with the back of my hand. "I'm a mess today, but *thank you*. I don't think Logan would survive without his brothers for long."

"Don't get me started on that," he clips, the coldness in his voice making me shiver again. "Why he thought we'd turn on him is fucking beyond me. What do you see in him? He's obviously an idiot."

A small chuckle breaks out of my chest. The tension, worry, and nervousness I harbored for weeks hiss out of me like air from a slashed tire. I must look comical, laughing with tears streaming down my cheeks.

"We'll always be there for him," Nico assures, tearing a piece of paper towel for me. "Same goes for you. You're a part of the family now. I'm sure I won't be your first point of contact if you ever need help, but you better put me on the list."

I dab my eyes dry, crumpling the paper towel into a ball. "Thank you. It means more than you'll ever know."

The ruthless coldness to Nico's features fades before my eyes. He's not changed one bit, but my perception of him has during the last ten minutes. I'm still not comfortable around him, still intimidated by the vicious energy he exudes, but my skin's not crawling right now, and that's big.

The door to the flat opens, and Logan lets himself in

without so much as a knock. His eyes land on me first, and two wrinkles crease his forehead. "What's wrong?"

"Nothing," I say, my voice breaking even though I'm smiling. "Happy tears."

Amusement tugs at the corners of his mouth, and his eyes cut to Nico. "You made my girl cry *happy* tears? Who the fuck are you?"

Nico pushes away from the cabinets, squeezing Logan's shoulder. "I'll leave you two alone." He crosses the room but turns back to look at me, his hand firmly on the handle. "Take care of my niece, Cass."

I'm not sure what surprises me more: that Logan told them I'm pregnant or that Nico's so certain it'll be a girl. Either way, I'm too stunned to do much else than nod.

Logan pulls me into his chest as soon as Nico shuts the door behind him. "What did he want?"

"He said I shouldn't be afraid of him and that they'll always be there for you and..." My voice shakes again because Nico's words hit the most neglected parts of me. "And *me*, too."

Logan stamps a kiss on my head. "He means that, baby. They all feel like shit as if me doubting them is their fault." He inches away, looking around the room. "Are you packed?"

"Two bags as promised."

***

"Open the door," Logan says, his tone amused. He yanks the door handle to the bathroom for the nth time. "Don't make me break the door down. He's in his pen, I swear."

"I can't stay here with that thing!" I yell, sitting on the edge of the bathtub, wrapped in a towel after Ghost entered the bathroom while I was in the shower. I screamed so loud half of the neighborhood must've heard. One octave higher, and the windows would've shattered for sure. My ribs are taking the beating now, hurting like nobody's business. I've got painkillers in my bag, but I don't want to take them even if they are pregnancy friendly. "Promise you'll take me home when I open the door," I whine, my pulse still on the quick side.

"*This* is your home. Open the door."

I've been here for six hours, but he already calls it *my* home, not just his. "Is he locked away?"

"Yes! I think you gave him a fucking heart attack screaming," he chuckles again. "Open, baby. Come on."

I turn the lock and crack the door open, scanning the bedroom through the narrow slit. My eyes come across Logan's face and his broad smile. "You need to take me home."

He pries the door open, forcing me to step back. "I've got a better idea." He tugs my hand, forcing me to step out of the bathroom, and sits me on the bed, a phone to his ear. "Do you still want Ghost?" he asks whoever's on the other side of the line. "I'd appreciate it if you could come get him tonight. Cass will end up sleeping in the bathtub if you don't." He crouches before me, one hand on my thigh and climbing higher. "Yeah, that'll work. Thanks."

"What will work?" I ask when he cuts the call and tosses the phone aside. "Who's taking Ghost? Is he going for good or just a sleepover?"

"He'll be gone for good. I could risk having him here when it was just me, but now that you're here..." he brushes his fingers over my tummy, "...and my baby's here, it's time to let him go."

"You really are happy about this..." I mutter, fascinated by the sheer joy shining in his eyes as he touches my tiny bump.

"Never happier, princess," he catches my lips with his and moves his hand lower, pushing it under the towel to stroke my pussy. "How sore are your ribs?"

"Pretty sore, but... *oh,*" I gasp when he circles my clit.

"Do you know that orgasms dull pain?"

I cock an eyebrow, fighting not to let my eyes roll back into my head at how good it feels to have his hands back on me. "I'm not sure how useful I can be."

He slips one finger inside me, eyes on mine, his dark and aroused, pupils blown. "You don't have to move a muscle. Feeling you come, seeing your face when you do..." he adds another finger. "...I need that." He hooks his finger between my boobs, untying the towel with one move, and grazes his teeth over my pebbled nipple. "Lay down, baby."

I arch back, bracing with both elbows before I move my hands to his head and force him higher until he hovers over me and dips his head for a kiss.

And for the first time, I don't cap what I feel for him. I don't hide it. I don't try to suppress it. I let the love consume me whole, and I transfer it into the kiss so he can feel how much he means to me.

"I don't ever want to be without you," I whisper, tracing the contours of his face with my fingers. "I'll always love you more than anyone ever could."

He opens his mouth, but I don't let him say a word, yanking him down for another kiss.

I don't want to hear *I love you, too.*

I don't want to hear *I'm falling in love with you.*

I want the three words in the simplest form.

I love you.

And for that, I'm willing to wait as long as it takes.

TOO WRONG

I weave my fingers through his hair and bask in how peaceful I am when he's close. How *wanted* I feel in this moment.

Dreams *do* come true, sometimes. And happily ever afters don't just happen once upon a time...

THIRTY-ONE

Logan

The monthly get-together won't start for four more hours, but here I am, knocking on the door to my parents' house ahead of time, on a mission.

It's been a week since Cassidy moved in with me, and my previous companion, Ghost, was evicted and relocated to Nico's house. I'm on cloud nine most of the time, enjoying the peacefulness of having Cass with me, holding and kissing her whenever I feel like it.

But it's not all glitter and sparkles. There's a side to Cass I hate seeing. She tries to hide her insecurities, but every day I get glimpses of how unsure she is about us... about *me*. Small things, like when I loaded her empty cup in the dishwasher the other morning while she was reading a pamphlet in the kitchen. I thought nothing of it, but she paled and started apologizing.

The same happened when she cooked dinner. I've been taught that when a woman cooks for you, you clean up afterward, but Cass lunged over the dining table to snatch a plate out of my hand so fast she hurt her ribs again.

She acts like I'll kick her out the door the moment she puts a foot out wrong, and it kills me every time. I notice how vulnerable she is now that she's with me most of the time. Now that we *talk* and spend time together outside of bed. I see how easy it is to make her doubt me and herself.

She's been opening up more, talking about her past, the alcoholic parents and foster families, the abuse, neglect, and fear.

And that's why I'm at my parent's house.

Cassidy is mine now, she's growing my baby, and I'll be fucking damned if I let anyone else hurt her.

Intentionally or not, it ends now.

I faced my brothers and came out on the other side unscathed. It's time to face my parents.

"Logan!" My mother chirps, flinging her arms around my neck. "I didn't expect you here so early."

I reciprocate the hug, then walk further in, inhaling the sweet scent of apple pie hanging thickly in the air.

Grandma must be here again.

My mother is a great cook, but just like Thalia, she can't bake. One more position on a long list of things they have in common. Too bad neither of those things brings them closer.

"Is everything okay?" Mom asks, the sixth sense she developed while raising a team of boys works without fail, as always. "You look worried, sweetheart. What's wrong?"

Nothing yet.

"Is Dad here?"

"Yes," she drawls, her eyes narrowed and full of contradicting emotions. "He's in his office."

"Can you go get him? I've got something to tell you."

She pales a touch, and her beautiful face twists with worry, but she nods, hurrying down the long foyer toward the back of the house while I head to one of the living rooms.

I don't sit down, too fidgety to stay still.

"Logan," my father clips in a firm but friendly tone, entering the room. "What brings you over so early?"

"I think you should sit." I lean against the grand piano, clenching and unclenching my fists.

They glance at each other but oblige, taking a seat on the white chesterfield sofa, close together, a united front in the face of potential problems.

My brothers and I take after them in that department.

Mom squirms in her seat, her eyes wide, and Dad takes her hand, holding it in his lap, gently stroking her knuckles.

"I want you to meet my girlfriend," I start, letting that piece of information sink in first. "But it'll either happen on my terms, or it won't happen at all."

My mother straightens her back in a defensive move, while my father remains impassive. His undeniable authority leaves no room to doubt who's in charge here. Years of political career mean that Robert Hayes remains in control of any situation even if he's not uttering a word.

He knows there's a reason for my opener, and I'm pretty sure he knows what the reason is too, but until I say what has to be said, he'll remain silent and study my moves and gestures before he assumes the role of a negotiator.

"What do you mean?" Mom asks, her cheeks glowing scarlet with annoyance that rings in her voice.

"Mom..." I come closer, plopping down in the wing chair opposite the couch. "Theo won't ever tell you this, but I will because someone has to." I take a deep breath, eyes on hers, my tone as gentle as possible given the situation. "I know you love us, and you're out of your depth now that we're adults and starting our own families, but you have to accept that the women in our lives will *never* replace you. Theo loves you just as much as he did before he married Thalia. Neither of us will stop because we're growing up, but—"

"But?" Mom clips, her lips in a thin line as she tears her hand from Dad's grasp and folds her arms over her chest.

She's got the berating look down to a T. She angles her body to the side and lifts her chin, eyes narrowed, and lips pursed. Despite her obvious defensive demeanor, the hurt in her eyes stings me more than it used to back in the day.

"Do tell me what the *but* is, Logan."

I rub my chin keeping my emotions in check. Hurting her isn't my intention. I'm just trying to help her see reason and realize that her behavior will cost her dearly.

"*But* unless you accept our choices, Mom, you'll see less and less of us. Theo will snap at some point if you don't stop treating his wife like the enemy. I'm surprised he's lasted this long."

"I do *not* treat her like an enemy!" Mom's cheeks grow even hotter, small torches swimming in her eyes. "I don't have to love her, do I? She's Theo's wife, not mine."

"You don't have to love her," I agree, not letting her anger get to me and light the fuse. "But what reason other than jealousy do you have not to even like her? She's been crawling out of her skin to earn your acceptance. She's amazing, Mom. She makes Theo happy. What more do you need? You should be glad he found her."

You should see the caricatures he used to surround himself with.

Dad wraps his arm around Mom's shoulders, pulling her closer as if to comfort her, but the look on his face is no longer impassive. He's an open book.

Today, he's on my side. He won't admit it aloud, though, supporting the united front of Mr. and Mrs. Robert Hayes.

"I love you," I continue, looking them both in the eyes. "Both of you. And I want you to meet my girlfriend, but I also love *her*, and she's been through enough." I rest my elbows on my knees, fingers knotted together. "That's why I'm here. To tell you that if you make her feel unwanted, even for a second, I won't bring her over here again. *I* won't come over." I inhale a deep breath, bracing to break the most important piece of news I'll ever tell them. "I hope you'll do your best not to act so hostile, Mom, because in February, you're going to be a grandma again."

A small whimper flies past her lips. I can't tell what emotion hides behind that sound. Whether she's happy, sad, or shocked, but she is *something*.

My father, on the other hand, is the epitome of calmness. Only his eyes betray that he's emotional.

"Oh, Logan! Why didn't you bring her over sooner?!"

Distressed. That's what she is.

"It's a long story. You do know her, though. Remember the girl that almost drowned at Theo's?"

"Cassidy?" Mom gasps and a knife opens in my pocket. "That photographer? *She's* the mother of my grandchild?"

My mom is not a snob. Not by a long shot. She's an activist. She owns a charity and loves helping those less fortunate, but wherever her sons are concerned, no woman is good enough, apparently. Maybe we should all be gay like Shawn. She sure loves Jack like he's her own.

I get up, disappointment spreading inside my mind like a contusion below the skin. "That's all I had to hear," I say, my tone reflecting how defeated I feel. I cross the room, my throat so dry it's painful to swallow. "Don't expect us today."

I enter the foyer and catch a glimpse of grandma retreating into the kitchen. She's always been on the nosy side, even though no one ever hid anything from her. We're quite an open family, rarely keeping secrets.

I veer off in the direction of the kitchen to at least say *hi* to her before I storm out of the house, but Mom's high-pitched voice halts me in my tracks.

"Logan, wait!" She rushes after me and grabs my arm in the middle of the foyer. "I'm sorry, I'm just…" her voice cracks like eggshells, and her eyes pool with tears. "All my boys left. It's just your father and me here, alone." She sobs, sniffling pathetically. "You have less time as it is, and with wives and kids, you'll be too busy. You'll stop coming over and—"

I pull her into a tight hug. "We're here, and we will always be here. We won't stop coming over just because we're starting families. If anything, we'll be here more often. You'll be sick of us, I promise." I kiss her head, wrapping her tightly in my arms. "This house might feel empty now but give it a couple more years, and it'll be full of grandkids. Thalia and Cassidy aren't stealing your sons. They'll give you another line of the Hayes, Mom. They make us better men and we want you and Dad to accept them."

She cuddles into me, holding onto my jersey and bobbing her head as if she's ready to say and do whatever it takes just to hold onto me and all her other sons, too.

Dad approaches, wrapping us both in his arms, the silent hero, saving the day with gestures more than words. "Of course, we want to meet her," he says, his tone controlled on the surface but laced with thick emotions underneath. "Congratulations, son. I'm proud of you."

And I know he doesn't just mean that I finally found someone worth my time, but that I was willing to tell Mom the cold, harsh truth that'll benefit us all.

"Please come over with Cassidy today," Mom pleads, inching away. "Please, I really want to get to know her. I mean it."

I press my lips to her forehead. "We'll see you at two."

***

Cassidy digs her nails into the back of my hand, squeezing hard enough to cut off my blood supply.

"You need to calm down, princess," I say, pumping my fingers around hers. "You're not doing my baby any good."

She inhales through her nose and pushes it back out past her lips. "I'm nervous. I've not been in one room with your family since Thalia's birthday, and that didn't go down well."

I pull her to my side and kiss her head because I've learned that my lips on her act like a soothing balm. "It's different now."

Truth be told, I don't know what the fuck to expect. We're only here because I couldn't stand the pleading note in my mother's voice. I didn't have it in me to say *no* to her when tears filled her eyes, but I won't trust her words until her actions confirm them.

I've not changed my mind. It won't take much venom on Mom's part to force my hand. I'll grab Cassidy and get her out of here without a backward glance.

She's my priority, and nothing will ever change that.

The door flings open. Once again, Theo waves a hundred in my face, grinning from ear to ear. "Nico thought Cass might haul your ass here sooner."

I roll my eyes. "He's got too much cash," I shoulder past him, pulling Cass with me. "We should find him a sugar baby he can spoil rotten with Chanel purses and Louboutin heels. Cass takes longer to get ready than I do."

"Do you?" He asks her, not an ounce of reserve in his voice. They cleared the air when he and Nico came over last week to collect Ghost. "No way that's possible."

Cassidy smiles small. "I'll let you in on a secret. Logan doesn't start to get ready until it's time to leave."

The house is oddly silent: no piano music in the air, which isn't common. Mom always plays when Nico's around. Either we're late for the concerto, or it hasn't yet begun.

"Whatever you did…" Theo grips my shoulder and pulls me in for a brief hug. "Thank you."

"What do you mean?"

He points at the living room windows, and curious, I head over there, peering out into the garden where all my brothers stand scattered around, talking and drinking beer. Little Josh is with Grandad, kicking a ball out on the tennis court; Shawn and Jack help grandma set the table; Nico talks to Dad by the BBQ, and the triplets are in the pool, lying on inflatable mattresses, dark shades pulled over their eyes.

It doesn't click straight away, but when Theo pats my back again, I spot what he's trying to show me. Mom's with Thalia on the three-seater swing, drinks in hand. They're immersed in chat. What's more, Mom sports a full-blown *genuine* smile.

"I told you she'll get over herself at some point. Why are you thanking me?"

"Don't act stupid," Theo clips, whacking the back of my head. "Mom burst out crying when we walked in through the door. I thought someone fucking died before she started apologizing. She mentioned you opened her eyes this morning."

Looks like I did because ten minutes later, Mom's crying again, hugging Cassidy to her chest, touching her stomach and whispering *congratulations*.

EPILOGUE

Logan

Cassidy's in the shower when I wake up. I praise myself for my cleverness in designing this house because, with the door to the ensuite open, the shower is in clear view from our bed.

I raise on my elbows, watching my girl lather her breasts with soap. Water cascades down her sexy body, dripping over the small bump.

At fourteen weeks, the alluring roundness of her tummy is *finally* showing under fitted clothes, which is why I don't let her wear baggy jumpers. I've been waiting for this moment too long to let her hide the bump under loose t-shirts.

I want everyone to know she's pregnant. Meaning taken. Claimed. *Mine.*

It's just past six in the morning, and it's the first time Cass has been up before me since she moved in. She's been sleeping more and more as the days go by. Thankfully, sleepiness is the only inconvenience associated with pregnancy.

She's not been sick, she's not swelling, and she stopped crying for no reason two weeks ago. The only craving she has is lemons. Better than pickles, I guess, but my jaw hurts when she peels the skin off and eats them like apples.

I get out of bed to join her in the shower.

"Morning," she says, eyes roaming down my body to stop at my stiff cock. "Oh good, you're ready."

I chuckle, pulling her to my chest. "Are you?" That's a stupid question considering she's wet for me twenty-four-seven lately, but I trail my hand down her stomach until I reach the mark, rubbing her gently. "That's encouraging."

She spins around, pressing herself to me and a small whimper leaves her mouth at the contact. She's already worked up, her boobs full, swollen, cheeks rosy, pupils blown.

There's nothing better than a woman ready and willing bright and early in the morning. I run my fingers up the side of her body, watching her shudder when the pad of my thumb grazes her pebbled nipple.

"You had another dirty dream, didn't you?" I ask, cupping her ass and giving it a gentle squeeze. She's been waking up needy from intense, erotic dreams for two weeks, and fuck if waking up to her lips working my cock under the comforter isn't a fantasy come true. "Tell me about it."

She pours a generous amount of my shower gel into the palm of her hand and rubs it over my chest and shoulders, taking her sweet time before she grips the base of my cock and pumps slowly.

"I'd rather show you," she says, her voice breathless when she shoves me further under the stream and drops to her knees, taking me in her mouth.

"I'd rather you show me too," I groan, my eyes rolling

back into my head when she sucks, gliding her lips as far down as she can. "That's it, baby," I grab a fistful of her hair. "That's good. Just like that."

Her lips are incredible, and it takes little time before I'm there, on the brink of an orgasm. As if sensing impending doom, Cassidy releases me with a soft pop and gets back up.

I grip her waist, scoop her off her feet, and then lay her on the bed, wet and needy. I used to throw her, but I learned to handle her a bit more carefully now that she's a two-pack.

I waste no time diving between her thighs, closing my lips on her clit. She smells fresh, like ginger and lemons. Turns out it's neither hair shampoo nor body lotion, it's shower gel.

"It must've been one hell of a dream," I say, looking up at her pretty, flustered face. "We're going to recreate it. Tell me what to do."

She chuckles softly. "I thought you didn't need pointers."

"I don't, but a brief description will help."

She moves her legs onto my back and weaves her fingers in my hair, yanking me down hard. "Lips," she utters, her eyes closing. "Two fingers."

"Three words," I whisper, then do as I'm told, licking her bottom to top as I slide two fingers inside. "Just like that?"

"Yes," she breathes. "Oh god, *yes*. Don't stop."

She palms her breasts, and another needy whimper leaves her lips. I don't think I deserve this, but pregnancy hormone Gods are definitely in my corner.

Thirty seconds is all it takes for the orgasm to rip through her body like fire in dry grass. She fists my hair and keeps me in place while her hips arch, and she rides her high, coming all over my tongue. I'm rock-hard watching her take what she needs. She's not done trembling before she tugs on my hair, forcing me to climb higher until she can reach my lips to kiss.

"That's the sexiest thing you've done to date." I brush her wet hair away from her face. "I want more of my needy princess," I whisper, biting her ear.

"I need you. Now," she says, her tone urgent as if she can't wait any longer. "And I want you to *not* be so gentle."

Not gentle? I've toned down the wild sex for now, too worried about hurting her or our baby somehow, but there's no denying that holding back fucking sucks.

She flips onto her tummy, pushing her ass out.

"You want it hard?" I position myself at her entrance, the tight space even tighter at this angle. "As you wish." With one stroke, I'm inside, and I lean over her back. "Hold onto the edge of the bed, baby."

She grips it with both hands when I pull out and drive back into her, the pace of my thrust fast and demanding to give her what she desperately needs.

This is *heaven*.

"Oh God," she moans when the bed starts slamming against the wall. "*Don't* stop."

As if I could. The angle is perfect, and knowing she wants and needs me to take her like this brings the primal instincts to the surface. A mist of sweat works its way onto my chest within minutes. I fight the urge to spill inside her hot pussy when her moans grow louder.

She props herself on her elbows, arching her back, then grabs my right hand and cups it around her swollen breast.

"Don't hold it," I rasp, slamming into her. "I'll make you come again. As many times as you need. Let go."

The second I take her hard nipple between my fingers, she gasps, and her walls throb around me, the orgasm so intense she's shaking, fisting the sheets, and writhing beneath me, pushing her hips back to take me even deeper.

"There you go," I say, rocking into her hard to prolong the sensation until she comes down from her high.

I don't ask for more pointers. I pull out, push my hand under her waist and pull her up like a rag doll, forcing her to kneel on the bed and grip the headrest with both hands. "You good, princess? You want more?"

"Yes," she utters. "I love you so much."

"Not more than I love you. Hold on tight."

I grip her throat, forcing her to rest the back of her head on my shoulder when I thrust in, forcing another needy whimper out of her lips. I swear her boobs grew bigger overnight, again. They no longer fit in my hand.

"Harder," she breathes between soft moans. "Please, Logan... *harder.*"

"Shh, it's okay, you need more, not harder," I coo in her ear, then dig my thumb into the dimple on her lower back, ramming into her like I'm on a fucking mission.

I slide my hand from her throat to her clit and use two fingers to rub tight circles.

It's still not enough, so I spin her around and force her to straddle me. My hands and mouth free to give her more while she rides me, dictating the pace.

It's frantic.

She needs the release so much she claws my back, rising and falling in a rushed, demanding tempo.

I rub her with my thumb and take care of her swollen breasts, grazing my teeth over her hard nipples. She moans, gasps, and I've never loved the look on her face more than in this moment when she's focused solely on herself.

TOO WRONG

When the third orgasm comes, I tip over the edge with her, pumping a few more times before I still.

We're both breathless, my muscles on fire, chest heaving, and heart racing as if I had just run a marathon.

"You're so hot when you come," I say, pulling out slowly, my lips on the back of her head. "You good? You want more?"

We can't go too long without sex, but I've been on dick duty two, sometimes three times a day the past two weeks. And today? That was the wildest ride since I found out she's pregnant. I regret it a little, knowing she'll most likely be sore all day but fuck if that wasn't hot.

"I'm good for now. I'm sorry, I—"

"Don't. Don't apologize. I'll give you whatever you need." I kiss her forehead. "Believe me, I'm more than happy about your sex drive."

"It's the hormones." She hides her face in the crook of my neck. "Dr. Jones says I should stop being so horny by the end of the second trimester. Maybe sooner."

"I sure fucking hope not." I move my hand lower, spreading my fingers over her bump. "When will she start kicking? I'm growing old here."

"You ask every day. *He* won't start kicking for at least another month, probably longer."

We're both sure about the baby's sex. Cass says it's a boy, but she's wrong.

I caress the bump with my thumb and tap my fingers along the middle to wake our little princess. Although all the rocking just now probably did the trick. "Kick," I whisper. "Go on, Ava, kick Daddy."

"Ava? You want your son's name to be *Ava*? He'll be bullied at school."

"It's a *girl*."

"It's a *boy*," she huffs. "What do your brothers think?"

"Well, one of them thinks I'm gay." I smirk and duck when she tries to smack my head.

"I meant the sex of the baby."

"That's beside the point."

A triumphant smile curves her lips. "They're team *Owen*, aren't they?"

"They're team *boy*. No fucking way it'll be *Owen*, though. Nico's the only one still on my side. His money's on a girl. He bet everyone a hundred bucks."

"Doesn't he lose like every time?"

"Shut up. It's a girl." I pull her to my side, kissing the crown of her head.

"I'll tell you when *he*, your *son*, kicks, so please stop asking every day. Also, you need to let me go."

I chuckle, moving my hand away. She's got the bladder capacity of a toddler these days, and I bet it'll only get worse.

Whatever. I'm loving this.

I love taking care of her. I love stopping at the grocery store every night to buy more lemons or whatever she asks for. I love holding her close and stroking her hair while we watch a movie.

And I. Love. Her.

So fucking much I can't breathe sometimes.

My phone pings on the nightstand a second after Cass locks herself in the bathroom. It's just past seven in the morning, but as it's Friday and they're getting ready for work or college, I'm not surprised to see a notification from the Hayes group chat.

Before I unlock the screen and open the app, five more pings sound in quick succession. The first thing that jumps out at me is a picture sent by Cody. Not just any random picture. It's a book.

More specifically, "Sweet truth" by Aisha Harlow. My face and abs are clear as day on the cover, my arm snaked across Mia's back, her face hidden behind a veil of wavy, blonde hair.

Cass showed me a copy of the book as soon as it was released weeks ago. I forgot all about it, but I should've known my brothers would find it sooner or later.

Cody: And the Model of the Year award for the picture titled LOWEST HANGING PANTS goes to...

I burst out laughing. From all the things they could've found wrong with that picture, the jeans hanging low on my hips—as per Cass's instructions during the shoot—showcasing the V on my abdomen is what Cody chooses to mock.

Not my glistening chest covered in baby oil.

Not the mess that my hair is, as if I just got out of bed because Aisha's a shitty stylist at best.

Not the way I'm glaring at the camera.

Nope. My *jeans*.

A bunch of laughing emojis and gifs litter the screen, and I scroll down to the next text message.

Theo: Logan. This is an intervention. Let us talk. We're worried about you.

Shawn: Firstly, you need to understand that we'll always love you, but...

Nico: Your narcissism is spiraling out of control.

Colt: Your obsession with baby oil isn't healthy.

Me: You're all assholes.

Cody: There's no need for name-calling, Logan.

Conor: Take a deep breath. We're trying to help.

I chuckle again just as Cassidy gets out of the bathroom, watching me with curious eyes.

"What are you smiling at?" She crawls in beside me, resting her head on my chest, one hand draped across my middle.

"My brothers only now found Aisha's book. They're staging a text-message intervention to tackle my narcissism and baby oil addiction."

I angle my phone, letting her read through the messages, but it's not even three minutes later that her breathing stabilizes, and she falls asleep again.

Careful not to wake her, I untangle myself from her arms to get ready for work. As much as I hate leaving Cassidy alone, I love coming back to her. That's the one thing I'll do for the rest of my life. I'll always come home to her.

Thank you

I hope you enjoyed *Too Wrong*. Nico is next, and you'll find the first chapter of his book when you flip the page.

Love,

I. A. Dice

ONE

Nico

Fucking college kids...

Cars line the curbs on both sides of the street: everything from flashy Ferraris, all-out American muscle to a baby-pink Fiat and even a yellow school bus some senseless moron parked at the bottom of the driveway, blocking the way.

Kids swarm the street, booze in hands, not enough clothes on their backs, and way too loud.

More are coming, flocking, fucking crowds of them.

Half the college football team strut up the driveway in purple jerseys, cockier than cocky, their arms around young babes in bikinis or miniskirts. It's sixty-five degrees outside, but cool evening air doesn't stop them from flaunting their lean bodies.

I rock back and forth in the driver's seat, looking through a narrow gap between the mass of bodies for any free space on my driveway.

There's none.

It's packed.

Twenty-odd cars are parked all over the place as if the valet for the evening parked them wearing a blindfold.

I inhale a deep breath, shift into reverse, and whirl around the kids, trying not to run anyone over, even though I really want to when a drunk prick steps into the middle of the street, his hands outstretched.

I have no choice but to stop.

Why did I agree to this again?

Instead of honking, I rev the engine. The deafening roar of the V8 startles a few babes, who break into infantile giggles, twirling their long, platinum locks around their fingers. Two even wink in my direction.

Don't fucking bother.

"Shit! Get off the road, you idiot." Someone yanks the kid off my spoiler. "You know who this is?" he says, his hushed voice still audible through my open windows. "Don't piss him off, dude."

At least they know.

Of course they fucking know.

Everyone knows whose garden they're raiding tonight.

They step aside, and I release the brake, reversing further down the street. Anger warms my chest until I'm talking myself out of reaching into the glove box for a pack of smokes. I quit four weeks ago—the seventeenth attempt during the last three years—but I ponder lighting one up twenty times a day.

Five minutes later, after leaving my shiny toy way too far from my house, I'm back on the driveway.

It cleared a bit.

Not of cars, though.

Fewer kids linger out the front, most in the garden by now, where a new-age techno beat pumps through a dozen tall speakers, making my bones shake. It took my brothers and the DJ the entire afternoon to connect the sound system.

I jog up the concrete steps to the main door but halt halfway there, catching movement in my peripheral vision... a porn clip in the making. One of the football jocks rams his dick into a drunk brunette who's spread-eagled on the hood of my brother's Mustang. Boobs, barely covered by a skimpy bikini bra, threaten to bounce out every time the obnoxious asshole rams into her like a machine gun.

He'll have a goddamn coronary if he keeps up that pace much longer.

I should tell them to get the hell out of there before they dent Cody's car, but if I say a word, he will, too. And that will count as an excuse to make him bleed.

I'm on a tight schedule. No time to throw punches this evening. My fuse has been way too short since I quit smoking. It's never long, but it's been almost nonexistent lately.

Better not to get involved.

If Cody didn't want his car serving as a fuck-bench for the night, he should've parked in the garage. Although, he probably pulled the short straw with Colt and Conor, who form two-thirds of the Holy Trinity: identical triplets.

The garage has five spaces, but I own three cars, so one of my brothers parks under the clouds. They don't complain. They can't. I let them move in with me the summer after they graduated high school, so they could spread their wings like teenagers should, away from our overprotective mother's watchful eyes.

That was two years ago. They're *twenty* now, and that sure

makes me feel old. I still remember the day they were born. They're turning twenty-one in a few months, but Mom still treats them like they're five at most. Maybe because they came as a surprise nine years after my parents decided four sons were enough kids to have.

Or maybe because they're wild.

I insert the key into the lock and take a deep breath to cool my jets before I turn it, rather proud I didn't smoke.

Stick to the plan.

Fifteen minutes. In and out. Shower, change of clothes, then out again, away from the mayhem till it passes, and my garden will be mine again by tomorrow.

I push the door open, and I'm fuming again.

Last year, after the triplets threw their first Spring Break Inauguration party, I remodeled the ground floor. Not by choice. The damage their idiot friends caused forced my hand, so this year, I set hard rules.

The main one: don't let anyone inside the house.

Looks like that's too much to ask for because the door to the guest bathroom down the corridor stands wide open. Conor is there, leaning against the frame. A puzzled expression taints his features, and he's cluelessly scratching his chin.

Colt's taking two steps at a time, almost flying down the stairs with a travel-sized bottle of mouthwash, toothpaste, and a toothbrush in hands.

And then, I hear it... someone's puking.

"What the fuck is going on?" I boom, halting Colt at the bottom step. "Why are you here?"

He shifts his weight from one foot to the other, an *argh, fuck* look crossing his face. "Sorry, bro," he says, but there's nothing apologetic about that *sorry*. "There's been a small incident, and Mia—"

"You brought a drunk chick in here to puke?!" I toss the keys into a decorative bowl on the side table by the staircase. "This is the last party you're hosting in my house. Get her the fuck out of here before I do."

He lunges forward, clamping his jaw as he drops everything he held to the floor to free his hands. He grips a fistful of my shirt, shoving me toward the living room, his eyes narrowed, chest heaving. "She's not drunk. She's *scared*, so you better shut up and let us handle it."

I glance at where he holds me, wrinkling the fabric. That's the first time he dared to get in my face. I can't decide if I'm proud he's got the balls to threaten me or if I'm pissed off he's got the nerve to touch me.

I think, most of all, I'm confused. "Scared? She's puking because she's *scared?*"

Colt nods, opening his fist before stepping away, his back arrow straight. "Just give us a few minutes to calm her down, alright?"

How scared does a girl need to be to throw up?

A few scenarios fill my mind. The anger stirring within me like a thunderstorm morphs into a full-blown tornado.

Maybe someone died: drowned in my pool, and the cops are on their way, led by my eldest brother, Shawn.

"What the hell happened? I swear, if you tell me someone died, you'll be packing your shit in five minutes."

"Died?" Colt's eyebrows shoot up, and he snorts a derisive laugh. "Drama Queen much? No one died."

"Then *what* got this puking chick scared?"

"Brandon forced her into his lap. She elbowed his face and broke his nose. Just get on with whatever you came here for. We'll calm her down and get her out of here."

I imagine a tall, overweight woman with a black belt in karate because there's no way any other woman could take on Brandon Price. He's a quarterback. Built like a true quarterback, too.

Relieved as I am that no one's leaving the party in a body bag, I can't draw a link between Brandon's broken nose and the girl's fear. She should be proud.

Colt's gone before I ask any supporting questions, and I realize that I don't give a fuck. My focus is on leaving the house as fast as possible without looking out the windows to assess the mayhem in my garden.

So that's what I do. My phone rings when I'm halfway up the stairs. I slide my thumb across the screen, pressing it to my ear. "I need fifteen minutes, Theo."

"Hurry up," he yells, excited like a kid on Christmas Eve. "We're on our way."

Since Theo married Thalia, Logan knocked up Cassidy, and Shawn adopted Josh, we rarely catch up. Now that we finally planned a night away from the usual bullshit, I'm buzzing at the thought of spending the evening with my brothers.

It's been too long.

I climb another flight of stairs to my bedroom. It spans the whole second floor of the six-bedroom house: my private bachelor pad with the largest bed money can buy, a showcase shower, and a stand-alone bathtub.

This space used to be a recording studio for some up-and-coming-never-made-it pop star, so it's soundproof. I hardly take advantage of that fact because I don't bring women home often but considering all the chicks my brothers fuck in their rooms one floor down, a soundproof bedroom is a blessing.

I hit the shower, then squeeze into a gray, long-sleeved t-shirt, pairing it with black jeans. A silver watch, bracelets, cologne, sneakers, then an AirPod in my left ear, my Spotify playlist soothing my mind on low volume.

My job—my *life*—is overly demanding. My thoughts rush at a hundred miles an hour, never stopping. Music is the only thing keeping me relatively sane. The only thing that keeps me grounded. Without it, I would've ended up in the looney bin years ago.

I force my hair into submission, raking my hand through it on my way downstairs. The second I exit the comfort of my soundproof bedroom, my temper flares, flashing bright red inside my head.

Someone's playing my piano.

The two hundred grand Model C Steinway in the living room. The piano my mother bought, hoping I'd keep playing after I moved out of the family home ten years ago. She has seven sons, but to this day, she claims only I inherited her musical talent. The story has it I crawled onto her lap before I could walk, watching her fingers glide across the keyboard.

I call bullshit. It's a tale my mother made up as a means of encouragement so I'd sit through those torturous lessons. I love the sound of a piano, but I hated playing, and when the time came to get my own house, I stopped.

Deep breaths, man. Calm down.

Yeah, as if that'll work. Anger dances in my gut, stewing like a wasp trapped in a matchbox.

My mother and the older gentleman who tunes it once a year are the only two people allowed to touch my piano.

Normally, I'd unplug the sound system, scream my head off at the triplets and kick every kid out of the garden, but before I reach the stairs that'll take me to the ground floor, the anger bubbling in my veins fades, leaving no trace.

A piano does that to me. It quietens my mind to the point where I don't need an earphone, and *this* song could drag me out of the darkest place.

The melody flowing from downstairs overwhelms the new-age electro beat blasting in the garden, and "Fantasy" by Black Atlass playing in my ear.

Whoever is there, touching my fucking piano, is talented. Each note wraps itself around my tortured mind, soothing my frayed nerves. Whoever is there plays better than my mother, and I never thought that anyone, save for the songwriter, could play this song better.

Ten seconds later, I'm in the living room doorway, the AirPod in my hand. Cody sits at the foot of the corner sofa, toying with his cell phone, wearing nothing but yellow shorts, his chest bare. Dark sunglasses are pushed on top of his head, digging into the man bun Colt and Conor mock daily. He tucks the phone away when he sees me resting against the doorframe, my attention centered on the girl playing John Lennon's "Imagine" of all songs.

"Hey, bro," he whispers, crossing the room. "Sorry about this. Mia needed to calm down. Piano does the trick."

Mia. The puking chick. Not a six-foot-tall karate champion. Far from it. She's petite, her face hidden behind a curtain of dirty-blonde waves cascading down her waist.

Normally, that'd be my interest down the drain, but I can't tear my eyes off her fingers gently skimming the keys, transitioning from one note to the next with effortless precision. A surge of liquid heat flooding my system eases the ever-present tension seizing my bunched muscles.

It's almost fucking unnatural not to feel my ribs cinched around my lungs, not to hold my fists clenched, not to lock my jaw and grind my teeth.

My body gives into the calm melody, switching off the high-alert mode I'm always in, and I pull down a deep breath, filling my lungs with ease for a change.

"*She* broke Brandon's nose?" I ask, mimicking Cody's hushed tone.

I don't want to talk. I don't want to disturb her, but I hope she'll turn around. She doesn't.

She doesn't acknowledge me in any way, as if she hadn't heard me... as if she's alone with the piano.

"Yeah," is all Cody says.

So helpful.

By the look of her, she's five-foot-nothing and less than a hundred pounds, making the nose-breaking incident hard to comprehend. Snapping a bone requires strength. I'd know.

"How did she manage that?"

A proud smirk crosses Cody's face as he turns to Mia, a warm glow in his eyes. The bitter stench of beer wafting in the air tells me he's had a few, but he's sober enough not to swoon. And yet, here he is, dangerously close to looking like a love-sick puppy. "We're teaching her some self-defense moves. She's getting good."

Good? Great, if you ask me. Taking on Brandon Price is an accomplishment. Especially for a pocket-sized girl like Mia. Bragging rights earned until the end of college and every reunion going forward.

"Where's Colt and Conor?" I ask, watching Mia's hands flit down the keyboard. She wears at least a dozen gold rings, some low where they're supposed to be, others higher, above the middle joint.

"They're kicking Brandon out."

As the song nears the end, I wait for Mia to turn around, but she morphs the melody into another: "Can't Help Falling in Love" by Elvis Presley. A nagging curiosity burns me up from the inside out, leaving a smoke of question marks behind.

Who is she?

A pastel pink skirt she wears, sprawled over the stool, falls to her knees, and the white of her blouse peeks between her thick, wavy hair. I glance at the cream rug where she rests her feet, dressed in pink heels with little bows at the back.

Seriously, *who* is she?

She's at a Spring Break party. Ninety percent of girls in attendance wear bikinis, and she's dressed in pink.

Fucking *pink*.

"What did Brandon do to scare her?"

"He's got a thing for Mia. She keeps shooting him down, so he's growing impatient. He forced her onto his lap, and she elbowed his face."

"Colt told me that much." My voice is almost a whisper. "I'm asking what got her scared enough to throw up."

"She always pukes when she's scared." He shrugs like it's not a big deal. "She doesn't do well with confrontation." He looks at her, his voice back to normal level when he says, "I'll get you a drink, okay? We should head out soon, Bug. Will you be okay to go back on stage?"

She must be one of the dancers hired for the party. It'd explain her pink skirt.

Cody grabs a bottle of wine from the drinks cabinet, pours half a glass, and tops it up with Sprite.

White wine spritzer at a Spring Break party?

Beer in red solo cups is what college kids got me used to. Mia might've soothed my agitation with music, but it's back twice as strong. I can't make a single assumption about her. It's unsettling... the not knowing. Curiosity sprouts inside me like a magic bean, growing fast until I think I'll crawl out of my fucking skin if I don't see her face.

Turn around, Mia.

"Last one," she utters quietly, the words like both a plea and a promise.

"Yesterday" by The Beatles reverberates through the living room. My skin breaks out in goosebumps as pleasant shivers slide down the length of my spine. She's too young to convey the emotions as if she's McCartney himself.

The melody is overcome when someone calls my cell. Mia doesn't startle, doesn't flinch, and doesn't stop playing at the interruption. Nothing calms my fucked-up mind like piano music, and that's probably why I remain rooted to the spot instead of taking the call out in the hallway.

"Rise and shine!" Theo booms. "You ready yet?"

No. I need to see this girl before I leave. "Five minutes."

"Hurry up, bro. We don't have all night! Logan's got a two am curfew, so move your ass. We're waiting outside."

I cut the call, watching Cody cross the room with purpose, shoulders tense, eyes not veering from Mia. The newly acquired muscles on his back flex when he pumps his fists. It's a nervous gesture. I know because I do the same fucking thing when I'm trying to compose myself.

He stops on Mia's right, a step behind the stool: an oversized shadow ready to protect her. The melody fades. The room falls silent save for the techno beat blaring outside, and Mia slowly rises to her feet.

TOO SWEET

Too bad Cody's blocking my line of sight.

Move, Cody.

I don't know why I want to see her, but I do. I want to see the face behind the talent. The face responsible for Brandon's humiliation. The face of a girl who wears heels with bows and pukes when she's scared.

"Is Brandon still here?" she asks.

Cody wraps his arm around her, and the single click of her heel on the tiled floor tells me he pulled her closer.

That's interesting.

My brothers don't usually date, but his hold on Mia clearly shows she's more than just another fuck. It's in his stance—the protectiveness.

"Conor and Colt are trying to get rid of him. Don't worry, even if he stays, I won't let him anywhere near you, Bug." He dips his head, and though I only see his back, I know he stamped a kiss on her hair. "Are you sure you're okay?"

Move, Cody. Show me your girl.

As if he hears my screaming mind, he lets go of Mia to fetch the wine, and finally, *finally*, I see her.

She looks like a senior... in fucking high school. Her white off-shoulder blouse is tucked into that layered tulle skirt sitting two inches over her knees.

It's modest.

It's girly.

It reminds me of candy floss, but somehow, it's inappropriate because my mind runs wild, imagining everything she's not showing.

She stands thirty feet away, yet her large eyes are so green the color is unmistakable. Skin like honey, small nose slightly upturned at the end, and those lips... natural, I can tell. Heart-shaped, bee-stung, so full it borders on ridiculous.

No fillers.

No makeup, either. Nothing. No lipstick, lip gloss, eyeshadow, or other stuff women use.

A soft glow of pink brightens her cheeks when she looks past Cody. She toys with her rings, tugging and twisting when our eyes lock. I have the urge to say *boo* just to watch her flinch. She looks afraid of her own shadow but holds my gaze despite her cheeks growing hotter. It's cute. I'm sure she'd rather let the ground swallow her whole.

"Hi." A hint, barely a suggestion of a smile pulls at the corners of her pouty mouth before she bites her cheek to keep it in check. "Thank you for letting me finish."

Words somehow fail me for the first time ever. I don't know what to say... *You're welcome? No problem?*

Nothing sounds right.

"You're gorgeous," comes out instead. I smirk internally when her lips part into an inaudible *oh*.

Cody's head snaps to me, a hard edge to his narrowed eyes. Yeah, I might've crossed a line, but fuck if that's not true.

Mia shakes off the initial shock, using both hands as she tucks dirty-blonde strands behind her ears. "Um, thank you."

"Don't thank me."

She blushes harder, tugging her bracelets, and shifts her attention to Cody when he catches her hand, interlocking their fingers.

"You ready? Six is probably growing impatient." He waits for Mia to nod. "Good. Say *bye*."

"Bye," she mouths, following it with an awkward wave.

Cody leads her out of the room, sending me a warning glare full of threats as if he's afraid I'll drag Mia upstairs to

TOO SWEET

fuck the shyness out of her system.

He should know better.

I don't waste time with college girls. Pretty and tight as they are, they're too young and too clingy.